Strike!

Julius G. Getman

Plain View Press
P. O. 42255
Austin, TX 78704

plainviewpress.net
sbright1@austin.rr.com
512-440-7139

Acknowledgements

Thanks to Allegra Young for her unfailing willingness to read drafts
and make suggestions. Thanks to Terri LeClercq for her marvelous
ideas, her careful editing, and great writing suggestions. Thanks to
Dick Markovits for careful reading, intelligent discussion, and editing
help. Thanks to Kay Graglia for reading an earlier draft and making
intelligent suggestions from a conservative perspective about how
to improve the novel. Thanks to Gale Hathcock for ideas, linguistic
suggestions and secretarial help.

This book is dedicated to all of the honorable hard-working people who have lost their jobs for exercising their right to strike

To Terri

Chapter 1

The papermakers rose from their seats and lifted their beer mugs. Tony Lucelli called out the toast: "To Bill Samson, the best damn local president in the union." The others clinked their glasses solemnly: "To Bill."

Bill Samson looked uncomfortable. It was great to have such loyal supporters, but he wished he was more worthy of their confidence. They had gathered on this cold March evening at the Anchor Pub to celebrate his re-election as President of Local 34. The Anchor, a venerable Maine tavern of sturdy wood beams, low ceilings, and hidden corners overlooking the fast flowing Panscott River, was Bill's regular hangout – the place where he went to relax. All of the bartenders and waitresses there knew him and liked him. Even though everyone knew that he was important, being president of Local 34, he never acted like a big shot. He was fun, a teaser, who loved to kid around, loved his beer, but never got drunk and always left a big tip.

During the course of the evening Bill was unusually quiet, joining only half-heartedly in the conversation that animated the others. Some victory they were celebrating. He had gotten 652 votes and Gary Sanborn, running as a "hardliner," had gotten 540. The campaign had turned nasty towards the end with Gary telling the members that "Bill is too busy kissing Tom Gillian's ass to realize that Consolidated Paper is trying to bust our union." Everyone knew that Gary was a bullshitter, still, a lot of guys had voted for him. They were pissed at the company, and Bill had always been known as a company man – even wore a Consolidated Paper Company jacket at union meetings. A few years ago, with wages high and lots of overtime, almost everyone was a company man. But that was before executive salaries went through the damn roof and stock options made already wealthy CP officials rich as Saudi princes. And to get the guys really pissed off, CP's new president George Watts was already issuing statements about the need to cut labor costs and make the mills more productive.

Bill took a sip of his beer and sighed deeply.

Ray Allair clapped Bill on the back. "Don't worry, Billy, they're just trying to scare us before negotiations begin. We're the best papermakers in the world, and everyone knows it. Why would Watts force us into a strike?"

"Damn right," Bill said, bringing his fist down sharply on the table and causing beer to spill onto his lap. They all laughed, but Bill's eyes remained down, focused intently on his beer.

"Come on, Bill, this is a party, not a funeral. Cheer up."

Ray Allair grabbed Bill's glass. "If you're not going to drink it, I might as well." He smiled. "You're going to have to arm wrestle me to get it back."

It was a challenge Bill could not refuse. It was a contest that he rarely lost. He smiled, showing the gap between his top front teeth. "You're on, you dumb son of a bitch."

The others cleared the table as Bill and Ray placed their elbows in the middle and clasped hands. "Ready" Tony Lucelli called out. They tensed. "Go!"

The battle was fierce but brief. Ray was young, well built, and athletic, but Bill had the biceps of a weight lifter, and he knew how to get almost all his strength into his downward thrust. Ray's arm was slowly but surely forced down till it touched the well-scarred wooden tabletop

Bill, short and balding, with a deeply lined, leathery face and tiny wrinkles emanating from the corners of his eyes, felt triumphant for the first time that evening. Almost 55 and still able to more than hold his own with the younger guys. But his thoughts soon reverted to the looming strike. I won because I know how to arm wrestle, but what the hell do I know about leading a strike? Almost nothing except that if it fails it's the local president's fault. I'll be the one who gets shit from all those tough talking pussies who'll race to cross the line if we're losing and look for someone to blame. Guys like to blame their giving up on somebody else. He had already learned that during his time as local president. Of course the four guys at the Anchor with him were not going to turn tail. Not a cowardly bone in the group. But there were 1500 production workers at the mill. And it was up to him to unite them and make sure they stayed united.

A year earlier, in the spring of 1988, Bill had attended a University of Maine labor education class on Strike Leadership. The instructor had stated several times that "The local president is the key." He had gone on to detail the president's tasks. Bill, trying to capture the essential ideas of the class, had taken notes, writing in his schoolboy script: "maintain solidarity," "stimulate rank-and-file involvement," and "make sure slogans reflect issues." Next to the last of these he had written "buttons and songs." When he returned home from the training sessions, he had placed that loose-leaf folder with his notes on the top shelf of his closet. It had remained there, untouched, until the morning after last week's election, when he had recovered it from beneath a pile of heavy woolen sweaters, gloves, and hats. He studied the notes intently for about half an hour. How was he supposed to "stimulate rank and file involvement" in a local where only a handful of members ever attended meetings? He shoved the notes back into the closet and slammed the door. The only songs I know are Country & Western: songs about faded love and slipping around. Lot of good they'll do in a strike. Sure, I know that Solidarity is the key, but right now the union is split. Some guys want to go to war, and most of them guys are scared to death we'll lose our jobs.

I wish I could make good speeches, Bill thought, but whenever I try to say something important, the guys look like they can't wait to get the hell out of the room He had once asked Ray Allair what was wrong with his speaking style. "You're too calm," Allair told him. "You need to get more excited about what you're saying." Bill tried to change, but all he could think of was to speak louder and use more profanity.

Although he was on good terms with most of the guys and had a group with whom he regularly played cards and drank beer (four of whom were now present), he kept his fears about leading a strike to himself. According to the unwritten code passed down from generation to generation in North Bethany, Maine men were expected to keep their fears to themselves. Bill had never heard his father express fear of anything, not even the torpedoes he faced crossing the Atlantic during World War II. Intimate conversations and discussions about feelings were almost as bad as showing fear. Men worked side by side for years and managed to limit their conversations to work, weather, women, and sports. The confused feelings of failure and mortality that tormented Bill as he got older were, of course, never mentioned to anyone.

Bill looked across the table at Tony Lucelli's handsome face. Was I ever that good looking? Not a chance. Maybe if I looked more like Tony I wouldn't have screwed up my life chasing women. It began with his first wife. I was going take over the damn paper industry till I met Bonnie. He smiled as he recalled her shapely legs and short skirts. She loved sex, would do it all day. And she'd try anything. I thought I'd died and gone to heaven. But I didn't think about consequences. What a fool I was. Three months later she tells me, "I'm pregnant." I thought we had to get married.

Bill usually avoided thinking about Bonnie. He'd been a lousy husband. A vision of a tiny studio apartment with a makeshift table and beat-up old chairs flashed through his mind. He thought of the constant angry arguments, the out-of-all proportion debts, and the baby crying his lungs out and never stopping just when Bill most needed sleep before a sixteen-hour shift. When they divorced, Bill was ordered to pay alimony and child support payments. It left him broke. He had no money, no plans, and no hope. His life was meaningless. He spent most of his nights drinking and whoring. He remembered waking up on at least three occasions with his head splitting while a strange woman made coffee. I was out of control before the guys on Number One elected me steward. I still don't know why they thought I could do the job. I sure worked my ass off to prove they didn't make a mistake. And then I started to like it. Got good at handling the guys' grievances. I wasn't a shouter but I knew the agreement better than anyone and I gave it all I had.

He had been successful negotiating grievances, even when he couldn't convince management that his interpretation was right, he could persuade them that a compromise settlement made more sense than a formal arbitration hearing. His record was almost clean. One arbitration case in ten years. Management came to respect him, and the guys elected him secretary-treasurer and then president of the local. But no one had to tell him that settling contract grievances was far different from leading a strike.

Two years ago he had been offered the chance to become a part of management. Tom Gillian, CP's Director of Labor Relations, had offered Bill a great salary and a fancy title if he would move to Boston and help develop management bargaining proposals. Bill was not sure why he didn't jump at the chance. It was not, as some of his friends speculated, to continue his then-new relationship to Shirley Lopatka, a young woman 17 years his junior who had never lived anywhere outside of North Bethany. In fact, Shirley was prepared to move with him and had actually urged him to take the job. "I wouldn't keep you from such an opportunity," she had told him gravely. "I don't feel tied to North Bethany, or the state of Maine for that matter. If you take the job and want me to go with you, I'm yours."

The idea of moving to Boston was a lot more appealing when he learned that Shirley was ready to go with him. But if they pulled up stakes and moved together, it would make his commitment to her much stronger, almost like getting married again. He felt a sudden stab of fear, and he remained silent when Shirley asked cheerfully: "When do we move?" He tried, in vain, to think of something to say, and finally realized that he did not want to leave North Bethany. "I don't want to get caught up competing with a bunch of young hot shots with fancy degrees. Besides, I like being a machine tender and a union president. That's who I am." She kissed him. That was OK with her, too.

They continued to live together, and Shirley quickly became a favorite with his friends. During the victory party they tried to lighten the mood by teasing Bill about the relationship – wondering where she was getting her sexual gratification now that he had grown "too old to get it up." Their teasing was meant and understood as a compliment. Shirley, lively and youthful with clear blue eyes, smooth skin, and the lithe body of a former cross-country runner, was quite a catch for a middle-aged paperworker. To conclude their tribute to Bill's sexual longevity, Ray Allair, who had a fine tenor voice, sang a couple of verses of the ribald Irish folk song, *Maids, When You're Young, Never Wed an Old Man.*

Bill's mood lightened. He laughed. "You guys don't know the half of it."

Thinking of Shirley was not an unalloyed pleasure. In the context of his upcoming birthday, it recalled his painful decision to turn down Gillian's offer. Had he taken it, perhaps his 55th birthday would not have reminded him of his failed ambitions. Life would surely have been more exciting in Boston. Still, he knew that he would decide the same way today. He wanted to live out his life in North Bethany, an old-fashioned mill town about 50 miles northeast of Portland, built on a flat stretch of land north of the tree-laden Shawmut Hills and just south of the cold deep waters of Lake Panscott. The fast-flowing Panscott River, stocked with blue fish and cod, marked its western boundary. North Bethany was home, the place where his family had lived for four generations.

The paper mill spanned the Panscott River just below the town's northwest boundary. Its huge, fenced buildings and towering smokestacks gave it the look of a medieval fortress. The inside of the mill resembled a giant, living organism that consumed and digested trees and spit out huge rolls of shiny paper. Roughly 1300 production, maintenance, and construction workers worked in the mill — bringing in logs; treating the wood; running and adjusting the huge, noisy paper machines, each as big as a building and long as a football field; disposing of waste; and providing the entire enterprise with power.

The members of Local 34, of whatever background, shared a common culture. They were socially conservative, family oriented, religious, hard working, and, until recently, unashamedly proud to be working for Consolidated Paper. When they spoke of the company, it was in the first person: "We make the best paper for magazines." "Our profits rose last year." They were not emotionally prepared for a battle in which CP would be the enemy.

Still, loyalty to CP was fading fast. When George Watts became CEO, his salary became the main topic of conversation in the break room. According to *Pulp and Paper*, Watts' salary and perks were worth over $5 million a year. And his stock options could double his salary if the company stock rose 10 points or more. No wonder he was talking about cutting jobs and closing mills. The Company's shares would go up. It meant more money for him and the other executives on the stock-option gravy train.

During the 30 years that Bill had worked at the Panscott mill, the last twelve as local union president, the possibility of a lengthy strike had seemed as remote as a Maine winter without snow. CP was a union-friendly company. "We settle our differences over the table, not at the picket line," Bill liked to say. But with Watts in control and his own rank and file angry as hell, he felt like someone trying to stop a fast-moving car with faulty brakes that was about to crash into a stone wall.

Chapter 2

George Watts knew that his appointment as CEO would raise both the price of CP's stock and the anxiety of its workers. He was a controversial figure. His admirers thought of him as the model of a modern major executive – disciplined, hard working, and shrewd. Watts was a leading practitioner of the "leaner and meaner" administrative style. He even looked the part — trim and small boned, no fat anywhere, with skin pale and smooth as a sheet of glazed paper. His opponents — unions, bleeding hearts, and radicals — described him as the epitome of ruthlessness and greed. But that only showed how little they understood him. Watts didn't take on daunting executive tasks to make money. His goal was to create viable profitable companies that made a contribution to the economy. He was, in fact, despite all contrary appearances, a romantic who considered reshaping inefficient corporations a high art form.

His greatest pleasure came from his work. He once confided to a female reporter from *Business Week*: "I study a balance sheet the way some people look at a painting or others read poems. It has a story to tell, and I can figure it out. I study income ratios and balance sheets, and from them I learn how a corporation is functioning. They tell me where to cut and where to spend and what needs fixing." As he was getting ready to leave, she asked whether he was anti-union. "I'm neither anti-union nor pro-union. But I am pro worker. I've saved thousands of American jobs by making sure that the companies I head are profitable and able to compete with industries around the world. I care about workers, and I care about America."

It led to a fine article. *The CEO Nobody Knows* — so favorable it made him blush when he read it. Watts refused to discuss his salary other than to say, "I earn whatever I get." And he had no doubt of the truth of his answer. When others were home with their families, he was busy planning, meeting with subordinates, negotiating deals, reading reports, sending out letters and memos. He had paid the price – a messy divorce and an angry teenage son.

Even before he formally took office in June of 1988, Watts had concluded that labor costs were the chief reason that CP's margin of profit fell below the 15% return on investment that he considered minimally acceptable. During his first week in office, he met with the company's financial and labor relations officials to develop a plan for cutting labor costs. The financial people were enthusiastic, but Tom Gillian, CP's long-time director of labor relations, had shown himself to be, at best, a reluctant warrior. "We've had great relations with the union, and that's why our workers have been so productive." He argued "If we try to cut wages or take away benefits, they'll strike, and strikes cause trouble and don't help anyone."

Watts remained silent, but he watched Gillian carefully. There was a history revealed in his heavy body and gnarled, working-class hands. Gillian was an up-from-the-ranks executive with old-fashioned views of labor relations. He was bound to be poorly educated. I've dealt with his type before — he identifies with the workers and he's proud that we pay such high wages. He doesn't really understand the market, thinks he's helping the company by buying labor peace. Probably he's one of the reasons our cost per unit of output is so high. We don't have to pay a premium for worker good will. Not today, when computers can be programmed to run the paper machines for precisely the right amount of time at the proper settings. I'll have to get rid of him and find somebody younger and better educated, somebody not afraid to take on the union.

○

Gillian, who was good at reading people, could tell that Watts had contempt for his approach to labor relations. They were not well-matched, that was obvious. He's an arrogant son of a bitch, and I'm probably on my way out.

Gillian shared his unhappiness with M.W. McLean, his young Deputy Director. "Board of Directors made a big mistake appointing someone who has never been inside a working mill, doesn't know our history, and doesn't understand the teamwork that goes into making good paper." Gillian's eyes, which normally had the color and shine of a fine olive oil, darkened. "It's not like CP's hurting. Profits are high again, and we're expanding." In the past Gillian had bragged to cohorts at other companies that CP was "an old-fashioned paper company run by old-fashioned papermakers." He had worked for CP for over forty-two years and had seen it grow from a small specialty papermaker to the second-largest paper company in the United States, with thirty-five mills in the U.S. and eight others scattered from Finland to Indonesia. He suspected that, under Watts's leadership, the term "old fashioned" would not be used as a compliment. When they met and Watts extended his unblemished and carefully manicured hand, Gillian had been repelled. Those hands have never done a real day's work, he thought.

There was a time when Gillian's ideas about labor relations were considered new and dynamic and when other companies did their best to lure him from CP. But that was a long time ago, before the thinning gray hair and the paunch that grew slightly bigger each year despite his continuing resolve to diet and exercise. Gillian's phone no longer rang with calls from executives trying to find if he was moveable or from reporters seeking to learn the secret of his success. He felt increasingly out of place with the company's young, dressed-for-success labor-relations executives with their Ivy League degrees and business school jargon. *They don't give a damn about the people who actually make our paper. I tell them that we need to work together with our unions, and they roll their eyes like I'm a senile old fool.* "We've got a bunch of warriors eager to battle as long as it's someone else's job at stake," he told McLean. "They'll be happier now that Watts is in command."

There had not been a serious strike at CP in fifteen years. To Gillian that constituted success. But he knew that the company's stock had dropped during the paper recession of the mid '80s, and its profit margin had decreased from 1984 through 1986. Although CP's financial position bounced back in 1988, the buzz among hardliners at other paper companies like Boise Cascade and International Paper was that CP had missed a golden opportunity in the '80s to cut costs and reduce their workforce.

It wouldn't be long before Watts replaced him and brought in his own people — younger, better educated, more aggressive and confrontational — to handle labor relations. *He's looking for Ivy Leaguers — the kind of people who drive foreign cars and drink imported white wine.* Gillian wondered where he could go if he left CP. When Mike Cavil, Director of Human Resources, himself significantly overweight, praised Watts for "eliminating the fat," Gillian had imagined a headline in the industry newspaper: "CP Cuts Excess Fat: Overweight Labor Executives Given the Axe."

○

In fact, Watts had almost fired Gillian after their first meeting. At the last minute, he decided to first discuss the matter with those of CP's senior executives whose toughness he trusted – the ones committed to the idea that companies work best when management power is least fettered. To his surprise, they all urged him to keep Gillian on. "Tom Gillian is straight and he is loyal," company VP Clyde Monks had argued. "He will support official policies whether he agrees with them or not. If he reaches a point where he can't go along, he'll quit quietly. The press believes him, and the unions and workers trust him."

Watts thought about it carefully. *He's got old-fashioned ideas, but if he's loyal he could turn out to be a real asset, help convince our workers and the press that we are not greedy villains trying to get rich at their expense. It's worth trying.*

In February of 1989, Watts hired Professor Sheldon Eastman of Barnett University Business School to undertake a thorough study of the company's labor policies. Gillian, when he heard about it, was not happy. Eastman, for God's sake, blames everything wrong with American industry on unions. But he knew that protest would be futile and told Watts that he would be happy to work with the professor.

Gillian and Eastman met on several occasions during the next five months. The meetings were not cordial — formal courtesy from Eastman, but no warmth, not even casual conversation. Eastman was almost bald. His scalp resembled in shape and color a large eggshell. He wore an expensive gray suit and fussy dotted tie, and sat stiffly at the small table, asking questions in an even, unemotional tone, and scribbling notes when Gillian answered.

In January of 1989, Watts scheduled a meeting of top executives so that Eastman could amplify his fifty-page report, *Reclaiming Management Rights and Cutting Labor Costs at Consolidated Paper*. Gillian had already received and carefully read the report. Eastman was critical of all the policies that Gillian had introduced — high wages and benefits, the effort to keep senior craftsmen, the constant willingness of the labor-relations staff to compromise grievances, and the general reluctance of management to fire able workers. When he had finished reading it, Gillian felt much as he would have felt reading a document criticizing his three grandchildren.

The actual meeting in the spacious, oak-paneled, executive conference room, with its picture windows looking out over Boston Harbor, was even worse than he feared. It began with Eastman smiling unctuously while Watts introduced him with effusive praise.

"We were students at the same great institution, and we have carried forward the lessons that we learned during our time together at the University of Chicago. We are both believers in the free market and committed to the ideas of Milton Friedman — ideas that have helped America to remain competitive. The more I have worked with Professor Eastman, the more I have come to value his knowledge, his expertise, and his commitment to the rights of management."

Eastman's message was direct. It was time for the company to take command of its mills, and the best way to do this was by demanding major concessions from its unions during the next round of collective-bargaining negotiations to begin in April with Local 34 in North Bethany, Maine. The union might threaten or actually strike, but that was no reason to change course. In fact, a strike would help the company, which could hire permanent replacement workers. After the strike they would vote to decertify the union. CP would no longer be required to bargain with it.

"That will scare the hell out of all the other unions," Eastman announced. The assembled executives laughed appreciatively. A few applauded.

Gillian had taken his seat at the conference table determined to remain calm and silent. But as Eastman described the benefits of hiring replacement workers, he found himself sketching a battle scene filled with diving planes, bombs, and devastation on his legal pad. His heart thumped and counterarguments filled his mind. When he could no longer restrain himself, he spoke up. "Sure, we can find replacement workers. Anybody can, but they won't be real papermakers like the ones we have at North Bethany. They'll make bad paper. And once strikebreakers start coming across a picket line, we'll be faced with violence and hatred."

Eastman's professional smile became a smirk of superiority. "Mr. Gillian, as I'm sure you know, the process of making paper is no longer the skilled craft it was. As for the issue of violence, we can deal with that by hiring special police. I suggest Blackhawk Security." Watts nodded in agreement. Eastman's pale skin colored. His smile became broader. Gillian wondered what it would take to wipe it from his face. He then made the mistake of continuing the debate.

"Making paper may be easier, but maintaining the new computerized equipment is more difficult than ever. In the long run, we'll need our experienced workers."

Eastman looked impatiently at his watch as though to suggest that his schedule was being unfairly interrupted with foolish questions. "The risks are far smaller than those your new CEO took to make Dearborn Electric more profitable." The latter statement was greeted with loud applause.

Gillian was tempted to ask how Eastman could be so confident about a process he had never experienced, but when he looked at the faces of his fellow executives, he realized that continuing the debate would be foolish. They didn't care about the soundness of his arguments. They were intent on showing their support for Watts.

Gillian decided to take his case directly to Watts, even though he had little hope of winning him over. The next morning Gillian entered the elegant CEO office, with windows on all sides and its sweeping view of Boston Harbor. How different it looked. When the office belonged to Eldon Leeds, Watts' predecessor, it was lively and slightly ramshackle, with papers and books strewn about, and the walls adorned with personal mementos. The walls were now bare except for a single photo of Watts shaking hands with Alan Greenspan. The desks and office furniture had been rearranged. Everything seemed less personal and more efficient.

Gillian got right to the point, arguing that Eastman had ignored the most critical aspect of labor relations, namely that industrial peace and mutual respect between labor and management were the best way to achieve high productivity.

Watts's eyes had become colder, the pupils now a frosty gray. "In the long run, productivity is a function of intelligent management, decision making, and the power to effectively implement." He produced an earnings chart. "If you study this chart, you will learn how the union is costing us money."

Gillian had seen many such charts. He had answers. He leaned forward to respond, saw the look of anger on Watts' face, and stopped. Gillian pulled his head and shoulders back a bit. He knows how I feel. No need to get him angrier.

Watts noticed Gillian's retreat and smiled. It's going to work. He wants to keep his job. "I'm sure, Tom, that you understand your obligation to whole-heartedly support our management policies."

Gillian's face took on a conciliatory expression. "I have always supported Company policy, and I will continue to do so."

"Good, you have a major role to play." Watts rose, indicating plainly that the meeting was over.

Gillian spent the rest of the day fantasizing about quitting and finding a position with another paper company. But his fantasies did not cheer him up. It would be almost impossible for him at his age to land another top level executive job. Besides, it was painful to imagine shifting his loyalty to one of CP's competitors. I wonder what Bill Samson will think of me when this is over.

Chapter 3

Jordan Marcon peered into the mirror. Not a reassuring sight. All he could see were lines of worry and fear.

He was not so presumptuous as to question God's plan, but why was he being tested now? These should be for him peaceful, contented years, but his life was in turmoil. It was all beyond his understanding. Jordan had led an honorable Christian life, tithed each month to the Church of the Redeemer, and never strayed from God's commandment to honor the sacrament of marriage.

Maybe he was paying now for his youthful indiscretions. Jordan thought back to his early wild, carefree days, mostly with shame, but also with a touch of nostalgia. When he first started at the mill, he was a youngster, not even twenty years old. He owned a hot rod Chevy with huge mag wheels that cornered like a European sports car. It was only God's grace that he never had an accident, even when driving drunk while making out. In those days he had a regular table at the Anchor Pub. Bill Samson was his favorite drinking buddy. They would order big mugs of New Castle draft beer and talk about work or sports or girls and listen to country music.

That was a long time ago. A month before his twenty-fifth birthday, in January of 1966, everything in his life was irrevocably changed. He could still picture it. He was on his way to the Anchor when he recognized Ann Hyatt, the twenty-year-old daughter of his high school baseball coach, moving towards him, exhaling soft wisps of breath with each stride. How beautiful she looked with her bright red cheeks and eyes that, even in the cold Maine wind, shone like polished amber!

She looks just like the actress who plays 'That Girl" on TV — only she's prettier.

He strutted, thrusting his hips forward when he walked. Would she realize how cool he was? Just as Ann came abreast of him, their eyes met. He stared so intently that he failed to notice a patch of ice on the path. Jordan stumbled, reached out, tried to catch his balance, failed, and bumped against Ann with enough force to knock her to the ground and send the religious tracts she was carrying under her arm flying.

"Oh, God, Ann! I'm so sorry! Let me get those papers for you. I'll be glad to pay for anything that I damaged."

She laughed, which made her high cheekbones stand out. The inviting curve of her mouth, the sparkling teeth, and the bright gleam coming from her eyes made the back of his neck tingle.

"Don't worry. These are from the church, and I can easily get more. All you've done is cost me a little time in distributing them."

He volunteered so earnestly to help her that she finally agreed. That little accident changed his life. When they finished handing out the leaflets, she urged him to come next Sunday to the Church of the Redeemer. "It would make me very happy to see you there," she told him, and his heart pounded as though he had just scored a touchdown..

He vividly recalled that first Sunday sitting in back of the small wooden church on the outskirts of town, feeling totally out of place. Everyone else knew the words of the hymns and sang lustily while he sat mute. It was a stupid mistake to come. Then Reverend Harmon, slim-waisted and narrow-hipped like a rodeo cowboy, gave his sermon on "The Joy of Christian Life."

What both attracted and frightened Jordan was the intensity of his deep, hooded, brown eyes. They looked as though they explored the hidden recesses of his soul. Reverend Harmon talked about his days as a sinner — how empty he felt before being touched by God and how rich his life now was. Jordan would later tell friends that it was God speaking directly to him, letting him know that it was time to become a man, give up his wild ways, and dedicate his life to family, friends, and religion. Jordan accepted God's command and felt at peace with the world..

It was only a few months later, walking home after a bible-study class on the story of Ruth, that Jordan and Ann acknowledged their love for each other. How blessed he was to hear tender words of love from her. They were married in front of the entire congregation on a beautiful spring day, just before her twenty-first birthday.

God had blessed their marriage. Their love had grown stronger and so had their loyalty to each other. She had given him three sons — all now teenagers — each one popular and athletic and religious. And he had a good job as a digester operator in the North Bethany paper mill. Sometimes the guys he worked with teased him about being a "saint," or a "born-again," but Jordan never got angry. "I'm lucky I've been redeemed," he would tell them, smiling because he meant it. He even enjoyed the half-hour drive to and from work each day. It gave him a chance to be alone with his thoughts and to appreciate the natural beauty with which God had graced this area.

Jordan generally worked the early shift. He would leave home about six-thirty, driving west on Route 1 before crossing the Panscott Bridge into Bethany. During the course of his daily journey, the smell of the air would change constantly. As he left New Harbor, he could smell pine and spruce from the nearby woods. As he crossed into Bethany, the air became redolent with seawater. When he reached the southeast corner of North Bethany, he was greeted first by the pungent aroma of farms and livestock. And finally, when he approached the sprawling landscape of the mill, he would smell, faintly at first and then powerfully, the stench of rotten eggs that came from the sulfur discharged by the process of bleaching pulp. Most people found the smell of the mill unpleasant, but Marcon actually enjoyed it. Those sights and smells that he encountered on his way to the mill were the same as those that had greeted his father, who had made a similar trip during the years he worked at a nearby paper mill. Without thinking too much about it, Marcon had always assumed that his sons would someday follow a similar path to their jobs at the mill. It was all-comforting and seemed to be part of God's benevolent plan.

But, as the Bible tells us, life changes quickly. And now heartbreak loomed and occupied his mind. What mostly worried him was Ann. She was always tired. She had lost too much weight, looked gaunt and unhappy. Something was wrong. Their family doctor had referred her to Dr. Manning, an internist at the Portland Medical Center, who had ordered a battery of tests.

"We want to make sure it's not something life-threatening, like cancer," the doctor had explained in a professionally calm voice that made Jordan tremble.

A month ago, Minister Harmon's sermon had been "why trouble comes in bunches," and sure enough, while Jordan was waiting to hear about Ann, a new problem arose. Strike talk spread through the mill like a malignant vapor. How could the guys talk about it so calmly? Peter Gay, a swaggering, godless man, seemed almost eager for a battle "to convince those anti-union sons of bitches who now run Consolidated Paper that we are as tough as they are and just as strong."

Jordan avoided him whenever he could. Thank God for the calmer voices, like Armand Ouelette, who assured him that things would work out. "Why should CP want a strike when they're handing out money and give big bonuses and stock options to the suits that sit up there on their asses? Why would they want to take it away from the people who make their damn paper?" Jordan hoped fervently that Armand was right.

Marcon was not financially prepared for a strike. His savings account was small — tiny, really. His wages barely paid his monthly bills. The boys are God's blessing, but they haven't learned the virtue of frugality, always asking for new things. Jordan hated to say no to them. And he regularly tithed about $350 a month to the Church of the Redeemer. The building committee considered his tithe as money in the bank to help pay for a new youth hall.

Even with his medical insurance intact, if God chose to test them further and Ann had something serious like cancer, Jordan would be pushed to the limit to pay for treatment and medicine. He was not sure what would happen in case of a strike. Do striking workers lose their insurance benefits? He wanted to ask someone but didn't really want to hear the answer. He could be facing financial ruin. His fear deepened as, every day, Ann's beautiful gray streaks in her hair lost their sheen. He prayed nightly for God's help.

Bill Samson had called a meeting for the evening of April 1, just after he and mill manager John Dunsford were to exchange proposals for amending the current collective- bargaining agreement. Marcon dreaded it. The union was seeking a raise and needed improvements. In the past week, a rumor had spread that the company proposals would be "ball busters."

Jordan wished that someone else were president of the local during this critical period. Not that Bill Samson was a bad man, or someone who placed his own interests above that of the membership. But he was not a serious Christian. He was hot-tempered, foul-tongued, and impatient. He lacked the subtlety and class that Jordan would have preferred, which was why he had voted for Gary Sanborn. Of course, he and Bill had been great buddies years ago when they went to bars and got into scrapes together. Back then, Jordan hadn't been afraid of anything. Sometimes he wished he could be like that again. But he was now more responsible, and more cautious.

"What would Jesus do?" Jordan had no idea.

The union hall, once a small rental property, was located off Highway 18 just south of the mill. Bill Samson had persuaded the local executive committee to buy it during the 1982 economic downturn. He had mobilized the skills of the membership to tear down walls and build a good-sized meeting room with an elegant speaker's platform at the far end.

When Marcon arrived around 7:15, the hall was already crowded, but Bill Samson was nowhere to be seen. A hum of animated conversation, punctuated by bursts of nervous laughter, filled the room. Marcon was surprised to see Charles French and Lloyd Sanborn, two machine repairmen who had bragged to him recently that they had never attended a union meeting. They stood by the door looking nervous and awkward, as though their presence at the union hall was accidental, or something they wished to keep secret.

A little before 7:30, Bill Samson arrived. The bright red veins in his neck stood out prominently. Marcon's heart sank. Bill was not bringing good news! Bill marched straight to the north end of the room and slammed several papers on the lectern. His whole face was anger-red. "Listen up," he shouted, and he put his fingers in his mouth and whistled loudly. It took a few seconds, but the crowd of 100 or so gradually fell silent. "The shit has hit the fan! The company proposals are an insult! And they're serious. First, no raise! Not a cent, nada. Second, they want to eliminate Sunday premium pay."

Marcon could feel his stomach muscles contract as though they were making their own protest. He was counting on a raise, and his premium pay for working the thirty-five or so Sundays a year was crucial. Without it, he probably couldn't pay his bills. I've earned that premium by all the times I haven't been able to go to church on Sunday, or haven't been there for my kids — the ball games I missed and the family dinners we didn't have, he thought bitterly.

Samson's voice interrupted Jordan's reverie. "Proposal Two gives the company the right to permanently subcontract out almost all the maintenance work now done by our members." Marcon felt a momentary sense of relief because his job as an electrician was not included. Just as quickly, he felt guilty. Both his brother-in-law and his uncle were in danger of losing their jobs.

An audible groan came from the crowd.

"Wait! I'm not finished," Samson called out. "When I have laid out the whole proposal, we can start talking about how to respond.

"Proposal Three is titled 'Project Flexibility.' It gives the company the right to assign anyone they want to most jobs, regardless of seniority."

Jordan was upset, but confused. He liked being able to exercise seniority rights that he had acquired during his 25 years at the mill. It made him feel "professional," and he liked the extra pay that came from his electrician's classification. "Still," he thought, "maybe they have a point." His mind fought to make the announcement acceptable. "Fewer job titles might give them more flexibility and help production. Perhaps Bill can compromise on that one."

Samson went on. "Proposal Four is to 'modify holiday language to provide for a company option to work on December 24 and 25.' In plain English — no more Christmas holiday."

Marcon's temper flared. How dare they! Christmas Eve was the only time he could count on going to church, and Christmas Day was the only day he could be assured of spending with his family. They must be cruel and thoughtless people to want to take away his Christmas. This can't be right.

Samson faced the crowd, feet apart, hands on hips, chest thrust forward. "Nice, huh? No increase, and major givebacks. We need to prepare for a strike."

"Send Dunsford a telegram: 'Fuck you, strong letter to follow,'" Jack Caret called out, and the room erupted in cheers. Jordan Marcon didn't like Caret's language, but he joined in the applause. He fantasized rising and stating firmly, "I pledge to strike until CP gives in, no matter how long it takes." The crowd would cheer.

But he was also terrified. He didn't want to strike; he didn't want to risk his job. He wanted to protect his family and keep his lifestyle. Forcing his breathing to slow, he tried to imagine concessions that the union could make to reach an agreement. But he knew that the union could not accept CP's proposals and keep the loyalty of its members.

As the seriousness of the situation sank in, the members became less boisterous and more businesslike. They elected a new local negotiating committee, consisting of Bill, Cindy Regan, Eric Miller, and Local 34 vice presidents Emil Jean and Tony Lucelli to accompany George Connerton, the national union's representative. Connerton, who came up through the ranks and was president of the state's largest paper mill local in the 1950s and '60s, could be counted on when things got rough.

At Bill's suggestion, Eric Miller was chosen as overall picket-line captain. Jordan voted for him, but it was not an easy decision. Eric had a well-earned reputation as a hot-head who sometimes let his temper outweigh his better judgment. Marcon voted for him anyway because he admired Eric's toughness. Nobody could scare Eric. A third-generation papermaker whose brother had preceded him into the mill, Eric had flown helicopter rescue missions in Viet Nam, won the Distinguished Flying Cross for saving his navigator's life, and wore his medals at parades and Fourth of July celebrations. Sometimes he reminded Jordan of the way he was himself before he got religion and had a family.

Finally, a new "unity" executive committee was elected that included the officers of the union, Gary Sanborn, who had opposed Bill in the election, and a few newcomers like Cindy Regan, who was known to be smart and independent. Marcon voted for all of them.

It was almost 9 p.m. when Marcon pulled into his driveway. He turned off the key and sat in his car, exhausted and depressed. What if there was a strike? What would happen to his family's health benefits? They would be crucial if Ann did indeed have cancer. "Surely the Lord won't add that to my burdens. My load is as heavy now as I can bear."

When Jordan opened the front door, he could see Ann in the kitchen waiting for him. She rose to her feet and came to the door to greet him, looking thin and tired, a far cry from the beautiful, rosy-cheeked girl he had accidentally bumped into almost a quarter century ago.

"Well, how's it look?"

"Not very good. Bill read CP's proposals to us. Very tough. Everyone thinks they want us to strike. I don't know why. CP's making record profits. But you and I have to be ready for a long period of testing. We have to stop spending and live as cheaply as possible." He hung up his jacket and spoke softly to the wall. "I could even lose my job."

"Oh, no, Jordan, don't think like that. The good Lord provides for His own." She placed her hand on his shoulder and patted him.

"Let's pray," he said suddenly.

She smiled and nodded. They went into the living room and knelt on the soft carpet together. "Lord, protect thy humble servants, and permit me and Ann to face whatever burdens we encounter during our coming period of trial and pain."

"Amen," they said in unison.

His life had already changed. From that night, in every one of his daily prayers, Marcon now asked the Lord to "soften the hearts of those who control CP and give wisdom to the leaders of our union."

Chapter 4

When George Connerton of the national union's staff agreed to postpone his retirement to continue as Local 34's chief negotiator, Bill Samson, not usually given to overt displays of physical affection with men, threw his arms around Connerton and clapped him on the back. He could barely restrain the impulse to kiss him.

"If George Connerton can't get those bastards to accept a fair agreement, nobody can," Bill told Emil Jean. What he knew about the intricacies of collective bargaining he had learned sitting at Connerton's side during the previous two negotiations. Watching Connerton's cool, professional bargaining style had been both inspiring and humbling. He's an up-from-the-ranks guy just like me, but he never loses his cool and he don't take crap from anyone. They can't bullshit him with big words.

Bill smiled, recalling the time a management lawyer had solemnly informed Connerton that "Under Section 8 (a) (5) of the National Labor Relations Act, your proposal is not a mandatory topic of bargaining." He had later described the incident to Emil. "George sits there calm as can be, like a guy ordering coffee, and says "So what?" The lawyer looks surprised, and angry too. Then he starts laughing, like it was the funniest thing he's ever heard. Then everyone starts to laugh, and before I can figure out what was so funny, we're shaking hands, and the agreement is sealed. But it was more than humor and toughness. He's a genius at listening. He always hears what they say, and he hears what they don't say, too! God, I wish I could do that."

Connerton's looks hid his intellect. His close-cropped brown hair, broad irregular nose, and narrow, flitting, gray eyes crowned with more scar tissue than eyebrow, made it easy to recognize that he had been a brawler and a professional boxer. It always surprised people to learn that he was also a reader, a thinker, a person knowledgeable about law, politics, and labor history. It was Bill who had bestowed on Connerton the nickname "Goodman," mainly as a teasing reference to Connerton's favorite compliment, "Good man yourself," an Irish expression he got from his father.

Bill owed Connerton big time for lots of things, but especially for defeating Gary Sanborn's crazy scheme for Local 34 to disaffiliate from the national union. A lot of guys really loved the idea. Bill was forced to call a general meeting to consider it. Sanborn's argument was simple. The local was paying out more in dues to the national than the worth of what it was getting in return. "The damn slow-thinking, slow-ass southern locals are like an anchor holding us back," he announced. "But if we were on our own, we could take off like a Maine eagle." The guys cheered.

Bill was so disgusted, he shouted: "That's a crock of shit!"

Gary looked at him as though Bill were a not-too-bright first grader. "Tell me one thing we get from the national union that we couldn't get better and cheaper on our own."

Bill's mind went blank. Legal advice? Too rare. Leadership training? Too few guys. What do we get from the national that the guys care about? Then he smiled. "George Goodman Connerton. He's the best negotiator in the whole damn country, and anyone who has ever been at the bargaining table with him knows it. He's a national rep."

Gary was taken aback, but only briefly. "We can hire him ourselves," he argued. Bill could see looks of confusion in the audience. But he had a simple solution. "He's right here. Ask him."

Connerton, to avoid calling attention to himself, had been sitting in the last row of the Civic Center auditorium. But when the members started chanting in cadence "Good-man Conner-TON, Good-man Conner-TON," he sprang to his feet like a boxer answering the bell and walked, bouncing lightly on the balls of his feet and swinging his arms, to one of the aisle mikes. His speech was short. "I've been a union man since I was a kid of fifteen and worked as a laborer. What I learned from my father is that union means solidarity with other workers — all workers — not just the people in your own local. If you vote to separate this local from other paperworkers because you think you're better than them, you won't be acting like a union. You'll be acting like a damn country club, and you can get yourself another negotiator." The hall erupted in cheers, and the proposal to leave the national union was dead.

Bill knew that almost a year ago Connerton had purchased tickets for a trip to Ireland for himself and his wife Kathryn, a trip timed to coincide with her 60th birthday. He had reluctantly postponed it to handle the negotiations. Over beers at the Anchor Pub, he told Bill that he was furious at himself and at the "damn union" for disappointing Kathryn again.

Connerton paused and looked down at his glass: "I even had a dream the other night about meeting my Uncle Timothy at a party. He looked young and happy, and he spoke in Gaelic. I couldn't understand what he said, but I knew he was welcoming us. And when he finished, everyone applauded. Then I woke up and realized it was a dream. I felt like a kid who just learned there's no Santa Claus. But like I told Katie, I can't quit now. The guys who have paid my salary with their dues for all these years need me right now more than they ever have before."

Bill wanted to say something to make Connerton feel better. "You're a good man yourself, George Connerton," was the best he could do.

For the last few weeks Bill and Connerton had been meeting regularly. Bill had lots of questions, but Connerton's answers did little to cheer him up.

"You think they want us to strike?" Bill asked.

"Can't tell. Wait till we've been at the bargaining table a few times."

"Are the guys ready to strike?"

"Not now." Connerton replied. "They're angry as hell. They know about Watts' salary and stock options, but they're scared. Lots of them are in debt. They don't want to lose their paycheck. And they still love Consolidated Paper. Tom Gillian's treated us fairly."

"You think he's still calling the shots?"

"Hard to tell. But from what I know about Watts, I'd guess that Gillian is on a much shorter leash than he's used to."

"What do we need to do?"

"Billy, you're the key. Not to the negotiations at the table. I can handle that. But to the solidarity of the members. If the guys are united, CP will know it, and maybe they'll think twice about pushing us to the wall. The rank and file needs to have confidence in the leadership. So if you're scared you can't let them know."

Bill's stomach clutched. He must have me confused with Vince Lombardi or Ronald Reagan? His throat felt as though a small baseball was lodged at its top. Maybe he was sick? No who was he kidding? He was scared as a schoolboy waiting in the principle's office. Maybe they could avoid a strike. If CP was willing to bargain in good faith the union would meet them half way and they would arrive at a new agreement.

On Wednesday, April 7th, 1989, negotiations between Local 34 and Consolidated Paper Company began at the Holiday Inn in Bethany, a tourist town separated by both a short strip of farmland and a way of life from North Bethany. Bethany was a tourist town bordering Panscott Bay, a well-to-do community with a large summer population made up of people from New York, Massachusetts, and Connecticut. Its houses and stores were bunched together near the shoreline, but, up in the hills, the homes were widely separated, with large picture windows looking down on the breaking waves of Panscott Bay. It was in the Bethany Hills that the mill executives, well-to-do professionals, and successful merchants lived. On Shore Road alongside the bay were expensive seafood restaurants, antique shops, bookstores, and art galleries. Bill never thought of Bethany as a real town. It did not produce anything. In the summer it was filled with people who did not know each other. It was empty in the winter when its elegant shops were closed.

North Bethany was an old fashioned mill town. Almost everyone was connected in one way or another with the paper mill. It had changed very little since the small housing boom of the late 1940s and early '50s when its modest colonial-style homes were built. Most of the stores were family owned. They were concentrated in the four block "downtown" area on the town's East Side — the only part of town that had sidewalks. The downtown also contained the town's one movie theatre, the Princess, which since 1982 opened only on weekends. The residential areas were spread out along winding roads that intersected at odd angles. The most impressive building in town was the civic center, built in 1972 on the site of an abandoned Quaker meeting house on the town's eastern boundary. Consolidated Paper Company had donated the funds for the renovation, and it had, after consultation with the union, hired a well-known Maine artist to paint a large mural on the rear wall of the auditorium showing various stages in the process of making paper. At the center's opening ceremony, the president of Consolidated Paper Company had announced to a cheering crowd that the civic center exemplified the mutual respect between Consolidated Paper and its workers.

The Bethany Commander Hotel, in which the negotiators met, was a newly built structure with a rooftop restaurant and balcony suites overlooking the water. It was flanked by expensive antique shops — on one side was "Exotic Imports," its carefully arranged display windows filled with vases and statues from Asia, Africa, and other far-away places once visited by Maine's seafarers. "William Adams Antiques & Collectibles" was on the other side, the front window arranged to resemble the kitchen of a nineteenth-century Maine farmhouse. It was a scene that might have been depicted by Norman Rockwell: old coffee urns, bread trays, and silverware set on rustic pine tables — all at prices that would have stunned the original owners.

A light rain was falling from a gray overcast sky when the union team arrived, but the air smelled sweetly of spring and early budding flowers. At Connerton's instructions, the union negotiators met at 8 at the coffee shop to eat breakfast and discuss bargaining strategy. It was as good a team as Bill could have wanted. Each member was an experienced papermaker, and each had a following within the local. Any contract that they agreed to was almost sure to be ratified by the membership. If they failed to agree and sought a strike vote, it would be overwhelmingly approved.

Sitting across from Bill, wearing his horn-rimmed reading glasses and gravely examining the competing proposals, was the local's vice president, Emil Jean. Emil, trim, light-complected, with smooth, round cheeks, and almond-shaped eyes, was a college graduate. He was, as usual, the most professional-looking in the group wearing a light brown suit and striped tie. No one who didn't know him would guess that he was either French Canadian or a paperworker. He represented the skilled workers, who had responsibility for maintaining and repairing the complex machinery with which paper was made. He was popular with the members. The majority liked his professional manner and trusted his judgment. Some of the skilled workers had urged him to run for president of the local. He had thought about it seriously before the most recent election but decided instead, to run for re-election as vice president. He was unopposed.

Like Bill, Emil was a self-proclaimed company man. Unlike Bill he was something of a dandy who regularly urged Bill to dress more professionally.

"Bill, you're our president. You owe it to our members to look as professional as possible."

Bill never seriously considered it. "We're papermakers, not fucking lawyers. What's wrong with looking like who you are?"

By Bill's choice, Emil was not part of the group that took him to the Anchor.

On Connerton's left was Eric Miller, slope shouldered and muscular, who worked in the boiler room and was added to the committee to placate the "radicals" — so-called not because of their political views (like Bill, he had voted for Reagan against Carter) but because of their determination to strike rather than grant concessions. Bill liked Eric. Everyone did. He was tough, generous, honest, and as loyal a friend as anyone could ever want. He was also a hot-head, too prone to battle, whom Bill sometimes needed to restrain.

On Bill's right, wearing a bright blue denim shirt, was Tony Lucelli, who represented the workers in the pulp mill. With his prominent, well-shaped nose, deep-set, dark eyes, and long, thick, almost circular, eyelashes, he was the handsomest of the union's members. Tony was also the only political leftist on the union's executive committee. He regularly suspected top company management of dishonesty, claimed that cooperative labor management programs were sell-outs, and subscribed to *Labor Notes* — a radical labor newspaper. He liked to tell stories about his great uncle Vittorio, an anarchist who had distributed leaflets with Sacco and had drunk wine with Vanzetti, on whose behalf he had marched, signed petitions, and wrote angry letters to the president and the governor in a futile effort to stop their executions. He was a decorated Viet Nam veteran who immediately after his discharge joined Viet Nam Veterans for Peace and never set foot in the Legion Hall.. Nobody agreed with him but everyone in the union liked him. And he was such a good worker and such a friendly person that his supervisors felt themselves blessed.

Bill thought it strange. How can a good guy like Tony be a radical? Labor radicals were assholes, always trying to stir up trouble. But Bill finally concluded that Tony wasn't a real radical. He just had a big heart.

Across the table from Bill was Cindy Reagan, the only one of the 20 women production workers in the mill who was active in the union. She was an attractive, wide-eyed woman in her mid-thirties who wore her hair piled high on her head and regularly came to work wearing tight, colorful clothes. The guys got a kick out of her earthy language and her quick wit. She was the local's recording secretary, elected to the post initially because the union's national leadership had told Bill that an executive committee of all white males could create legal troubles for the union. There was a lot of hard feeling and talk of reverse discrimination after she was elected for the first time. But that was long past. No one ran against her in the most recent election, and Gary Sanborn, one of her early opponents, had made a point of praising her dedication and competence.

Bill wasn't sure how tough CP meant to be. Tom Gillian was a fair guy and remained CP's Director of Labor Relations. CP was making record profits. As Bill told the guys, everyone would be better off if they settled. "Even Watts has to understand that Tom Gillian knows a hundred times more about labor relations than he does. Tom will convince him to be reasonable, and we'll reach a fair agreement like we always have."

Emil nodded approvingly. Tony shook his head sadly in disbelief.

Cindy Reagan laughed. "Billy, you're too old to be such a romantic. Consolidated Paper and Tom Gillian are getting ready to break your heart." Her tone was serious but her expression remained friendly, her smile warm and inviting. Bill enjoyed flirting with her even though he knew that she was happily married. Flirting with sexy women was something he did as a matter of course.

"Cindy, give me a chance and I'll show you how romantic I can be. Hey, when the meeting ends, we can go straight from here to the Pines Motel. I hear they have a great honeymoon bedroom. We could rent it for an hour."

Cindy tried to look appalled. "Billy, you're a lawsuit waiting to happen. In case the news hasn't hit Maine yet, sexual harassment is illegal." She leaned forward, giving him a view of her lacy bra. "Besides, I don't do anything that quick. I just start to warm up in an hour if I'm with a real man."

She got a huge laugh. I guess everyone is as nervous as me, Bill thought when things quieted down.

Connerton reminded the team to keep their emotions in check, not to look too eager for agreement, and not to act too upset by company statements. "Our main goal for the first day is to find out whether CP wants an agreement. Are they willing to compromise on their proposals?"

Bill nodded his head firmly. He would resemble one of the guards he saw years ago at Buckingham Palace. He knew how to conceal his emotions. A challenge to his self-control of a different sort, however, soon presented itself when he noticed their waitress approaching with a large pot of coffee. *Wow! I didn't know that Farrah Fawcett had moved to Bethany. Her face, with large, soulful, almond-shaped eyes, would melt the heart of a statue. And her long, shapely legs and milk-white breasts that rose majestically from her blouse — the top buttons of which were opened — would cause it to pant with longing.* George Connerton was saying something — perhaps something important — about the negotiations, but Bill had no idea what. *She's smiling like she knows me. Might as well smile back. God, she's lovely.*

"You probably don't remember me. I'm Sherry Meserve, Maurice Meserve's daughter."

Maurice Meserve. Sure, a good guy, a strong union man and a good worker who had retired about five years ago after mangling his index finger in a wood yard accident. I don't remember a daughter. I must be getting old to forget someone this beautiful, he thought.

"I was just a sophomore in high school when we met," she said in an explanatory tone, well aware that few men who met her these days would forget her. She smiled again and took a deep breath, her breasts pushed against her blouse. *I'm just like Jimmy Carter,* Bill thought, *lust in my heart.* The thought of the former president admitting to the press — "I have lusted in my heart but not with my body" — tickled him. *Who hadn't?* His mind turned to Shirley and her small, wiry body that he lusted after in his heart and with his body. He would have a drink with her when he got home. He'd even tell her about Sherry. Then they would make love. After lovemaking, she would lie on her side, her body curved so that her rump pressed against him. He would kiss her shoulder and whisper sexy words into her ear — outrageous things that she later said were "awful" but that he knew turned her on. Bill was in love with her, no doubt about it, even if he continued to have brief affairs with other women — they weren't even affairs, just secret meetings with sex. As union president and town selectman, he had too many opportunities for any real man to turn them all down.

Bill was drawn back to reality by the sound of Eric Miller sucking in his breath in awe. "Sherry Meserve," he said in a voice that conveyed both surprise and delight. "When you were in junior high school, you used to babysit my son, Ric."

"Oh, Mr. Miller, I didn't recognize you. You look so young and so distinguished wearing a tie. You were always one of my favorite parents."

Eric's eyes obviously traced the lines of her figure. "You were a girl then. Now you're a beautiful woman. I won't mind too much if we have to keep coming back here."

Sherry blushed, her face becoming more animated and even more beautiful. Eric beamed. His intense pilot's eyes focused on Sherry's face as though she were first prize in a lottery he had just won.

Sherry poured them another round of coffee and then patted Bill softly on the shoulder. "We're all counting on you."

Bill sighed. "So damn many people are depending on us, and we don't know if we can protect them." The others nodded solemnly.

Just before nine, Connerton paid the check, and the negotiating team walked to the meeting room, passing a row of reporters with cameras flashing and microphones at the ready. Following tradition, they ignored the shouted questions from the reporters and filed inside, seating themselves around the large oak table with Connerton at the center, flanked by Bill and Emil.

The company negotiating team had not yet arrived.

Chapter 5

By 9:30 Bill was seething with anger. He rose to his feet and started gathering his papers. "They're treating us like we're unimportant. Making us wait. What a childish damn trick. We'd be fools to sit here like a bunch of sheep. Let's walk the hell out of here. What a bunch of fucking…."

Connerton raised his hand dismissively. "There'll be plenty of time for us to show how tough we can be. As long as we're here, let's go over the company's proposals and our final positions." Bill put his papers back on the table and sat down. As he did so, the door opened and the three-person management team entered the room. Led by M.L. LeBlanc

It was an insult, that's what it was. Mel LeBlanc! Son of Bitch! raised in North Bethany and left as soon as he could. I remember when he worked at the mill. Tight ass. All the time scheming. When they made him a supervisor he acted like a prison guard. Everyone hated him. That's why they had to move him. Bad enough they brought him back, but to have that slimy bastard as chief negotiator. I can't believe it. Can't show how much I hate him. I promised George to stay cool.

LeBlanc's face was flushed with excitement, but his eyes flitted from person to person on the union team with little indication of recognition. A self-satisfied smile that he did not try to hide played about his lips. The other members of the management team were Jack Dunsford, the mill's general manager, and Edward White, Director of Human Resources.

Tentative handshakes all round, faces glum — a far cry from the friendly joking that served as a preliminary to negotiations in past years. Dunsford and White smiled emptily to the union contingent and took their seats. Bill unfolded his copies of the bargaining proposals and looked out the window at the dark, menacing rain clouds. He wondered whether his anger was apparent. He turned his eyes back to the management team and noticed the sneering look on LeBlanc's face. That same sneer was visible when, many years ago, after a fruitless grievance negotiation, LeBlanc had asked him if he knew why the Black paperworkers were located in the South while the French Canadians were in the North. Bill admitted he didn't know. LeBlanc's sneer became more loathsome. "It's because the South had first choice."

Bill didn't know why the story had bothered him. French Canadians often laughed at themselves. He himself had joked about French Canadians at family gatherings. Was it the sneer that made LeBlanc's joke different? No, it was the nastiness. Just like him to tell a joke that insults everyone, Bill thought. And now he's in a position where I have to pay attention to the son of a bitch. Thank God for George!

The negotiation turned out to be worse than Bill or any of the union negotiators expected. Connerton later described it as the most humiliating negotiating session of his career. "I kept probing to see if some compromise was possible. I offered to accept Operation Flexibility if the union were given a role in administering it. Not interested. I proposed to tie wage increases to productivity. He didn't even give me the courtesy of a reply. Twenty minutes into the negotiation and he was daring me, to my face, to strike. I had to hold myself back. Otherwise I would have grabbed him by the throat." The wrinkles around his eyes had become more pronounced.

For once, Bill got no pleasure watching Connerton negotiate. He was like a man trying to pet a snarling dog.

Leblanc did not even try to win them over. It was all about power. "Your members will have to work Sunday. Big deal. People all over Maine work on Sunday and for a lot less. If I put an ad in the paper, I could get thousands of people to work at the wages your people get, without Sunday premium pay."

Connerton tried a novel approach — one that he had carefully planned. He asked LeBlanc what percentage of profit on investment he thought adequate for the company's needs. LeBlanc had heard Eastman state that the company needed to try for an annual return of 15% on investment. "We gotta have at least 15%."

Connerton was ready. "Suppose we put into the agreement that if profit at the mill falls below 15%, the union will make some of the concessions that you are seeking."

A few seconds of silence before LeBlanc's supercilious sneer returned. "George, you don't get it. These are our proposals now, and these will be our proposals whenever the negotiations end. You're not going to get any big concessions from me. Mr. Watts needs the resources to get the company going again."

Tony Lucelli couldn't restrain himself. "If Mr. Watts thinks the company needs money, why doesn't he donate some of his five million dollar fucking salary?"

"Mr. Watts' salary is not your concern," LeBlanc snapped, turning his angry face to Tony. He quickly shifted his attention back to Connerton. "Let me make it clear and simple. You need an agreement. The company doesn't. I can replace your people within a week if I have to."

Connerton took a deep breath and turned his gaze toward the window, looking out at Panscott Bay. Bill followed his gaze and noticed that the sun had come out. The air was bright and clear, the sky a stunning blue. He could see a gull swooping gracefully towards the water, which glittered with reflected sunlight. Directly ahead, Bill watched a large sailboat floating effortlessly out to sea. A middle-aged couple lounged on the deck. He thought about the trip to Ireland that Connerton was giving up in order to be in this room, the target of LeBlanc's taunting. He turned his gaze back to LeBlanc who seemed to be smirking at Connerton

"God damn it, you miserable prick. George Connerton gave up his trip to Ireland to help us reach an agreement, and you don't even have the decency to treat him with respect." Bill leaned forward, his fists clenched. LeBlanc recoiled, for a moment, as though he were avoiding a blow. But he quickly recovered his composure and turned towards Connerton.

"George, haven't you explained the rules of collective bargaining to your assistants? Bill Samson hasn't gotten any smarter over the years, has he?"

Bill lost all control. He awkwardly grabbed for LeBlanc, clutching at his arm. LeBlanc easily avoided him by moving back.

As he righted himself, Bill could see the shocked expressions on the faces of the other management negotiators and Connerton's look of unhappiness. The only person who seemed poised was LeBlanc.

"The meeting is postponed for a week," LeBlanc declared. "You're lucky that I'm in a forgiving mood. Any similar behavior and Mr. Samson is fired permanently and charges will be filed with the Labor Board." He and the other members of the management team gathered up their papers and left.

When the door closed behind them, Bill felt like a prize idiot. He had played into LeBlanc's hands. "George, I must be the stupidest person in the union, and here I am the president. Don't even have the brains to keep quiet."

Connerton walked over and patted Bill on the shoulder. "Hell, Bill, we weren't making any progress, and in another five minutes I would have probably taken a swing at him myself." Connerton paused and then smiled. "Of course, being Irish and a boxer, I would have flattened the son of a bitch."

The laughter of the team made Bill feel better. Not good, but better.

Bill returned home feeling anxious. He did not want to tell Shirley about his screw up at the negotiations. She doesn't need to know the details, he thought. When he opened the door Shirley was in the kitchen. He could smell the pork roast cooking in the oven. She handed him one of the two gin and tonics she had prepared and took the other for herself. Cheese and crackers were set out on the coffee table in the living room.

"How did it go?" she asked as soon as he sat down.

"Not good."

"How not good? Will you have to strike?"

"It's not clear. We've just begun negotiating but we need to get prepared."

He had to press his lips tightly to keep them from trembling.

Why isn't he acting angry, she wondered. No curses, no details of any kind. Maybe I should just let him be. No, there's something he needs to get off his chest.

"Who was the chief negotiator for the company?" She had heard the rumor that it was going to be someone local this year and not Tom Gillian or one of his assistants as had been the case in the past.

"Mel fucking Leblanc."

"Oh that's terrible. Did he negotiate in good faith?"

"Are you kidding? He wouldn't know good faith if it bit him in the ass."

"That must have been terrible for George…and for you."

"Worse than terrible. Here's George, calm and reasonable, making lots of good arguments about what was wrong with their proposals, and that little prick just sat there, practically laughing in our faces. He's still got that 'fuck you' sneer that made the guys call him The Joker. All I could think was how I'd like to wipe that look from his face. I don't know how George was able to stay so calm. I acted like an idiot. Tried to grab the son of a bitch by the throat. I missed him and he cancelled negotiations for a week. Said if I try something like that again he'll file charges. The worst thing is, he can do it. I feel like an idiot."

Shirley stood up and walked to the other side of the table where he sat looking wretched. "Don't beat yourself up. You're a good man, and you're fighting for your people."

He put his arms around her, and suddenly, before he knew what was happening, he began to weep.

Chapter 6

On April 5, Bill drove to Augusta to meet with Ed Makum, president of the state AFL-CIO, at its headquarters in a once-fashionable office building that now housed mainly marginal businesses, small-time lawyers, and aging dentists. He was looking for help. The union's national president had authorized him to hire an additional organizer to help prepare members for the upcoming battle with CP. Connerton was too busy with negotiations to do the job himself.

Makum, once secretary-treasurer of the Carpenters Union, was a charmer, a shrewd observer with a great supply of stories. Bill got right to the point. "Ed, I think we are going to strike. I need a good organizer to help get us ready."

Makum looked doubtful for a few seconds, but suddenly his small, quick gray eyes lit up. "Billy, I may have just the guy for you. His name is Don Foreman, and he's an old-fashioned labor agitator who happens to be looking for a job."

"Who's Don Foreman? I never even heard of the guy."

A look of troubled candor replaced Makum's customary expression of professional cheerfulness. "Foreman's a piece of work. I think he's an organizational genius, but he can also be a political nightmare. He's a radical — you know the type — shows up without being invited at open meetings, asks lots of questions, and makes lots of suggestions."

Bill was doubtful. "Does he know what he's talking about?"

"A lot of his ideas are risky. Some are wild, but some are damn good, the kind of ideas that make you wonder why nobody else thought of them. He's got imagination and cojones the size of basketballs." Makum laughed. "He doesn't think too highly of guys like me. Told me to my face that I'm too busy protecting my job." Makum laughed again. He tugged at the corner of his sports jacket. "He's probably right, and no one else around here is willing to tell me.

"I hired him to help out with the Converse strike because our guys were getting their asses kicked and we were out of ideas. He changed things fast. Organized the local into teams, called them 'truth squads,' sent them out around the state, even used wives and kids. They got a lot of great publicity, and when reporters asked them why they were striking, he had them ready with 'fact sheets' that told how much profit Converse was making and how much they were paying their top execs. After a few months Converse came to us, and we worked out a settlement."

Makum poured out two cups of coffee and handed one to Bill. "A lot of my people don't like him. I understand why. He has this 'I-Know-Everything' style that up-from-the-ranks guys like us hate. Sometimes he lectures me like I'm a school kid and he's the teacher. He's a left-winger and a self-declared expert on everything. But he's almost as good as he thinks he is, and that makes him pretty damn good."

Bill sat silently for a while. This didn't feel right. Why would someone as sharp as Ed Makum support hiring a radical? Troublemakers, that's what they are. Always causing dissension and stirring up workers against management. Of course, his guys were stirred up already, and Makum made him sound like a guy with ideas. Organizers like that were in short supply. "Eddie, I don't like left-wingers. I'm an old fashioned, try-to-get-along-with-management guy — usually. But right now I'm pissed, and my members are pissed. I don't care if he's left-wing, right-wing, or chicken-wing. If he can help us, I want him. These goddam negotiations are going nowhere quick."

Makum smiled, then put his hand on Bill's shoulder sympathetically. "Don't worry, Billy. Your negotiations can't be tougher than the ship-builders' negotiation at Bath Iron Works. That one was really a war. The caucus sessions got so angry that Gary Bickford, the local's chief negotiator, collapsed right at the bargaining table. Stared straight at the damn management lawyer and then fell over — heart attack." Makum's face was grave. "When Bickford woke up the next morning, he was in a hospital bed. The first thing he saw was a big vase of flowers. He went over to read the note. It said 'Wishing you a quick and speedy recovery.' The Negotiating Committee, by a four-to-three vote.'"

Bill burst out laughing. Makum slapped his knee and smiled cheerfully as though he was looking forward to the next stage of the struggle, which was sure to be filled with more stories for his retelling. But soon Makum's expression became serious again. "I have a feeling Foreman'll do a good job for you. Why don't you talk to him? You can meet him and decide after if you want to hire him."

Bill drove home, using the quiet ride to think about Don Foreman. He wavered back and forth, and then decided to interview Foreman the following Monday. He thought he'd ask both Emil Jean and Tony Lucelli to join him. If he hits it off with them both, I'll know he's the right guy.

That night Bill called Tony and asked him what he had heard about Foreman's work during the Converse strike. Tony had been enthusiastic but not specific.

"The guys I hung out with at Converse thought he was great. Said he gave them a whole new idea of what unions could be. But I don't know if everyone agreed. He made some enemies at first, but by the end of the strike they say he could have been elected local president. He may be just the guy to turn this local into a fighting outfit."

Bill blinked. He didn't want a rival who'd change the local, just someone who would take orders and help him.

Maybe I'm being an asshole. If he's as good as Tony thinks, we'll be lucky to get him.

He also met with Emil at the union hall. He had not heard of Foreman, but when Bill described him, Emil's nostrils flared, as though he smelled something unpleasant.

On Monday morning, at 7:30 a.m., a tall, slim, intense-looking man with dark, curly hair and a full beard was waiting at the union hall when they arrived. Wearing sandals and "Workers Unite!" t-shirt, Don Foreman reminded Bill of the Viet Nam war protesters who used to wave banners and chant slogans outside the recruitment center in Portland. It was not a pleasant memory. Bill, a Korean War veteran, still bristled at their attitude of moral superiority as though old-fashioned patriotism and willingness to serve were something to look down on. Those damn grubby-looking, self-important assholes.

Bill could tell that Emil's reaction was also negative. I should just thank him, tell him we have decided to stick with our own people, and send him home. But Ed Makum had recommended Don. Shit, Ed doesn't like radicals any better than I do.

Don seemed oblivious to Bill's reservations and Emil's hostility. He smiled broadly and extended his arm. They all shook hands. Firm handshake, Bill realized. A tiny circle of lines radiated from the corners of Don's eyes. He's not a kid, must be over forty. Bill poured coffee and ushered Don to the small president's office in the back of the hall.

"Ed Makum tells me that you are a good organizer."

"I like to think strategically. There are strategies that can turn a typical business union into a fighting force. It's not that hard once you get the hang of it."

Bill wondered what changes Don had in mind for Local 34. "How did you learn about organizing?"

"I started in the civil rights movement, organizing voting drives in the '60s. Then I did political organizing for Democrats — community organizing for Common Cause and the Clamshell Alliance. But when I got a chance to work with unions, I jumped at it. I always believed that unions were more important than do-good liberal groups. I learned that from my parents. They were union organizers back when it was tougher to organize than it is now."

Emil's expression remained hostile. "Have you ever had to do real factory work for a living — not as an organizer but as a rank-and-file worker?"

Don laughed. "Good question. I wouldn't trust an organizer who never worked. I've earned my own money since I was 17. I worked as a carpenter's assistant in Lewiston while I was in college, then I worked as a plumber in Canada. When I came back to the States, I worked for two years at Mellon Paints, where I was a trimmer. Then I worked union at Bath Iron Works. I was shop steward before they fired me."

Bill relaxed. He's a worker, not a damned student radical. He asked something that was really bothering him. "Don, what's gone wrong? In the old days, management was afraid of strikes. Now we are."

Foreman sat down and immediately stood up again. "That's a good question, Bill, and the answer is complicated."

Bill suppressed a smile. Makum was right about one thing. The guy likes to lecture.

Foreman raised his index finger "First off, management is better organized. Second, the law is against us." Bill nodded in complete agreement. Foreman, now holding up three fingers, continued. His tone became more emphatic. "Third and most important of all, unions don't use their members right. A lot of union officers are afraid of their own members. They don't realize that mobilizing the rank-and-file membership has always been the key to union success. It wasn't leadership, but membership, that made unions strong in the '40s and '50s. We all need to remember that. Think of the sitdown strikes in the auto industry and the mass picketing in steel."

Emil shook his head. "Our rank and file don't know about strikes, and the last thing they want to do is take on CP. What unions need today is professional leadership, not anarchy." He set his lips firmly, as though Don's mistake should now be evident.

Bill thought there was much to Emil's point. I wonder if Foreman ever tried to involve guys who earn good money, work lots of overtime, and want to spend their free time enjoying themselves.

Foreman sighed audibly. "Look, I realize you guys don't know me, but I can help you win a strike against CP. I'm a damn good organizer. Just let me hang around for awhile. I'll talk to your people, I'll learn about the issues. I'll get people involved, and I'll develop a strike plan." Turning to Bill, he said: "Strikes are different today. You don't win them at the picket line. To win, we — you — need to put pressure on CP, and you need allies. We're in Maine. Maine is filled with environmentalists. If we can get their support, CP might have to explain their record of polluting the water and fouling the air."

Bill took a long, slow gulp of his coffee and smiled. The environmentalists! Obvious, now that Foreman mentioned them. He placed his coffee cup on his desk. "Give us a few minutes alone, Don. This whole business is new to us, and Emil and Tony and me need to talk about it."

Don walked outside to the pebbled parking area in front of the small A-frame house that served as Local 34's union hall, where he began pacing impatiently back and forth.

Bill wondered if Emil had been won over. He turned to face him. "I know he's got Tony's vote. But what about you? It's your choice too."

Emil's expression was unyielding. "I say get rid of him. He's gonna be more trouble than help. He's too sure of himself and too radical. I know he's done work, but he's not a real worker, not like us. Work is our life. His life is being an agitator and causing trouble."

Tony's eyes shone fiercely. "Damn, Emil, that's dumb. It's agitators like him that made the labor movement great in the '30s. We're lucky to have a guy like him to ready to help us. If we don't hire him, we'll be sorry."

"If we do, we'll live to regret it. He's the kind of guy that works people up. Some of our members will do something stupid because of him. He'll get us all in trouble, and when we've lost because of him, Foreman will just walk away."

Bill's face showed his indecision. "I sure wish it was unanimous, and I damn sure wish I was more certain." He pulled on his lip for a few moments then brought his hand down firmly onto his desk. "We need to go for it, take a chance and hire him."

Tony nodded happily, but Emil's cheeks reddened as though Bill had struck him. "Mark my words. He'll get everyone stirred up, and we'll pay for it." Emil walked out the side door to avoid being part of the group that welcomed Don to his new position.

During the next few weeks, Bill recognized that Don had several key virtues that he himself lacked. He was sure of himself and was a model of organization, kept careful notes of his responsibilities, and never failed to do what he promised to do. Don also had a knack for spotting abilities in others. When he learned that Cindy Regan's hobby was making comic strips for her kids, he quickly enlisted her skill as a caricaturist in adorning picket signs. He read something that Jill Carter wrote, decided that she had a way with words, and got her to serve on the media committee. Don had lots of ways of relating to the members. He could talk slants and belly plays with the football fans, and he could speak knowledgeably about angles and joints with the construction workers.

Don also had a way of making enemies needlessly. Sometimes his New York roots showed. He was not patient like most people from North Bethany. He wanted everything done immediately and was far from understanding when his deadlines were not met. He was feisty and demanding. Once, when a local bank teller refused to cash his government check, Don got furious, berating her for her "small-town bureaucratic" approach. She made the mistake of telling him the rule was for "your protection."

"My protection!" Don yelled. "How can it be for my protection to not give me my money? Are you trying to be dumb, or does it just come naturally?"

He apologized.

Emil Jean's initial distrust of Don grew stronger. He insisted that Don was an impractical dreamer. "He's like Ralph Kramden on the Honeymooners. Full of big ideas that will never work!"

"He sure did a great job for the Rubberworkers," Bill answered.

"I know about that strike, Billy. It wasn't him. It was the national union that won the strike by threatening to run a corporate campaign against Converse. And what we need is not to send a bunch of amateurs around New England in a van but to get Jack Elder and the national union to use their clout with CP. Let Jack tell them he won't sign off on any more agreements till we get a decent contract, and they'll come around."

Bill's face tightened. "He won't do it, and if he did, it wouldn't work. These 'amateurs' are our best hope."

"Have it your way," Emil said, "but don't blame me for the trouble he causes."

Chapter 7

Bargaining resumed after a week and continued through the month with the union and management teams getting together at the Commander Hotel two or three times a week. A few minor agreements were reached but no real progress towards a new contract. With each meeting, Bill's emotional state grew more precarious. He was tired all the time, even though he was mainly sitting on his ass. By the end of the day, he felt emotionally and physically exhausted. It was LeBlanc.

"I can't stand the sight of the guy," he told Tony during a break. "His superior sneer, those cold eyes. He reminds me of a fucking undertaker, but it's our funeral he's preparing." Tony laughed. It was an apt description of LeBlanc, who was tall and thin, had a prominent adam's apple, and came to all the bargaining sessions wearing a navy blue suit and a dark tie that he never loosened. The only thing different was that LeBlanc was more aggressive than your typical undertaker — not even a pretense of compassion.

"Bargaining is a matter of power, and we have it," Leblanc announced sneeringly, during one particularly unpleasant negotiating session..

This can't be legal, Bill concluded. LeBlanc must be violating the law.

"Aren't they supposed to bargain in good faith?" he asked Connerton. When Connerton nodded, Bill exploded.

"Well, how can they be in good faith if they don't agree, don't explain, talk to us like we're peasants and try their best to get us to strike?"

"If the law made sense, you'd be right. I'll file charges with the Labor Board this afternoon. But don't expect anything to come of it. CP's probably made enough changes in their proposals to get by."

Bill spat from the gap in his front teeth. "It's all bullshit! They don't want an agreement! And everybody knows it!" Bill was beginning to realize how little protection the law actually gave workers. I'm like a deer in hunting season surrounded by guys with assault rifles.

Minor agreements were reached during the bargaining sessions when mill manager John Dunsford was the company spokesman. Dunsford had been an executive at the mill for almost 20 years, working his way from labor-relations trainee to overall manager. He was a cautious, formal man who wore button-down shirts and striped ties to work and whose statements to the employees were precise and loaded with qualifiers. Bill liked him. He does his job. He's a straight guy who treats us with respect.

Dunsford negotiated with unmistakable earnestness, regularly altering minor aspects of his proposals, offering technical explanations of CP's positions, and listening carefully when George Connerton spoke. "I don't agree, but I'll meet you half way" was his common response to Connerton, and he quickly became known, almost affectionately among the union negotiators, as "Meet you half-way Dunsford." He doesn't want a strike anymore than we do, Bill thought. He's a papermaker like us. But he doesn't have real power. If CP wanted an agreement, he would have been their chief negotiator. But even when Dunsford spoke for the company, the negotiating process served to increase Bill's feeling of inadequacy. He was living in a world of words — hostile, confusing words that seemed to change personality like treacherous humans. He had no ability to control them.

How nice it would be to be back in the mill where everything — wheels, belts, motors, and controls — was understandable and worked in harmony to produce a gleaming, useful product. Bill's mind refused to stay focused on the bargaining. During one meeting, while Connerton and Dunsford discussed conflicting proposals, he found himself estimating how much paper he could have made during the time he sat idly by.

Connerton scoffed at Bill's contention that, if Dunsford were the principal negotiator, an agreement would be easily negotiated. "It's not LeBlanc, it's Eastman's plan that Watts has bought into. If Mother Teresa were on the other side of the table we wouldn't reach a fair agreement. CP's playing good cop, bad cop, using Leblanc to get us angry and Dunsford to protect their legal position."

He's right, Bill thought, but that doesn't make listening to that sneering, look how important I am, son of a bitch any easier. Why would a guy want people in his own community to hate him? I wonder if he has any friends? Each meeting was the same as all the others. Bill would leave the hotel with his head throbbing and his fists clenched.

The hatred he couldn't express at the bargaining table never left him. It erupted at inappropriate moments toward the very people who were trying to help him — friends, supporters, members of Local 34, and their families. One evening, as he sat on the couch watching a ball game on television and grumbling to himself, Shirley came up behind him and gently stroked the back of his head.

"Goddammit! Can't I have any time to myself!" he exploded. As soon as the words were out of his mouth, he felt profoundly embarrassed. What an asshole! But he said nothing.

He even reacted angrily to members who called, asking about the state of negotiations.

"Look, anything important happens, I'll call a meeting. And if you have questions, don't call me at home! Call the union hall!" He knew he was piss-ing people off. If we had another election right now, I'd lose by a landslide. Well, too fucking bad. They're stuck with me. They were stupid to elect me anyway. I'm too old. I'm tired all the time. I don't even care about sex. I know Shirley has to be wondering about me.

Bill hated the very sight of the Commander Hotel . His unhappiness was shared by all the others except for Eric Miller, always the first to arrive and always easy to locate in the coffee shop flirting with Sherry Meserve. Sometimes, when Mel was at his most insulting, Bill would look over and see Eric smiling to himself. Lucky for him, to have someone that lovely to think about. But it damn well better end right there. I need him focused, and I don't need to have every damn member of the Meserve family on my ass.

On Tuesday, just before the strike-vote meeting, Bill and George Connerton left the negotiating session together. "I'm ashamed when I think how I used to respect CP management," Bill said bitterly. "I used to tell everyone that Tommy Gillian was the great white hope. Now I realize he's just like the rest of them — a two-faced, lying, side-stepping, union-bashing son of a bitch."

Connerton shook his head. "No, Bill, he's still a good guy. But he isn't in control any more. Eastman is running things, and he wants to show us who's boss. We'll have to strike, no doubt of it. And our guys need to come out fighting."

Easy to say, Bill thought. But how do you do that when you're on the defensive and exhausted?

The strike vote was scheduled for the evening of Sunday, May 30. The weather was unusually hot and sultry for Maine. When Bill arrived at the town civic center, the parking lot was nearly full. Almost all the cars were of American make – Chevrolets and Fords, mostly, with a few Plymouths and Pontiacs. He parked his car on the building's east side next to those of the identical blue Chevies of the Noel brothers. Floyd's license plate had a POW sign, and Jack's showed a Purple Heart. They were good guys, who would vote to strike and would stick to the end. When they were teenagers, Bill and Floyd Noel used to go hunting together. But once he came home from the POW camp, Floyd never wanted to hunt again. "I know exactly how that rabbit feels," he told Bill. It was only in the past few weeks that Bill had any inkling of what it was like to feel like a hunted animal.

By 7:30, when the meeting was scheduled to begin, the auditorium was packed. Lots of guys stood pressed together in the rear. About half of the members were of French Canadian heritage. The other half were a complex mixture of various ethnic stocks, mainly Scotch, Irish, English, and Italians. They considered themselves a diverse group and were not troubled by the small number of women and the near total absence of people of color. The great battle for ethnic tolerance in North Bethany had been waged between the Yankees and the French Canadians. And it was long over. The groups had melded into a single community, happy to share each other's ceremonies. Seated near the rear were the two non-Caucasian members of the union, a Korean woman named Dhang Wa Kim and Anthony Yamashita with his egg-shell coloring, who was half-Japanese. In 1984, two African American men from New York had been hired. Good guys, well liked. But after two years of harsh Maine winters and the isolated life common to the community, they applied for and were granted transfers to warmer places, with a greater black population.

The room was stifling — the air was hot and moist. Bill, itchy from sweat and insect bites, could see sweat pouring from the mostly dejected-looking faces of his members. The damp summer heat made circles form under his shirt sleeves, and his good wool pants stick uncomfortably to the inside of his leg. He dispatched someone to open the casement windows on each side of the auditorium. Along with a slight breeze came hundreds of just-hatched mosquitoes. They arrived with the angry buzz that made them sound like a hostile military force about to launch an attack, which is what they proceeded to do, swarming in complex formations, diving and stinging the audience so mercilessly that they might well have been sent by CP to disrupt the meeting.

Bill, tight-faced and grim, joined Emil Jean and Jeff Baker, the local's young, sad-faced lawyer, at the podium. He scanned the audience. Not a re-assuring sight. They're scared just like me. They know CP is out for our ass. They got the money and the know how. We're just a bunch of papermakers who don't know shit about striking. To his right he could see Terry Boyle, a round-faced, heavy-set, recovering alcoholic whose murky green eyes flickered with the desperation of a person already heavily in debt. Over on the far edge was Jordan Marcon, looking down at his shoes. On the far of the auditorium he watched Jerry Langlief, a paper-machine repairman with twenty years of seniority, slapping at a mosquito, his normally pleasant features distorted by anger and frustration. Langlief's job would be in jeopardy under the company's plan to subcontract work. Poor bastard.

He sat hunched forward as though he were trying to avoid a stiff wind. So many lurking tragedies! So little choice!

After a few announcements, Bill turned the meeting over to Jeff, the only person in the hall other than Emil Jean wearing a suit and tie. Jeff's dark, serious eyes, long thin nose, and thin, professional smile made him look like a minister at the scene of a tragedy. He summarized the company's final proposal, which differed slightly from those Bill had read to the members nearly two months earlier.

Bill stepped to the mike. "Anyone think we should accept CP's proposals? This is your chance to say why."

Silence.

The members were to cast two votes: whether to accept the company's proposals and whether to strike.

Don Foreman, an outsider, wasn't eligible to vote, so he just paced back and forth behind the last rows of seats. Not that he doubted the outcome of the vote. What concerned him was the lack of a noticeable fighting spirit, the sense that many of the members felt beaten already. Like Bill, he could sense their fear and confusion. Don knew from past experience that, if the strike failed, he would be an easy scapegoat. *Here I go again.* Why did he continually subject himself to such emotionally threatening situations? He wasn't sure himself. He had become a professional agitator. His life was isolated. No home base, no real friends. It would be comforting to believe that he was motivated solely by a desire to help the downtrodden. That was part of the answer, but, he knew, only part. He got most of his pleasure from doing battle, from smiting the unjust, from leading, and from educating. Many years ago a therapist had told him he was running away from intimacy. *Just the usual psycho crap,* he told himself. Right now he wasn't so sure. *Maybe I should have been a lawyer like my father wanted.*

He had entered college with the idea of going to law school. He was a good student. At Bates, even though he devoted most of his time to the football team, he had gotten high grades. But somehow the course of events leading from a summer in the civil rights movement had led him to the role of perpetual outsider — a fighter in other people's struggles.

When Bill called for a vote on the company's proposals, a chorus of "no's!" reverberated through the room. Almost everyone was on his feet. The members knew that they had taken an important step, and Bill could see the gravity of the situation reflected in their expressions. Some looked defiant, some confused, and others fearful. Some smiled sheepishly as though unsure of their ability to sustain the struggle. Foreman stopped pacing and allowed a quick, tight smile to momentarily lighten his intense expression.

There was plenty of discussion before the second vote, a vote that no one in this room had ever taken before: Strike! Several members argued that the union should simply continue working without a contract. Jordan Marcon, speaking for many, asked, "What happens if we just reject their proposals but don't call a strike?"

"They will be able to implement their proposals without our agreement," Jeff Baker answered. "That means they can take away premium pay, install Project Flexibility, make you work on Christmas, and subcontract work whenever they want to."

Howls of anger and disbelief erupted all over the hall. "You mean all these rights we thought we had aren't worth anything?" someone yelled.

Jeff Baker shook his head. "I wish I could honestly tell you there's an alternative, but there isn't. You have two choices: accept or fight." Baker took a slow breath. Law school hadn't offered a course in Breaking Bad News to Angry Groups. "And as soon as you go on strike, as you know, management has the legal right to hire scabs to take your jobs — permanently."

Anxiety enveloped the room. They were papermakers. What kind of future could they have without the jobs so central to their lives and their sense of self? Don felt he could reach out and touch the fear. Somehow it had to be dissipated if the strike was to be effective.

Suddenly Eric Miller stood up, his fists clenched, his eyes blazing with anger.

"Lots of us are scared. I'm damn scared myself. We don't know if we can win this strike. All we have is each other and our faith. They have the money and the right to hire scabs." He paused and looked down at the floor as though seeking inspiration. "I risked my life for this country, and I'll fight just as hard for my union. I may be scared, but I won't run, and I won't give in. The people in this union are my family." He clenched his fist and raised his arm over his head. "CP has declared war on my family. Okay, you sons of bitches! Let's fight!"

The hall erupted in cheers.

Bill raised his arm next to Eric's and, almost without realizing what he was doing, shouted, "Fight!"

The chant "Fight! Fight! Fight!" was taken up by the members who repeated it over and over, louder and louder, stamping their feet in rhythm with the chant, sending their message of defiance out through the casement windows into the hot Maine night. Don looked at Eric, and his eyes moistened. He was watching Winston Churchill in jeans. When the chanting finally ended, many of the members solemnly shook hands — a few even hugged. The strike vote carried unanimously. Even Jordan Marcon voted for it.

During the week before the strike deadline, little paper was made. Most members, who knew that their labor was being used to prepare CP for the strike, followed Bill's advice and made sure they followed every safety rule and inspection procedure. Management distributed a bulletin stating that each worker was required to complete a detailed job description. The union sent a flyer encouraging its members not to complete the descriptions. "They want us to create handbooks for the scabs. Don't do it." The company threatened to fire any worker who refused to complete a job description. Most of the workers prepared ambiguous, confusing descriptions of their jobs that would be of the least possible use for replacement workers.

A few of the foremen tried to get as much work as possible out of the production workers before the strike. They had schedules to meet. They threatened immediate discharge. There were others, though, like foreman Tommy Parker, whose son worked in the wood yard, who made no secret of their pro-union sympathies. When they walked through the gates together early one morning, Parker told Bill, "Hang in there. You're fighting for me and my whole family."

As anger increased, so did the informal slowdown. The workers stopped for breaks frequently, abandoned the work floor for the bathrooms three and four times a shift, and made more mistakes in a week than most had previously made in a year. No longer feeling part of the CP family, they treated the intricate and expensive paper machines with disdain, as though courting accidents. On June 5, two days before the strike was to begin, the local papers carried ominous news items. CP was placing ads in papers all over the country for replacement workers. The work level slowed even more, the level of anger rose to new heights.

Rumors of a "job action" on the final pre-strike shift circulated through the mill. Some told of a planned attack on a wood room supervisor, Roland Lavoy, who had taken to taunting the production workers for their lack of productivity. Some anticipated an assault on Mel LeBlanc. Others referred to sabotage and even talked about a bomb rigged to go off under one of the massive paper machines shortly after midnight.

Bill picked up the rumors third-hand. Whatever was in the works, he was being excluded from it — probably so that he could truthfully deny knowledge. The idea of sabotage didn't trouble him. Why should he act to protect those bastards? But how would beating the shit out of a supervisor or destroying property help the strike? I think something's up, but I don't know what, he admitted to Tony Lucelli. Why is Tony smiling like that? The son of a bitch is in on it. Well, screw it. If it happens, it happens.

The only person who seemed really upset by the idea of sabotage was Don. If he gives me one more lecture on the importance of nonviolence, I'm going to punch him right in the fucking mouth and fire him.

The last pre-strike shift ended at midnight on June 6th. Bill entered the mill for his last workday as nervous and as suspicious as the company security guards, who roamed the mill grounds in teams. By 11 p.m., Bill began to relax. He allowed himself to turn his mind to the local newspaper, wondering if it would carry the press release he and Don had prepared. It was a doozy: it detailed the salaries and bonuses of CP's top executives, and it contrasted them with the salaries of the paperworkers. The gap was enormous.

Bill's attention was wrenched back to the mill when suddenly the mills' lights — thousands and thousands of them — went out. Immediately, curses from the guards and laughter from some of the workers mixed in the total darkness. Bill, who was hard of hearing after years of absorbing the noise of paper machines, thought he heard something being broken and was immediately afraid that papermaking machines were being vandalized. He shouted out, "Don't be stupid! They want to make us look like thugs."

After a moment of silence, a voice he half-recognized but could not place responded, "It's better to be a thug than a coward!"

The lights came on within minutes as security guards marched through the mill and stationed themselves by the paper machines. A company spokesman announced over the intercom system that the mill was officially closed. In an angry voice over the loud speaker, he ordered everyone to leave immediately.

Bill did not know what had happened, but he could see a knot of security guards over by the Number 2 machine scurrying about importantly. He helped his co-workers to shut down his machine and quickly joined the flow of angry workers leaving the mill. As they got to the gate, many turned, some with fists raised and others pointing their index finger in the air, whether to claim victory or declare hatred he could not tell.

The strike had begun.

Chapter 8

The union hall buzzed with nervous laughter and excited conversation. But for the smell of freshly brewed coffee and the haze of cigarette smoke, it might have been a locker room just before a big game. At 6:30, when the first streaks of dawn appeared, the picketers — over a hundred men and 20 women — arranged themselves into a long column with Bill and Eric Miller at their head and marched four abreast to the mill entrances. Most were wearing blue T-shirts that displayed a raised fist over which the word "strike" was written in bold white letters. Cindy Reagan and Jill Carter wore their T-shirts over short skirts that showed off their legs and drew the expected compliments and teasing. Many marchers carried picket signs. "Local 34. Whatever it Takes for as Long as it Takes," "Workers United Can Never Be Defeated," and "Show Watts What's What."

The picketers traded conversation and jokes for the first few minutes. Then, as they crossed Highway 18, Eric Miller began to chant in military cadence:

"I don't know but it's not funny.

Watts is making too much money."

The chant got picked up by the marchers, who fell into step as they chanted. Don Foreman added a verse:

"We've been fooled and we've been had.

All it does is make us mad."

And a few minutes later, Ray Allair came up with a new chant that was repeated enthusiastically.

"Said it before, going to say it agin, 34 is bound to win."

Bill could hear Tony Lucelli's fine baritone voice leading the chanting from the rear of the march, where he had stationed himself to act as a goad to stragglers.

As they reached the South Gate, the workers were happily chanting the combined verses. The mood reminded Bill of the tailgate parties he had attended at a Patriots' game in November. Emil Jean, marching behind Bill, did not seem to share the general upbeat mood. "They're acting like this is a party," he told Bill. "I don't like it."

Don Foreman, marching behind him, snorted in annoyance, "There's a name for what you're complaining about. It's called 'solidarity'!"

Emil's thin lips contracted. "We'll see," he said.

Without rancor, the pickets yelled, "Go home and do some real work!"

to the supervisors they passed along the route of march, and, when some of the supervisors flashed them thumbs-up signs, they cheered enthusiastically with fists raised skyward. They did the same when truck drivers, delivering lumber in huge 18-wheel trucks, honked their horns in a show of support. It was at West Gate, where replacement applicants were lined up waiting to be interviewed, that the atmosphere changed dramatically. Bill felt his hatred rising and looking at the faces of the other strikers he could see his own rage echoed. The strikers formed a dense line that seemed to strain against the police barricades as if to charge the applicants and do physical battle with them.

Ed Allen, who had fought at the Inchon Reservoir during the Korean War, stood in the middle of the line, swinging his picket sign like a baseball bat. When Bill walked over to him, Allen admitted, "I feel like I'm back in Korea. I'm scared, and I want to kill the enemy."

Eric Miller and Jordan Marcon were on either side of him. Miller was bellowing obscenities and threats in quick and endless succession. His face was flushed, and his eyes sparkled with hatred. Eric's enthusiasm was contagious. Most of the other fifty strikers also screamed insults and shook their fists at the applicants, who pretended to ignore them.

But not Jordan Marcon. Marcon stood motionless on the fringe of the massed strikers — a study in depression. He did not curse. "Go home, we don't want you," he kept repeating, in a voice so low and devoid of feeling he might well have been talking to himself.

Bill approached him and patted his shoulder. "Give 'em hell, Jordan."

Marcon smiled weakly. "I keep wondering which one of these guys is going to take my job. Billy, I really need that paycheck."

"Hell, we all do. That's why we have to stick together — so we can go back together."

"I know, Bill, but I've got special problems. My wife is sick, maybe real sick. She may have cancer, and I already have medical bills to pay."

Poor son of a bitch. No wonder he looked so sad.

"Hey, Jordan, we're a union. If you need extra help, we'll find a way to give it to you. Come down to the hall, and we'll work this out."

"Thanks, Bill." Marcon was obviously embarrassed. He spoke softly despite the roar of anger all around them. "I need to know you guys are there for me."

Bill reached out to shake Marcon's hand, changed his mind and hugged him. "We'll be there as long as you need us." Talking to Jordan was sobering. Bill was on a high, but he realized that he could not take the fighting spirit of the local for granted. The strike vote meeting was a refreshing shower for the spirit. But showers have a way of wearing off. The spirit, like the body, needs constant attention.

When he returned from the picket line, Bill reached eagerly for the *North Bethany Sun*. The front-page lead, in 72-point type, was SABOTAGE CAUSES HEAVY DAMAGE TO CP MILL PROPERTY. Bill read the first part of the story. "On the night before a strike by 1400 union members, mill officials reported that hundreds of thousands of dollars of vandalism was done to costly equipment."

Hundreds of thousands, what bullshit! But people who weren't there and just read it will believe it. Damn, damn, damn! I warned the guys. He noticed that a separate article was devoted to an interview with mill spokesman, Joseph Timowski, who professed to fear even greater violence. Timowski claimed that company officials and supervisors had received threatening phone calls — some containing death threats and others threats to the families of mill officials.

Goddam CP! Liars! The newspapers lap it up. He looked in vain for the information in his press release, but it was not there. Bill angrily rolled up the paper and slam-dunked it into a wastebasket.

That was only the beginning of what everyone in Local 34 recognized as an anti-labor news bias. The *Sun* ran a series of articles, based on company press releases, focusing on minor acts of misconduct at the picket line and company allegations of vandalism and harassing phone calls. The local TV news stations seemed to have developed a particular liking for the phrase, "Another violent day at the North Bethany picket line." Bill met twice with the media committee.

"Do something! They're whipping our ass," he pleaded.

It was Don who cooled him down. "Give them a chance, Bill. They're doing their best, which ain't bad and they're learning." Based on Don's advice, Bill was regularly available to reporters. Almost all of his time, however, was spent arguing with them. "You're focusing on the petty shit and ignoring the big picture. Don't you understand? CP is trying to distract you so you won't write the truth. They're trying to bust the union."

The reporters listened; some even seemed to agree, but the constant flow of unfavorable articles continued. Tom Gillian seemed to be all over the TV screen, explaining CP's position in a calm, reasonable voice. How the hell can George Connerton defend that lying son of a bitch, Bill wondered. He's not a good guy. This is one time George Connerton is wrong. Look at him in his $200 suit, smiling and joking. He's enjoying every minute. Showing his power. Even if we settle the strike, I'll hate the bastard from now on.

Bill was wrong.

The day after the strike vote, at a major meeting of top management and labor relations experts, Gillian had unsuccessfully urged the company to come forward with a generous new proposal.

"I remind you that, when the union had the economic leverage, they didn't hesitate to escalate their demands," Eastman said.

"Professor Eastman, you weren't on the scene in those days. I was. The union never asked for everything they could have gotten, and whatever pay raises we granted were more than made up for by price increases."

"Yes, I know that you used to pass on wage increases, but in the new global market that's impossible." Eastman's thin lips curled. "No offense, Mr. Gillian, but perhaps you would feel more comfortable as a member of the union's team." This remark led to a burst of general laughter that was quickly ended by the look of displeasure on Watts' face. Gillian reddened and his eyebrows rose ferociously at Eastman's comment and the laughter that followed. Damn them all, he thought, they're treating me like the company fool. The arrogant, self-important bastards! He faced Eastman with no effort to hide the anger that radiated from his eyes.

"I put in time defending this company's interests long before you even knew there was a paper industry." He was ready to quit.

Eastman's tone became more conciliatory. "Mr. Gillian — er, Tom — we all recognize that you have given the company years of devoted service. I hope my comments were not understood as denying that fact. But you must admit that the times have changed, and the Company would be foolish not to take advantage of its bargaining strength. We believe the market provides the fairest way to set wages, and that is all we are trying to achieve."

"Let's not argue further," Watts had stated. "The first week of the strike, we need to win over the press and the TV reporters. That's where Tom has been so valuable up to now, cultivating reporters and business analysts. I anticipate responsible coverage for once, not union propaganda masquerading as hard news."

Eastman, his lips tightly pursed, nodded and smiled at Gillian in a not very successful effort to convey respect.

Gillian was reminded of a self-congratulatory copperhead.

"I trust the strikers will be given an adequate opportunity to compromise and return before we permanently replace them," Gillian said. He tried to remain calm, but his voice quivered with emotion.

Eastman's gloat of triumph was not difficult to discern. "I must remind you, Tom, that if there is a strike, we don't want the strikers to return. We want to be rid of them and the union. We must stick to our guns."

"It's a bad plan morally and tactically," Gillian insisted. "Not only are we repaying loyalty with firing, but we are almost guaranteeing violence."

"We are going to have plenty of security forces employed to protect lives and property. Of course, in the long run, violence by the strikers will help us win the strike."

"Under the law, it's the union's job to keep their strike peaceful," company counsel Sandra Levin added.

Watts clapped his hands together. The room fell silent. "Tom, you are our point person, and a damn good one you've been. You must continue your good work, in the same honorable fashion, explaining our decision to hire replacements." He favored Gillian with a look of benevolent understanding.

Gillian was aware of conflicting impulses. He was angry — annoyed at being used and manipulated — but comforted. "I guess my job is safe for a while," he thought, then felt deeply ashamed.

When the strike began, it was Gillian's job to explain CP's new aggressive labor policy to the press. His reputation for working well with unions made him the ideal person for the job. Bill Serrin of *The New York Times* told Jeremy Gross of *Newsweek* that "If it wasn't coming from Tom Gillian, I'd sure think CP's statements were pure bullshit and that George Watts and his crew of young hot shots were trying to hide some old-fashioned union busting."

Gillian understood his role and hated it. "They're keeping me on," he told Laura, "because the key reporters and people in the field know me and trust me. But I'll soon destroy a reputation it has taken me years to build. And I'll deserve it for trying to put a fancy lid on a sack of worms."

For the first time in his life, Gillian had trouble falling asleep. He had become an outsider at CP with no real voice in setting policy. It was Eastman who had the final say on negotiating strategy. Gillian had received anguished phone calls from George Connerton and National Union President John Elder, and another from the union's New England vice-president. Each left him heartsick. It took all the self-control he had not to confess that CP's new labor policy was adopted over his helpless protests.

The evening after his call from Elder, Gillian headed straight for the kitchen where Laura was busily preparing dinner. His unhappiness showed on his face.

Laura took his hand. "What's wrong?"

"I've become a puppet. Eastman is pulling the strings. They don't ask my opinion. All they want me to do is lie to the reporters, keep them from seeing that this is a union-busting operation. What bothers me most is, well, it's that I've gotten pretty good at it."

He changed to a more pompous tone mimicking himself talking to the press. "We are attempting to explain to the union the competitive context in which we are currently operating. The company owes a responsibility not only to the current employees but also to succeeding generations, and most of all to the shareholders, who have placed their trust in the current leadership."

He put his hands on Laura's waist, a sardonic half-smile on his face. "I've gone from being a good papermaker to a cowardly shoveler of bullshit. I was once a union leader, and now I'm a union buster. I should quit — that's the only decent thing for me to do."

Her expression reflected his pain. "Tom, your quitting will just make things worse. Stay. You will get your chance yet."

"God, how I hope you're right. Right now I feel like I'm doing commercials for the Ku Klux Klan."

Gillian's success with the media increased the strikers' anger. Bill kept fending off recommendations for violent actions like storming the mill or beating up Mel LeBlanc. Bill argued with them as he argued with the reporters who continued to ignore the unfairness of CP's contract proposals.

The situation grew worse when, on June 20, the company announced that it would begin hiring permanent replacement workers to take the jobs of the strikers. The company's decision was reported in full by the *North Bethany Sun*. Mill manager John Dunsford was quoted as saying, "The decision was made reluctantly and only because we had no reasonable alternative," a claim particularly infuriating to Bill — who had watched the company turning down one alternative after another that could have led to agreement and prevented a strike. The company's press release blamed the union's "unwillingness to come to grips with current economic reality" for the strike. And in what seemed to Bill a final insult to the strikers, CP's press release praised "the high caliber" of the applicants hired. "They are experienced, talented, American working men and women. We feel confident that within a short time they will be able to produce paper similar in quality and quantity to that produced by our striking workers." The release ended with an ominous backhanded threat. "We hope that the union will recognize the importance of this step and call off their strike. We stand ready to welcome back any of the strikers whose jobs have not been taken."

Shortly after that announcement, four more former strikers crossed the line and returned to work. Everything was going wrong. The company, the law, and the press were working together to defeat the strike. Bill later told Shirley that "being ambushed in Korea by the Chinese was a picnic compared to the first three weeks of the strike."

Chapter 9

Travis Green was living in an apartment just off Amsterdam Avenue and 125th Street in New York City when he read Consolidated Paper's ad promising good pay and excellent career opportunities for replacement workers at the Panscott mill. An 800 number was provided. Travis marked the ad carefully. Then he put the paper down and tried to focus on the Knicks game.

A few minutes later he turned off the game, picked the paper up again, and reread the ad. It brought back memories of almost 20 years earlier when he had applied at International Paper's Mobile paper mill and been turned down. A smooth-talking guy from mill personnel had told him that he was one of the last people on the list of applicants to be cut. "If I were you I'd apply again early next year. That's when we're going to be expanding the mill's work force and training people like you." the guy had told him. Don't piss on my feet and tell me it's raining.

If they really wanted to hire him in the future, all they had to do was keep his application on file. Come back later. It was an old racist dodge. He never followed up.

But times had changed, maybe now, up in the north, things would be different. The CP ad specifically stated "no experience necessary." The ad also said that he would have to cross a picket line. He visualized himself confronted by angry pickets who were shouting "Die, scab, die!" Not a pleasant thought. He sure would hate it if he were on strike and scabs were hired.

But what did he owe these union people who had always gotten the best jobs and earned the most money? What had they done for him or other black people? I don't like being a scab, nobody does. But it's a chance to have a real profession, and it's time I was making something of myself. He called and asked for the application, which he promptly filled out and sent in. On Thursday, June 27, he received a phone call asking whether he could report for work on Wednesday July 5th. He thought for a few seconds Why not? "I'll be there," he said.

The next day he told his employer, the owner of Charlie Dyson's Body Shop, that he was moving to Maine. Dyson, a round-faced man with mahogany-colored skin, who had moved to New York from Jamaica, looked at him with disbelief. "Mahn, that's stupid. Brothers don't live in Maine. You'll be so lonely in a week that you'll want to rush back to Harlem. What you gonna do, mahn, on Friday nights? Go square dancing? Those people got no rhythm. One, two, one, two, one, two, maybe one, two, three — that how they dance, mahn. You feel like you trapped."

Green laughed and shook his head. "I don't know what I'll do when I'm not working. Maybe I'll just stay home and count my money. This is my chance to be a paper worker and earn good money. I'm taking it."

"Travis, you dreaming. You know nothing about paper."

"I know I don't have enough green paper. And I know that paper mills pay good. Hey, give me a chance, and I can learn to make anything."

Dyson shook his head. "You going to be a scab, mahn, a black scab. Them strikers will want to kill you. You know those Maine people; they a tough breed."

Travis laughed. He was a chunky, muscular man with ebony colored skin and strong features softened by a wide, almost constant smile. "There's plenty people in New York who don't know me and hate me anyway. And it's not like I'll be the only scab. I'll have lots of company. And once I learn about making paper in Maine, I can do it anywhere."

"What's wrong with New York, mahn?" Dyson asked. "Plenty of black people, lots of fine-looking women, and lots of excitement. Smahtest thing I ever did, moving here."

"I hate New York. Too dirty, too many brothers hustling me, too many white people looking at me like I'm going to mug them. I was happier in Alabama."

Dyson hesitated for a moment. Then, rubbing the grease from his hands onto his jeans, he smiled at Travis. "Well, I can see you mean it. So I'm going to pay you off, and here's something extra for when you get lonely in Maine and want to call me. You're a good guy even if your head don't work so good." Dyson wrote out a check for $700 and handed it to Travis, who looked at it with astonishment. They shook hands, hooked thumbs, and hugged.

On Saturday, July 1, Travis packed his clothes into his '81 Chevy and began his trip from New York to North Bethany. He was nervous — far less sure of the wisdom of his decision than he pretended to be in his discussion with Dyson. But he had always been a chance-taker. He had taken a chance when he joined the army and another when he left Mobile for New York when he quit school. This was another chance he had to take. Once out of New York, he found his way easily, traveling up Interstate 95 and turning east on Highway 1 — twenty miles north of Portland.

The CP woman on the phone had given Green the option of living rent free in a trailer on the sprawling mill property along with other replacement workers, but he wanted to live far enough away from the mill to have some privacy and learn a little about Maine. The bright July sun was still high in the sky when Travis crossed the Panscott Bridge into Bethany. On either side of the bridge, he could see the calm waters of the Atlantic inlet that edged the town. The tall churches and the winding roads set at different levels along the high, arching hills looking out over the Panscott River, where birds lazily criss-crossed, made him feel like he was in the middle of one of those travel videos on television. He drove around Bethany for an hour and a half, looking for an apartment he could afford. Nothing even close. He drove into North Bethany, where he discovered that any inexpensive rental would require him to live within the unpleasant smell of the mill. Finally, about three-quarters of a mile east of the mill, he saw a sign in front of a pleasant-looking duplex surrounded by flowers. "Home for rent $250 per month." It seemed perfect. "I wonder if they'll go into shock when they see my black face?"

He approached the house and pressed the doorbell.

A slightly plump, middle-aged woman in a half-buttoned polka-dot housedress, round-faced with sleepy eyes, came to the door. After looking at his car, her eyes opened wide. "What can I do for ya?"

"I noticed your sign, and I'm looking for a place to rent."

Her expression was far from friendly. "Your car license is from New York. Why are you looking for a home up heah?"

"I've got a job, and I'm moving up here."

"Wheya?"

"Working for CP at the mill."

"You're a scab. We don't rent to scabs. Never have, never will. Weah union people."

He was so surprised and disappointed that he blurted out angrily, "The law says you gotta rent to me."

She turned her back. "Nick, there's a scab here who won't take no for an answer. Says he's gotta legal right."

Nick, built small and muscular like Travis, came to the door wearing jeans and a union t-shirt. "Nothing in the law about renting to scabs. I wouldn't obey if there was. And don't think your black skin makes any difference to me." His voice grew louder and angrier. "I don't hate black people, I hate scabs, white and black. So get the hell out of heah and don't come back!"

Travis turned and walked back to his New York car. He says "scab" the way crackers say "nigger," Travis thought. He was turned down twice more — once by someone who had worked in the mill, and once by a schoolteacher who told him she didn't want any trouble. Travis eventually drove to New Castle, about twenty miles away from the mill. There he rented a small cottage in a scenic, wooded area from someone who assured him that he didn't care where Travis worked as long as he paid his rent.

Travis Green was one of the two hundred new replacement workers who crossed the picket line on Wednesday morning accompanied by gun-toting security guards, as TV cameras rolled and state police cleared a path through the angry massed pickets and onlookers. The replacement workers were met with shouts of hatred so raw and menacing that most moved closer to their swaggering protectors. Others simply put their heads down, as if they were trying to stay dry in a downpour; a few responded in kind, returning curse for curse, insult for insult.

Trying to ignore the shouts, threats, and stones directed at him, Travis raced through the barrier of angry strikers with his eyes fixed on the CP insignia just inside the mill entrance. He heard a woman calling out, "You're not an African American — you're just a dumb nigger who can't tell his friends from his enemies."

Once inside the gate, he followed handwritten signs to the personnel office where Mel LeBlanc and Ron Beleveau greeted him and the other replacement workers. LeBlanc began by assuring them that the company appreciated their willingness to work under "rather unusual circumstances" and that it would do everything in its power to make the experience a good one. "You will always have a job with Consolidated Paper as long as you work hard. We know that most of you have never worked or even been in a paper mill before, but we intend to show the union, with your help, how quickly willing workers can become first-rate paper makers." Travis felt a little better.

They were given a tour of the mill and a brief run-through of the process by which logs of different types were transformed into paper. Travis watched intently as the logs were debarked and then fed by conveyor belt to the chipper, a huge machine with powerful blades that cut the stripped logs into chips an inch and a half long. The chips were stored in huge vats, bleached, treated with chemicals, and turned into a viscous mass that was treated with air and chemicals. Then it was pumped onto fine-mesh screens and fed into computerized paper machines. There, the rolls of wet pulp were pressed together several times to remove water and produce huge rolls of different colored paper, which were then picked up by a forklift and transported to the loading dock. It was hot, noisy, and dangerous, but it was also impressive to have so much power so finely tuned to a single end.

Travis was handed a map of the mill and instructed to report to the number one paper machine. He wasted no time getting there. When he arrived, he stood in front of a complex, computerized control system that reminded him of his days in the Artillery, until he was approached by a sad-looking man with graying brown hair and thick, wire-rimmed glasses. His badge identified him as supervisor Armand LeClerc.

"Name?" LeClerc asked him, looking down at his pad.

"Green, Travis Green. Sure nice to be in here away from the crowd."

"You're heah to work, not engage in small talk."

"Just trying to be friendly, for god's sake."

"Mr. Green, I have to train you, but I don't have to be your friend. My friends are out on the picket line. In heah, we will be strictly business."

By the end of the first morning, he learned that, while some of the supervisors welcomed the replacement workers enthusiastically, others viewed them with contempt. The whole morning was stimulating and confusing. The instructions about operating paper machines were complex, but Travis was a quick learner with a feel for machines. It was interesting work, even though the area in which he was stationed was oppressively hot. By mid-morning, the heat and the noise began to take their toll.

He was glad when it was time to go to the mill cafeteria for lunch. He walked to a table with four other replacement workers: three men and a woman, all wearing name badges. The person directly across the table was John Ballinger, a balding, middle-aged man with thick, horn-rimmed glasses, neatly pressed khaki pants, and a white shirt. To his right was Edith Kent, a nice looking, slightly overweight woman in a pants suit. She had strawberry blonde hair, which she tied back in a ponytail. The person to Travis's right was Ed Young, who looked to be in his early twenties. His almost-white hair came almost to his shoulders, and he had watery blue eyes, thin lips, and badly discolored teeth. The man next to Travis was Charles Springer, whose pasty complexion and round pie-face reminded Travis of the bank loan officer who had just rejected his application.

"Boy, I'm glad the cops were there," Springer said. "Those people were like animals. They would have killed us if they had the chance." His accent suggested to Travis that he came from somewhere nearby.

"Daim those strikers!" Young exclaimed, shaking his head vehemently. "No why I'm gonna feel sympathy for them." Travis guessed from Young's twang and his long vowels that he came from Alabama, where Travis had grown up. "They give up they jobs and then blame us for taking them. If they haidn't been so stupid and greedy, they wouldn't haive to scream at us."

"I understand their being angry with us," Ballinger answered quietly. "I've worked union before. If the shoe factory I worked at had went on strike, I woulda been just as angry at scabs as those people were."

"If you liked working union so much, whah did you laive?" Young asked with a sneer.

"The shoe factory closed, took our jobs to Taiwan," Ballinger replied.

"That shows how much protection unions give you," Young said contemptuously. "I shore don't have any sympathy for these greedy fucks."

"Neither do I," said Springer emphatically. He paused for a second, then added, "If them damn union guys try to stop my car, I'll run it right at them. I carry a gun, and I'm not afraid to use it."

Nasty motherfuckers. Being a scab is going to be like war, and you don't get to pick the people in your foxhole, Green thought.

"I sure hope it doesn't come to that," Edith Kent said in a broad New England accent. "I don't want to fight. All I want is to earn some money to help my family. I'm sorry to take someone's job. But my husband's been out of work and — well, I — we have medical bills and I have no choice."

"I feel the same as this young lady," Travis said. "I don't hate nobody, but I always wanted to be a paper worker."

Edith Kent smiled at him in a friendly fashion. Young and Springer looked at each other and grimaced.

The rest of the day passed quickly. Travis was beginning to understand how to start the paper machines and when to stop. There was something profoundly satisfying about the whole business. He was glad that he had taken the job.

On the way out of the plant, he once more had to pass through a gauntlet of angry, shouting pickets. The group massed outside the gate was larger and, if anything, angrier than the earlier group had been.

On the drive to New Castle, he concentrated on the gigantic trees, the curving roads, elegant houses, picturesque apple orchards, and carefully mani-cured lawns. In Alabama, his family hadn't had money or time to make their yards pretty. And in New York, everyone lived right beside everyone else. No one had the wide-open spaces that even the old houses near the center of town had around here. He was happy to be in Maine.

During the next few weeks, his pleasure in the job continued. He especially enjoyed working with Edith Kent. He liked her calm way of speaking and her good humor. She was a good worker, just like him, a nice person — not a hater like Young and Springer. They regularly had lunch together. After the first week, she had confided to Travis that she needed to earn money because she was pregnant. "If I wasn't, I wouldn't have to be a scab."

Chapter 10

Bill walked the picket line like everyone else, so did Cindy Regan. They both hated it.

For Bill it was an ordeal of helplessness, standing in the humid summer heat shouting helplessly while shift after shift of hated scabs crossed the line.

By the beginning of July, the strikers were hurting financially. Strike benefits from the national union ($500 a week), together with unemployment checks (another $500), totaled less than half of their former take-home pay. Those paying off cars and credit-card debt were stunned at how quickly they were forced to reach into their savings. Hardship became widespread. Many of the strikers began looking frantically for jobs as fiscal emergencies loomed. Local 34 established a relief fund. The national union contributed $50,000 to it for emergency aid.

Bill set up a committee of three to allocate the money and invited Jordan Marcon to meet with the committee the last Friday in July. Marcon, Bill, and the committee members sat on folding metal chairs arranged in a circle around a small wooden table in the rear of the union hall. Jordan looked profoundly embarrassed, worn out, and frightened.

Bill tried to put Marcon at ease. "We don't have much money, and that's a sad fact, Jordan. But we want to make sure that no one needs to scab to take care of his family."

Marcon kept his head down, staring intently at his shoes. When Bill asked him to explain his special need, he did not look up but spoke slowly in a low voice, almost a whisper.

"I need help — need it bad. I have big bills to pay off, and my wife's real sick. Day before yesterday, she had a stomach biopsy. They're hoping it's just a bleeding ulcer, but they don't know yet. I had to give them $200 cash, before we went in. And then the pharmacy took almost $100 more. She needs the big pills so she can even move. Her pain is terrible. No one knows better than me what we're striking for, but the Lord says that a man's chief responsibility is to his family."

Two committee members conferred in hushed tones, then one whispered to Bill, who addressed Marcon. "Can you get by if we give you a thousand dollars now and an extra hundred-fifty dollars a month until the strike ends? We'll find a way for the union to pay your health premiums so your family won't get dropped."

For the first time, Marcon lifted his head and a faint, thin smile momentarily eased the look of pain that had distorted his normally handsome face. "Very fair, Bill. Very fair. You won't be sorry. I'll never forget this. You can count on me to do my part."

Bill's a good man, even if he hasn't been redeemed, Jordan thought. He left the meeting, prepared to do his part for the strike. He rushed home, eager to tell Ann of the good news. She was in the living room lying on the couch. Her face was tight. She had been crying.

His lips started to tremble. "What's wrong?"

"I just got the call from the doctor. It's cancer."

"Cancer," he echoed dumbly.

"He says that they can operate and get rid of it. How we can afford the operation and the treatment? Jordan, I'm scared to death."

Lines of worry seemed to have been newly etched on her face. "I don't want to lose our house and everything the Lord has blessed us with."

He tried to be calm. "Don't worry, Ann, I just met with the union committee. We're not going to lose our medical insurance." But he watched tears flow down the trails on her cheeks, and his right hand, held clenched at his side, trembled. He put it quickly into the pocket of his khaki pants. He was not quick enough to escape her notice.

That night, before going to bed, he knelt by his bedside, feeling empty and helpless. He prayed fervently for guidance. Afterward, his sleep was troubled. He kept waking up, his face covered with sweat. Ann was turned away from him, drugged into a silent stillness. Just as dawn was breaking, he awoke again, this time conscious of a calming presence in the room with him. It was Jesus, a halo of light around him, his face sad and his eyes filled with compassionate tears. He spoke softly to Jordan, repeating over and over: "I will not give you a burden you cannot bear."

Jordan fell back into a short and untroubled sleep. When Jordan finally awakened, he had no doubt that he had received a personal message from God. He went downstairs to call Reverend Harmon, who surely could help him understand it better.

Chapter 11

Early in August, Bill decided to give Eric Miller a break and replace him for a day on the picket line outside the main gate off of route 4. It had been over a week since he last walked the line and he wanted to know the mood of the pickets. He arrived about an hour before the scheduled afternoon shift. The sun, low in the sky seemed to cast a glow over the surrounding countryside. The air was brisk, almost cold. Some of the maple trees that lined the east gate had already started to turn color, and above them he could see a flight of geese in military formation flying south. The pickets dressed in fall jackets were quiet, no chants or songs, just a low hum of conversation until the scabs began to arrive for work. At that point the pickets formed a line marching in military cadence back and forth across the road that led to the gate. As the scab cars came through the road, the strikers gave way grudgingly, shouting threats and insults while shaking their fists. A few of the scabs stared directly ahead of them avoiding eye contact with the pickets, but others looked as angry and returned insult for insult. Some raised their index fingers as triumphantly as football fans signaling a victory.

A few minutes later, morning shift workers leaving the mill came across the line. Some of the replacement workers were escorted by security guards. Several scabs waved their paychecks; some laughed ostentatiously at the strikers, most of whom looked glum as though they wished they were somewhere else. The somber mood on the line was a far cry from the party atmosphere of the first days. Bill wondered what he could do to lift the spirits of the pickets. Poor bastards feel helpless. Anybody would. No way they can chase the scabs away. Pretty sure of themselves, surrounded by the damn security guards with their pressed uniforms and their cameras ready to take pictures of anybody who so much as bends down like they're thinking of picking up a rock. He led the pickets in shouting "Scabs out Union in," all the while thinking how meaningless it all was. The line was like a sieve. Anybody who wanted to work or make deliveries got through. The only bright spot came when a huge truck filled with logs stopped before crossing the line. The driver, a stocky, middle-aged man wearing a Teamsters jacket, got out of his truck and gave the strikers the thumbs up sign. They cheered loudly, for the first time showing real spirit. But 10 minutes later, Larry Gats, a supervisor, came out of the mill. The truck driver handed him the keys and Gats, quickly and efficiently, drove the truck to the wood yard. By the time Gats came back, the disheartened pickets had disbanded. A few pickets walked aimlessly waving their signs, along the road. Most of the others seated themselves silently on camp chairs. Bill could think of nothing to say to break the bitter silence.

Pretty discouraging, Bill realized. And it's gonna get worse when the really cold weather begins. The poor guys on the picket line. They'll be freezing their asses off without doing us any good. Thank God we have Eric Miller in charge of the line. I couldn't do what he does. He's got more guts than a butcher shop. Nobody crosses the line without him saying some shit to them. You can hear him all over town, daring the scabs to come out and fight. No takers so far. He's still got that linebacker style. Bill smiled for the first time that morning, his mood lightened by the recollection of Eric's days as a defensive lineman in high school. Eric, with his broad beam and thick, muscular legs, wasn't the fastest player on the North Bethany team, not by a long shot. Speedy players could sometimes run around him. But no one ran over him. Even the scabs could sense his fighting spirit.

Scabs! What scummy so-called humans they are. Bunch of misfits from Alabama, drinking and smoking dope instead of working. It's a good thing I don't have a weapon. Be tempting to take a shot at the sons of bitches strolling across the line. Don Foreman says we shouldn't hate them. Says we should think of scabs as "the unorganized part of the labor movement." Easy for him to be noble. It isn't his job they're taking!

At the union rally held on August 10th Bill could sense that tempers were running high, Strikers kept interrupting his report on the week's developments to shout their hatred for CP and the scabs. Our people are sick of watching the scabs cruising into the mill every day. So am I. The damn newspapers don't help always printing CP's side of every story. Just this morning the *Sun* had published a story headlined "Replacement Workers Doing the Job." Some story! — a bunch of scabs telling about how much they like working at the mill. The article included a long quote from Mel Leblanc saying that the scabs had become "first-class paper makers." Bill guessed that almost everyone had read the story. When Cindy Reagan mentioned LeBlanc's name during her report on the state of the union's treasury, the hall erupted in shouts of rage.

It was Peter Gay who suggested that the strikers drive around the mill honking their horns after the meeting. "Let's show the supervisors and the scabs that we're still here and we mean to stay right on their ass." He got a standing ovation. Bill was not sure what good it would do and he worried that maybe some guys meant to do more than honk their horns. He was always explaining why storming the mill was a bad idea. But it was clear that most of the strikers were going to participate. I'm the President, I better go with them, he concluded.

It was an unfortunate coincidence that the drive-by coincided with the end of the mill's main shift, which had been extended for two hours that evening because of a rush order. When the strikers arrived, cars carrying supervisors and scabs were still coming out of the parking lots. Bill could see guys shaking their fists and giving the scabs the finger. Some of the scabs were yelling back. He noticed Peter Gay and Dennis Oullette in Peter's Ford pick up truck, pass a Chevy car carrying scabs. Peter pulled in front of the Chevy and slowed to a crawl. The scabs tried to pass but too many cars were coming the other way. They moved the Chevy on to the highway's right shoulder and tried to pass, but the pickup cut it off as another striker car came up along side. The scabs were surrounded and forced to stop. Peter and Dennis quickly parked along the shoulder of the road and jumped from their car. One of the scabs, a tall guy with hair down to his shoulders, got out of the Chevy swinging a baseball bat. Bill saw disaster looming and quickly parked his car near some trees alongside the road. Other cars were parking. Groups of strikers were running towards parked cars belonging to scabs. Bill watched Peter Gay charge the guy with the bat. The scab swung the bat in a downward motion, aiming for Peter's legs. He missed and Peter tackled him, knocked him to the ground, and wrestled the bat from his hand. Dennis punched the guy's face. Other strikers were racing to the scene shouting. Bill almost panicked. Stupid bastards! This can fuck up the strike. The scab's nose was gushing blood. Bill raced over and grabbed Peter just as Don tackled Dennis. "Are you crazy?" Bill said furiously. "This is the worst thing you can do." Peter raised his fist, then shook his head and dropped his hand to his side. Don administered rudimentary first aid to the scab. Bill guessed that his nose was broken.

About twenty yards ahead Bill saw another group of strikers who had left their cars. They were picking up stones. This could be a disaster. Someone could be killed. Suppose they injured a supervisor. Forget solidarity then. It would split North Bethany for years. He didn't know if he could stop them. The guys were angry enough to go after the Little Sisters of the Poor.

Travis Green left the plant about 10 p.m. for his trip back home to New Castle. He was shocked to see the road filled with strikers, some driving slowly in their cars honking their horns and others in groups alongside the road. A little way in front of him the car of one replacement worker was surrounded. Strikers were trying to open the door. Others standing on the side of the road were shouting encouragement to them. Then someone pointed to Travis's car, and a group of tough-looking men gave him the finger. He could hear the chant growing louder: "Scabs out! Scabs out! Scabs out!"

Someone shouted, "We'll get you bastards," and out of nowhere, an egg smashed into his windshield. His arm muscles tensed. Immediately, several rocks hit the side of his car. Someone behind his car screamed "black bastard!" Another egg hit the windshield, making it hard to see the white line on the road. Damn them! They weren't going to scare him away! He heard the welcome sounds of police sirens. Strikers already in cars left the scene, and those standing along the road jumped into their cars and left quickly.

For the first time, he actively hated the strikers.

When he drove into his driveway, he sat very still until he felt calm enough to get out.

Later, trying to fall asleep, he tried to put himself in the strikers' place, watching outsiders coming to work their jobs. It was difficult. All he could think was that once again his chance for a decent job was being threatened by people who hated him without knowing him.

LABOR RIOT: REPLACEMENT WORKERS ATTACKED was the headline in the *Portland Press* the next morning. The lead story described how a union rally at the mill gate led to a general melee in which eight replacement workers were hurt, three seriously. Two had been struck in the head with rocks thrown by strikers, the other had been hit with a club. The riot was big news all over Maine. Anyone who read a newspaper, watched the local news on television, or listened to the radio was likely to learn about it. It was the subject of editorials from Bangor to Kennebunk and even attracted comment in a lengthy and despairing article in the *Boston Herald*. During the next week, letters to the editor were filled with angry criticism of Local 34. Scores of letters arrived at union headquarters with no return address, savagely attacking the riot and Local 34. A letter supporting the union signed by a group of clergymen was not released on schedule because several of the signers withdrew their names.

At Don's desperate urging, Bill quickly issued a statement condemning the violence and promising that the union would make sure that in the future the strike was "carried on in the spirit of non-violence," Bill announced a closed meeting of the local for Monday. They would have to take steps to keep this from happening again. The meeting was far more cantankerous than he expected. The strikers were angry, not repentant. Lots of them didn't think that a public apology was called for. "They only got what they deserved," Eric Miller declared to loud applause. Bill was incensed. Pointing his finger at Eric, he almost shouted. "How dumb can you be? It's not the scabs I'm worried about. It's the strike. We can't win this strike without public support and if this happens again we can forget it. Even the union people will be against us.

Bill's statement got some applause but lots of the strikers kept their hands in their laps. A few even shouted their disagreement. Bill Pratt, the next speaker, argued that "If we cause enough trouble the government will step in and force a settlement." He got at least as much applause as Bill did. Many of those who took part in the violence insisted that they had nothing to be ashamed of and that they had sent a message to CP and to the scabs. Tony Lucelli got the biggest hand of the night. He condemned the violence but concluded with an emotional defense of those who had attacked the scabs. "I'm not going to deny my brothers and sisters whose anger was righteous and just. It's a far worse thing for a company to hire scabs, and for those disloyal to their class to earn his money from their fellow workers' misery than it is for a loyal union worker to express his anger with the only weapon he has — his hands."

Bill felt the tug of Tony's argument. I wish I could join the guys cheering. I know just how they feel. I hate the scabs as much as anyone. But I'm the president of the damn local and I can't give in to my feelings. Don's right. The riot helped CP, not us. Once the cheering ended he asked for a strong resolution condemning violence.

The argument raged for almost two hours before a motion, proposed by Tony Lucelli supporting Bill's leadership and the current policy of non-violence, was passed. Bill was less heartened by the support than worried that nearly a third of the membership had voted no. The outcome reminded him of Ed Makum's joke about the union bargaining team voting four-to-three to wish the chief negotiator a speedy recovery. This time the joke did not make him laugh.

After the meeting, Bill got into his car and headed for the union hall where Don Foreman was, as usual, busily working. Bill could barely keep his emotions in check when he described what had happened during the meeting. "Our people are so fucking angry, Don. The riot only made them madder. They want to hit someone, and they — a lot of them — are not listening to me when I tell them why violence hurts the strike. Maybe it's me. I don't know how to control our members like I should."

Don's expression was solemn. "It's not you, Billy. A company in bad faith, scabs crossing the line, no paychecks, and no end in sight. Why shouldn't they be angry? And the only way that most of them know how to fight is to hit out. With all my experience, I couldn't have handled it any better than you did, probably wouldn't have done as well. It's never easy to get angry people to accept non-violence. We had some of the same problems in the Civil Rights movement."

Bill expression eased a little. He looked more interested and less troubled. "How did you do it? Must have been a hell of a problem."

"It was, and it wasn't. Some people rejected non-violence and broke away — formed their own movements. But for most of the people, it was a spirit of righteousness that came from listening to Martin King speak or hearing Mahalia Jackson sing. Just looking at Rosa Parks would give me goose bumps."

"We don't have Rosa Parks or Martin Luther King. We have Bill Samson, and I couldn't inspire a football crowd to cheer for a touchdown."

Don laughed, but quickly stopped himself when he saw the hurt look on Bill's face. "Billy, you're a leader, a damn good one. You know how the guys are feeling. You speak their language and you never forget it's their strike and their union. Good local leaders are the key to winning a strike. You can always bring in orators, but you can't bring in leaders from outside."

Bill was grateful but confused and worried. How can Don be so calm? I wish I could be like him. If we lose this strike, it will be the worst thing that ever happened to me and to all of us. Not even Shirley knows how scared I am. Maybe I should resign or something. How can a guy scared out of his mind lead a strike? Should I tell Don that I know I'm not up to the job? But what good would that do? He'd just think I'm a phony, telling everyone we're going to win but not believing it myself. Bill tensed. He could feel his face color. What to do?

"Tell me something, Don. Do really good strike leaders worry about losing?"

"All the time. It's the fools who don't — or who won't admit it. Hell, I'm scared too."

"The thing is," Bill admitted, "I feel like I'm on trial. I don't want to be the guy who people blame for losing."

Don's expression was solemn. "I'm a radical, Bill. I don't think that fighting for a good cause and losing is the worst thing that can happen to people. Letting themselves be pushed around by a bunch of greedy arrogant bastards is much worse and that isn't going to happen here. You're the leader who is making sure it doesn't. And you have to make sure the fight isn't corrupted. It's a hell of a tough job, I know. But let's face it, you don't have a choice right now, you have to fight." His voice took on a slightly pedantic tone. "The strike is ready to turn a corner. More and more members are getting active, learning how to fight with their minds and their hearts. That's the key." Don smiled. grimly, "Of course if we lose, the members will still blame us both, and explain to anyone who'll listen, how we would have won the strike if we only followed their suggestions."

Bill felt relieved. He wasn't sure why. "You're a dumb bastard, Don. You don't know enough to be afraid of CP or of losing the strike and having all the Monday morning quarterbacks blame you. You're not what I expected when Ed Makum told me you were a labor radical. You understand how regular workers think. The radicals who come to our state meetings aren't like you. They like to talk like workers but they don't work and they don't understand guys who do. You're kind of like Tony Lucelli. How did you become a radical anyway?"

Don laughed. "Sometimes I ask myself that same question. I know a lot of radicals are bullshit artists. I don't want to be like them. But there are things in this country that need changing basic things. Things like…."

"But America is the greatest country in the world. Who's got a better system than we do?"

"Bill, being a radical doesn't mean you're not a patriot. I love this country. If my grandfather hadn't come here from Germany in 1904, I wouldn't be alive. I have relatives that stayed in Europe and were killed in the Holocaust."

Bill looked thoughtful. "Anyway, how'd you go from being a football player to spending your life trying to change things?"

"Well, partly, it's my parents. They were communists when they were young. I got a course on current political problems with almost every breakfast. They analyzed everything. I never really told this to anyone but the truth is I hated it. I hated marching in May Day parades. Hated going to summer camp where they sang phony folk songs and collected money for strikers in Mexico. I wanted to be like everyone else—live my own life, play football and ignore the rest of the world. But when the Baptist church got bombed in Birmingham, I knew I had to do something. And from there, well, one thing followed another. I don't want to sound too noble, but I was brought up to believe that it's my duty to fight injustice." Don paused and sighed. "The truth is, I enjoy the struggle. Solidarity with guys like you makes me high as smoking pot. It makes me think that my life has meaning."

Bill's response was equally grave. "I'm not a radical — not yet, anyway. I never wanted to educate people or change the world. I can't be like you. Making good paper is all the purpose I need. I want to win the damn strike — kick CP's ass so hard they never fool with us again. I want to go back to being a company man." He paused, smiled, and patted Don on the shoulder. "But I'm beginning to understand why the rest of us need radicals. The guys will be coming by soon. We better stop bullshitting and get back to work."

Chapter 12

Eric Miller stood outside of Bill's closet-sized office. His feet were slightly apart, hands clasped in front of him. His head was down. He made no move to enter, even though the office door was wide open. "Bill, can I come in? I need to talk to you." His smile was boyish, ingratiating.

Why was he smiling nervously like a kid waiting in the principal's office? Why didn't he just walk in and start talking the way he usually did? What trouble had Eric's passionate nature gotten him into? A fight, Bill guessed. But Eric didn't look like he had just come from beating up a scab or a crossover, and if it had happened earlier, Bill would have heard about it. Maybe women? Of course! That stupid bastard.

Bill motioned him to a chair. "It's Sherry, isn't it?"

Eric's eyes widened. He looked confused and worried.

"What have you heard?"

"Nothing, yet, but I've got a brain." Bill's swallowed. This meant trouble. At the very least, it would mean Eric would pay less attention to his duties to the strike. Bill pictured Eric smiling benignly while the rest of the team were trying to control themselves during the negotiations. That hormone-driven indifference didn't mean anything, because the whole damn negotiation was a sham. But the picket line was for real, and he needed his picket captain on the job.

"Damn it, Eric, couldn't you wait till the strike was over?"

A crimson flush came over Eric's face. His penitent expression was quickly replaced by a fierce, angry glare. "Don't I remember that everyone was telling you to wait when you started living with Shirley, and wasn't I the one who said 'tell them to go fuck themselves?' And didn't you thank me for being a friend in need?"

He's right, I owe him for that one, but we weren't on strike then. I'm not going to let him make me feel bad about putting the good of the union ahead of his damn sex life. He's a married man, for God's sake, and she's got relatives all over the place

Bill pounded his right fist into his left palm in frustration. "I don't want to sound like a damn minister, Eric, but the last thing I need right now is my picket captain being a dickhead. Suppose Joyce finds out, or Mo Meserve, or Larry Dickens who walks the line three times a week and still has the hots for Sherry. There's a time and place for everything, and this ain't the time and it ain't the place. She's a kid, for God's sake. Of course, you being a war hero and everything, and paying attention to her, she's going to be flattered and fall for whatever line you're using, but you're married, and it's not right."

Eric's color deepened. Bill could tell from Eric's frosty "mind your own business" look that his lecture wasn't working. Better try another approach. Bill smiled his toothy, man-of-the-world smile. "You got good taste. No one can deny that. A blind man could tell that she's sexy by hearing people gasp when she walks into a room. But I need you focused like a fucking laser beam on the strike." He clasped Eric's shoulder. "You're too valuable to the union."

Eric's stony expression did not soften. "Bill, you don't know what the hell you're talking about. She's the best thing that's happened to me since I came back from Nam. This isn't a casual screw. I'm in love. I won't stop seeing her for you, for Don, or even to win the strike."

Seeing the passion on Eric's face as he spoke made Bill even more uneasy. Eric was volatile enough when he wasn't stirred up. He can't really be in love. She's a kid, for God's sake, even if she is a great looker with tits like ripe melons. Of course, Shirley's young, too, but that's different. At least she was pretty grown up when we decided to live together. And Eric has a wife and family. It's because of the strike and his blood being so hot right now. He's in a good mood now, but what happens if they get into a fight, or she finds someone else? He'll go out of control. After the riot, a bad incident on the picket line means that we lose the strike.

Eric had no intention of ending his affair with Sherry. In the reticent, privacy-protecting culture of North Bethany, no one had realized how miserable Eric had been in the days before the strike. He had been living a lie, pretending to be satisfied with his job and his marriage but constantly fantasizing about running away and starting a new life. Now a new life had walked right up to him, and he felt like he did before Viet Nam. What Bill didn't understand was that Sherry made his work for the union possible, stirred his heart as much as his loins, and let him know life was still out there, waiting to happen.

Every evening, after shouting insults and threats to the third-shift scabs, Eric would drive to the union hall where he kept a change of clothes, put on his favorite aftershave, and leave for Bethany where Sherry was just finishing her waitress shift. They would have a drink in the hotel bar, and she would tell him about her day.

Sherry had aspects to her personality that Eric would never have imagined when their affair began. She was a born storyteller. She could engross him in the details of her life as she described the lonely, elderly women who used the coffee shop to add human contact to their day. She told him about the customers who tried to get special treatment and the wealthy ones who bragged about their own days waiting tables in high school or college. Through her stories, he could picture the quiet customers who left large tips and the loud, abusive ones who did not. Reluctantly, she even told him about the men who flirted, patted, teased, and propositioned her. He thought they had great taste. She had stories about women who wanted to introduce her to their sons, and the ones who treated her like a rival or like a brainless bimbo.

Being with Sherry brought brief moments of peace and of hope to Eric's tortured mind for the first time since he left Viet Nam. When her daily stories ended, they would drive in Sherry's car to a wooded area on the outskirts of North Bethany, where Tony Lucelli had a cottage that he had made available to Eric with no questions asked.

Eric liked to take off Sherry's clothes, always starting with the buttons on her blouse and working his way down almost reverently. When she stood before him naked and smiling, he would kiss her and then draw back and look with such pleasure on her young, beautiful face and body that she would blush and preen. He would pick her up and carry her to the rug in front of the fireplace. Eric would lick her face, her nose, then her lips, her neck, and finally her breasts. When his lips touched her nipples, she would moan and quiver with delight until Eric could feel his pulse race and happily let his body take control of his actions. Generally, after their lovemaking, Sherry would fall asleep in his arms. He would wake up in about half an hour, tickle her or kiss her awake, and the sex and love play would begin again. He would slide silently into his home about 2 a.m.

His wife Joyce never asked where he had been.

Joyce was his high-school sweetheart. They were married before Eric left for Viet Nam. From the beginning, he was a good lover but a terrible husband. Apart from lovemaking, Eric and Joyce were badly matched. They did not converse easily, did not like the same kinds of music, and disagreed fundamentally about basic issues of child-rearing. Eric wanted the kids to be tough and self reliant, and Joyce wanted them to feel protected. They argued, and over the years their disagreements became passionate and nasty. At times, Eric found himself reacting to Joyce with rage. Sometimes he was beset by fantasies of violence. To keep the family together, they began to live increasingly separate lives.

Joyce was a teacher and counselor at the high school in nearby Westin. She worked with eager, confused, vulnerable Maine adolescents, and it was to them that she devoted much of her passion and tenderness. Eric knew that she never stopped caring for him, and sometimes, as by a gift of grace, their love re-emerged, and both would feel, for a time, that they could go back to the way they used to be. But the moments of tenderness were separated by long periods of anger and isolation. By the time of the strike, Eric knew that

Joyce knew that Eric had discreet but constant affairs. By then, it no longer bothered her. In truth, his escapades sometimes brought peace when relations between them reached an intensity that foreshadowed another round of bitter argument and accusation.

○

On August 15, the union held a potluck dinner. Most of those present were middle-aged couples. The men, their faces lined by the stress of work and the skin-damaging effect of the harsh Maine climate, had worked for CP since high school or separation from the army.

Most had solemnly pledged to their wives on the way over that they would not spend their time at the dinner talking about the strike, but of course they did little else. Almost as soon as they arrived at the hall, the strikers congregated by the Coke machine, sharing gossip and arguing about tactics. A circle of strikers quickly circled around Bill, who thought it necessary to express confidence that he did not feel. "They'll never make good paper with those fucking scabs. I hear that most have trouble finding their way to the men's room. Our guys are hanging tough. Only two members, Charley Brashear and Joe Kannel, crossed the lines last week. I didn't think Joe would have stay out this long. He's always been a me-first son of a bitch."

Tony Lucelli glared angrily. "Two more line-crossers! Worse than the damn scabs! Betraying their friends, their class, and their family like that! Charley Brashear! It's hard to believe I taught him how to run the Number Two machine." Tony's voice dropped. His eyes took on a look of melancholy. "He not only voted to strike, but told me how he was prepared to stay out as long as it took." Tony thrust out his jaw. "He better hope his path and mine don't cross."

Floyd Noel suggested that they post the names of the crossovers, labeled "Super Scabs," on the bulletin board. Bill agreed. Let everyone know who these sons of bitches are.

On a table in the corner of the hall, a 16-inch Sylvania TV was playing. The sound was barely audible, and a small group of strikers was aimlessly watching. After a few minutes of national news, Jennifer Clay, the news anchor on Maine Channel Eight, announced in her typically calm announcer's voice: "Things have taken a turn for the worse again in the Consolidated Paper strike. This afternoon both sides engaged in rock throwing, and only a strong police presence prevented serious violence." People from all over the hall moved closer to watch as scenes from the picket line flashed on the screen. A group of strikers was shown surrounding a replacement worker's car, their faces contorted with hatred. Some banged their fists on the hood, and someone spit onto the front windshield before police could intervene. Someone turned up the sound, and the whole crowd, which had grown to about fifty, focused on the screen.

Jennifer Clay's attractive face with its unchanging, I don't even think about how pretty I am expression, returned to the screen. "And some more bad news for Local 34. At least three more union men decided to abandon the strike. Mike Rafferty spoke with one of them, Jordan Marcon, this evening shortly before broadcast time."

A handsome, heavy-set man, shirt open at the collar, replaced Jennifer Clay on the screen. "Mike Rafferty, Channel Eight Eye-Witness News reporting from the strike-torn community of North Bethany. Given the mood in this town, it takes courage for anyone to abandon the strike, but three more strikers made the decision to return to work today. One of them, an electrician named Jordan Marcon, has agreed to be interviewed. Thanks for talking with us. Jordan, I'm sure this wasn't an easy decision for you. Are you worried about the reaction of your union brothers to your decision to go back to work?"

"Not really, Mike. I'm well known in this community. I coach the under-sixteen baseball team, my sons are on the high school team. People in North Bethany know that I have large medical bills because of my wife's illness." Jordan was wearing a form fitted blue shirt. His face was solemn.

"Did you vote to strike back in May?"

"Yes, I did, and I even walked the picket line a couple of times when the strike started. I've always been a good union man."

The union hall, which had been silent as a church service up to this point, erupted into furious catcalls and shouts of disbelief.

Rafferty leaned forward, his expression concerned and sympathetic. "Jordan, can you explain to our viewers and perhaps to some of your union brothers and sisters why you decided to quit the strike?"

"I'm a religious man, Mike, and I came to the conclusion, with the help of my minister, that God was testing me and that the best way for me to meet my Christian obligation to my family was to return to work. You see, I heard the voice of Jesus telling me that He would not abandon me. My minister helped me to understand that He was telling me to reclaim my job."

Rafferty seemed momentarily rattled. "Well, I guess interpreting God's will is a minister's job," he added somewhat lamely.

"Jesus has never let me down, and Minister Harmon knows His will."

"Well, whatever happens, things will never be the same. Jordan, thanks for talking with us and good luck. That's it from North Bethany."

Bill struggled to control his hatred. "Damn Jordan Marcon! What happened to him? I used to think he had balls. This very union offered him more money than we could afford. Turn off the damn TV before I put my fist through it!" he shouted. Someone near the set immediately did so.

"Religion!" Bill said derisively. "It gives a cowardly bastard like Jordan Marcon a chance to screw his union brothers and sisters and say it's God's idea."

He could see the blush of anger spread over Louise Adams's face. "Bill, don't be stupid," she retorted. "It's not religion that's to blame. That's what Jordan wants people to think. The truth is, we are the ones who are following God's commandment to care for one another, but we can succeed only if we follow what Jesus said and love one another, even Jordan, in His name. We have a cross to bear, just as Jesus did."

Bill felt abashed. "I didn't mean to insult you, Louise. I know that you would never betray us as Jordan Marcon did." Bill's look of contrition was so like a little boy's that Louise laughed.

"You're a good man, Bill. God knows it, and I know it — even if that hot temper of yours makes you say and do dumb things sometimes."

Cindy Regan, her brightly dyed blond hair piled high on her head, suddenly walked to the front of the room, her hips swaying from side to side with each step. She turned to face the crowd. "Everyone knows I'm not a hater."

"You're a lover," Ray Allair called out, getting a laugh.

"I am, and I'm not ashamed of it, but I hate that Judas Jordan Marcon like I hate sin. I swear before all of you that I will never speak to him or anyone in his family again."

Bill Samson put his arm around Cindy's shoulder. "This sister has more balls than Jordan Marcon, his sons, and his father." He paused for a moment and added: "I wonder what Jesus will tell him to do after we win the strike."

Don nudged Louise. "Solidarity Forever?" She nodded.

Louise's strong, pure voice suddenly filled the hall singing to the tune of Battle Hymn of the Republic.

When the union's inspiration through the workers' blood shall run,
There can be no power greater anywhere beneath the sun.
Yet what force on earth is weaker than the feeble strength of one?
But the union makes us strong.

Bill found himself holding Louise's hand in his right hand and Don Foreman's in his left. Soon almost everyone was holding hands and swaying to the music.

"Solidarity forever, Solidarity forever, Solidarity forever. But the union makes us strong."

Afterwards, people looked at each other and smiled self-consciously, surprised and slightly embarrassed. The group began to fade away as the summer light faded and the cool Maine breeze swept away the lingering fog that had filled the parking area. Eric drove to see Sherry, ready this time with a story for her.

Listening to the singing and seeing the members' faces light up with hope also inspired Bill, but he privately wished it had been his idea and not Don's. "I'm the president of the local, but I'm not the leader of the strike," he later told Shirley. "The really good ideas are coming from Don and the spirit from Eric and Tony. I'm just standing around trying not to screw things up too badly."

Chapter 13

"Strikes are a lot different than I thought." It was the next to last Monday in August and Bill was relaxing sprawled out on the sofa with a Miller Light in his left hand and his right arm draped over Shirley's shoulder. "It's not the picket line or even the leaders. It's the membership — the strike committees — working their asses off that make us strong," he told Shirley in a tone of rare satisfaction. "We have some great committees, and Don's the guy who's taught me how to use them "Our media committee is teaching the reporters what the strike is about. They are beginning to tell our side of the story, not just CP's. Our Thursday night meetings are going great! Good speakers, good music. Our members like being there. And the outreach committee is doing a hell of a job making contact with other unions and finding supporters all over the place. Don's great at picking the right people for the committees. Only thing I don't understand is why he's high on Arthur Poland."

Shirley was surprised. "You mean that real big guy who lets his wife do all the talking? Don't tell me Don has him involved. His wife told me he was too shy to speak to their son's grade-school class."

Poland, a fourth-generation paper worker, was a powerful man. His shoulders and chest were broad and his arms muscular. His head was oval shaped, smooth and thick. Bill, who didn't like Poland, thought it resembled a watermelon shell. Poland's jet black eyes were set wide apart and he seemed to glower at the world from beneath his thick brows. Despite, or maybe because of, his powerful appearance, Poland was pathologically shy. His nickname was "The Dark Shadow." Bill thought him creepy — an odd, dull, friendless man more likely to bore or annoy people than to inspire them. But Don Foreman saw something far different. "He's got a lot of passion that he hides from everyone, and he's damn smart. He's tough and emotional. He has the ability to say things in a way that's all his own. It's a gift we should try to use."

Bill Samson would have laughed contemptuously had anyone else said flattering things about Arthur Poland, but he had come to trust Don's judgments so he invited Arthur to join the outreach committee.

Poland was suspicious.

"Why me?"

"Because Don — and me — think you will do a good job, and this team is pretty damn important to us."

"I won't have to give speeches or anything, will I?"

"No, not if you don't want to. You can talk to people privately if you want. There'll be a lot of other things you can do. You can call around and help set up meetings, as long as you're really willing to work your ass off."

"Okay, Bill, I'll give it my best shot…and Bill, thanks for having confidence in me."

A few days after his conversation with Shirley, Bill asked Arthur to go with him to a fundraiser in Providence, Rhode Island to be staged by Local 213 of the Hotel and Restaurant Employees Union (HERE). It was understood that Arthur would drive, take pictures, and work the sound equipment. Ed Plant would speak to the audience. Bill would say a few words and meet with the leadership of the HERE local. The meeting was well-publicized. Bill was excited to discover a large crowd. Over 250 people packed in the state AFL-CIO auditorium. After local president Dominic Sirabella called on the crowd "to stand shoulder to shoulder with our brothers and sisters in Maine," he turned the meeting over to Bill, who was greeted with loud, rhythmic applause.

Bill handed the mike to Ed Plant, who grabbed it eagerly and looked out at the crowd. Ed was a great talker, a guy with lots of good stories. The crowd's steady beat of applause continued. Ed started to speak, but erupting cheers from the crowd made him stop. Suddenly, beads of sweat ran into his collar. His right hand, which was holding his hastily scribbled notes, began to tremble. Ed cleared his throat. "Union men," he began in a trembling voice that had more vibrato than an Aaron Neville solo. Bill winced, noticing that most of the audience were women. Ed must have noticed. "And you ladies." The trembling stopped, but his voice sounded weak. "It feels good to be among friends. Sometimes it feels like we don't have too many friends, like unions had in the old days. It's not easy to win a strike when these damn scabs keep crossing the picket line. It's a terrible feeling." He paused. Bill looked on nervously. "I don't know what to say except that Bill here won't let us punch them in the mouth like they deserve." There was a nervous titter in the audience and a smattering of applause. He fell silent for about fifteen seconds that seemed to Bill an eternity.

"I'm real proud of our president Bill Samson, who will tell you the real story." Abruptly, he handed Bill the mike.

Bill had prepared a short speech that began, "Now that Ed explained what it's like on the picket line, I'm going to tell you why we need money." Damn! What should he do, now that Ed hadn't explained? "Well, it's hard to explain what it's like on the picket line," he finally said in a voice devoid of passion.

"We know, brother. Some of us were on strike for a year against the Marriot Hotel." This got a cheer from the audience, and Bill wondered what could he tell this group about the need for money that they didn't know already?

"We need your support," Bill stammered, and then he paused, waiting for inspiration which did not come. "Oh, shit, what a fiasco." His face must have shown his confusion and annoyance.

Arthur Poland walked up behind him. "Bill, is it okay if I say something?" Bill gratefully handed him the mike.

The crowd began to applaud once again, waiting for Arthur to speak. "I'm a mill worker and a part-time farmer — not a speaker," he said in an effort to explain his earlier silence.

Someone in the first row with a Hispanic accent and cadence called out, "We understand. Somos trabajadores como tu!" Arthur was glad he had studied Spanish. "We are workers like you!" Several young women in the audience smiled at him reassuringly. Arthur suddenly felt light-headed, the way he used to when he jumped from the top of his grandpa's barn to the floor below. He cleared his throat, and the crowd fell silent. "As a married man with three children and a very large mortgage, the last thing in the world I needed was to risk my job. But the risk of voting 'no' was a worse risk. If I voted against striking, I would have voted against my family and my neighbors, the people who gave their time and their hearts to forge a union. So, I voted to strike to keep faith with my father, who lost his fingers on a paper machine in an accident, and with my grandfather, who fought to unionize the Otis mill in 1921. I'm the union son of a union father, and both my grandfather and my wife's grandfather lost their jobs in 1921 when they wouldn't abandon their union brothers." He took an audible breath.

"And I voted to strike to keep faith with my son who, God willing, will have a chance to work in the mill with dignity. And I will stay on strike to keep faith with my union brothers and sisters who are fighting for the rights of working people all over the country." He suddenly found himself caught up in a rhythm of affirmation.

"I'm proud to be a member of Local 34, proud of my union brothers and sisters." He paused, and his eyes became watery. He swallowed hard. Bill wondered if Arthur was about to cry. But Arthur collected himself and continued. "Our union is like an oak tree, able to bend with the wind and rain. Our members are like the leaves of that tree, and the food and water that comes from you and our other friends will make sure that our tree cannot be toppled, uprooted, or cut down. We are in this battle for ourselves and all the other trees in the forest. 'Like a tree standing by the water, I shall not be moved.'" He almost sang the last line.

Arthur paused for another deep breath and had to wait until the applause stopped. When he finished a few minutes later, the crowd stood up and cheered. Someone up front waved his hat several times and then put some dollars in it. He held it high again, then passed it to the woman next to him. Several others passed their hats up and down the aisles, as if it were a tent revival. Arthur looked like a man who has just found God.

Later, when the money was counted on the trip back to the Local 34 hall, it totaled almost $800.

◯

The morning after Arthur Poland's speech, Bill Samson sipped his coffee without expression and stabbed at his eggs mechanically. Shirley fingered the edge of her flowered chiffon robe, open at the throat, plenty of cleavage showing. Bill stared at her morosely. What ever happened to his sex drive? She used to brag about it to her friends even if it was through hints rather than description. He was so easy to be with in those days but now few smiles, little sex, and no playfulness. Bill placed his coffee cup on the small, formica-topped breakfast table. His manner suggested that even the coffee was an almost unmanageable burden.

It wasn't like Bill, even during a crisis, to pick at his food. "Something wrong?" she asked sympathetically.

He stared intently at the rivulets of yolk on his plate for a few seconds. "I'm not the guy to lead this strike,"

"What makes you say that?" Shirley asked, startled by Bill's tone of defeat.

"Everything. Every day I realize that I don't have the skills to be a strike leader. A really good union president knows stuff, all kinds of stuff, stuff I never even heard about. He knows labor history. He knows how to give speeches that get people excited and raise their morale. I'm like a quarterback who can't throw a ball 20 yards. Yesterday was the worst of all. I went to a rally in Providence with Arthur Poland. Arthur fucking Poland, the Dark Shadow! I got tongue-tied, and just like Don predicted he made this killer of a great speech. Damn near took the place by storm."

Shirley showed surprise. "Good for Arthur. And good for you that you gave him the chance."

"But you don't understand," he spoke rapidly. "I didn't choose him. It was Don who insisted I pick him for the committee. I didn't want to. I thought he was an asshole. But Don was right. He made this really great speech. People were near tears.

"There's so much I need to know that I don't know, like talking to reporters or making speeches. I get angry all the time. I get frustrated and I get depressed. I wish I could be like Don Foreman. He may be the best fucking organizer in the world. He understands how to get strikers working together, who to call to set up rallies, and how to deal with the press. I'm the damn union president, and he knows ten times more than I do."

"How did he get to know so much?"

"He's been everywhere, done all kinds of things. During the '60s, he lived in Georgia and Alabama registering black voters. He learned to live off the land, hustling free rooms.

He's the guy who made the Converse Rubber strike a success by sending the road warriors out to meet with unions all over the state. He got Ed Terry elected to the state senate — first union man elected from this district in thirty years. He's always thinking. Reads all the time. Told me that no matter how hard he works, he can't fall asleep at night unless he's done some reading."

Shirley's expression reminded Bill of someone who has just remembered a crucial phone number. "Why don't you ask Don to help you? He already gives you ideas, but he can also give you books to read, books about unions and strikes."

Bill's face registered abject fear. "I don't ... I couldn't ... I mean, I wouldn't even know how to begin."

"It's not hard. You just get yourself some books, open them to the first page, and start reading." Her expression was now tender. "Don probably has some labor books with him. If not, he can tell you where to get some."

"You know how slow I am reading. It would take me too long."

"Bill, you're being as stubborn as a teenager, which means that you're scared." She laughed softly. "You look like my little brother used to look when he had to take a math test. But as you always tell me, you don't know what you can do till you try."

Bill's face showed the resentment of a man falsely accused. But his brow suddenly wrinkled with thought, and he took on the expression of a truant caught leaving school. He started to laugh. "Damn, Shirley, you know me too well." His face brightened. "Maybe I'll try it. It can't make me any worse." He took a large bite of his egg on a piece of toast, put his dish in the sink, and kissed her rather absently on the nose as he left.

The image of Shirley in her flowery robe returned unbidden as he drove to the hall. I'm a lucky man. She's sexy, and she's twice as smart as me. It was Shirley who insisted that they live frugally in this small, poorly designed house, with its tiny kitchen and old-fashioned stove on the outskirts of town. Three years ago, Bill, despite years of earning a high salary, was almost broke and had considered filing for bankruptcy. Two divorces and a chronic indifference to money matters had cost him his home and left him with a three-digit savings account and over $4000 in debt. She had changed all that. Now they saved. Before the strike her salary as a saleswoman in an antique shop on Route 1 went directly into a joint savings account that Bill knew was not to be touched. Twenty-two thousand dollars was in the account. With Shirley controlling their expenses, they should be able to get through the strike pretty well. I sure couldn't have done it by myself.

When he reached the union hall, he found Don as usual making notes on his index cards. Bill was too agitated to wait until Don finished his work. "I've gotta talk to you." Don looked up, surprised at the urgency in Bill's voice. "If I'm going to do a good job leading this local, I need to know more about unions and strikes, and I need you to teach me. I've got to learn how to organize people, how to plan strategy, and how to make good speeches."

Don could not have heard words that pleased him more. He was, after all, the son of teachers, and he was regularly frustrated by the lack of intellectual curiosity that made so many union leaders contemptuous of, or even hostile to, learning. He had suspected that Bill might be different, and now he felt vindicated. Helping him to learn would be fun.

That afternoon, Don gave Bill a carefully marked copy of Jeremy Brecher's book, *Strike*.

Bill took small snatches of time during the next three days to read the marked passages carefully. He was fascinated but confused by Brecher's description of spontaneous strikes and of the ambiguous role of union leaders.

The stories brought to mind the drive by riot and the times when he found himself vetoing suggestions for illegal job actions proposed by members who were angry at supervisors or mill officials. But what was the moral? What new understanding was he supposed to gain from these stories of uprising and repression?

"I don't get it," he confessed to Don after three days of the most intense reading of his life. "I'm not sure if my job is to stir the guys up or calm them down."

He noticed Don smiling broadly.

"What the hell is so funny?"

"You do get it, Billy, and you have to do both. We can't win unless the members are stirred up and ready to fight with everything they've got, but you as the leader have to provide direction and sometimes you have to hold guys back."

"I gotta make sure they fight but not let them throw bombs or kill that miserable prick Mel LeBlanc. Simple job. Stir 'em up and hold 'em down."

Don laughed. "You get an A."

"Go fuck yourself," Bill replied, but for the first time in awhile, he smiled broadly.

The next day, Don showed up at the office with a copy of John Steinbeck's classic, *In Dubious Battle*, the story of a '30s strike by migrant apple pickers in California. Steinbeck's leading characters, Mac and Jim, are radical agitators who instigate the strike and then sacrifice themselves, their comrades, and the strikers to promote anger at the owners and the capitalist system. Bill, who could not remember ever reading a novel for pleasure, became engrossed. He stayed up till midnight and finished it the next day.

Mac and Jim were fascinating characters, radicals of a different age, but like Don, totally committed. Mac was sharp. He could stir workers to action. He knew what to say in all kinds of difficult situations and he was fearless. He was also ruthless, willing to sacrifice anyone for the good of the cause. Bill wondered at Don's reaction to the characters who, like himself, were outsiders and radicals. He decided to put the question directly. "Are all professional organizers like Mac and Jim? Do organizers learn to distrust the people they help? Should I try to be like them?"

"No, these guys weren't really organizers. They were manipulating everything themselves. I reread the book every few months to remind myself how harmful that can be. They were brave, no doubt about that. Committed, too, and smart, but that's not enough. A leader has to let leadership come from the ranks, just like you're doing."

"Do you think the apple pickers could have won that strike?"

"No, but they did have the chance to compromise. Mac killed any hope for a deal, and he knew just what he was doing. Sometimes a good union leader has to support a compromise, even when the people he likes and admires want to turn it down. That's really a hard lesson for me. It's tough to end a strike without being able to claim a clear victory, even when you know it needs to be ended."

Bill hoped he would not have to face that problem.

A few evenings later, partly inspired by Bill's positive reaction to stories of labor history, Don held a showing at the union hall of *Matewan*, a factually based movie by John Sayles about a strike by a local of the United Mineworkers in the 1920s. To help make it important to the audience, they charged admission: a dollar to the strike fund or a donation to the food bank.

The movie tells the story of a union organizer who is committed to nonviolence, a self-described "red," Joe Kenehan. When a black replacement worker wants to join the union, the company-spy villain, C.E. Lively, calls him "boy" and tells him he will be lucky to get out of the area alive. The miners seem confused and divided about how to respond until Kenehan bursts out, "Union men, my ass! See that man. He's a worker! ... Any group that keeps him out ain't a union; it's a goddamn club."

Bill got excited. He remembered George Connerton making the same point in almost the same words.

After watching the movie a second time at home with Shirley, Bill asked Don for more books, this time some examples of strikes that the union won. Don gave him *Building Bridges*, by James Green, describing the Mineworkers' strike against the Pittston coal company. He also handed him Taylor Branch's classic study of the civil rights movement, *The Parting of the Waters*.

Bill read both books with growing enthusiasm. He was stirred by the words of Dr. King and by union vice-president Cecil Roberts's speeches to the Pittston strikers. He was beginning to appreciate the moral power of non-violence. How had Cecil Roberts, a guy much like himself, become such a fine orator?

Only slightly self-consciously, Bill began to practice speech-making before his mirror. When he noticed Shirley watching him with a bemused, affectionate smile, he told her, "I feel silly, Shirley, but I'm going to get the hang of it before the strike ends!"

He spent more and more time with Don. Maybe because he knew Don would be leaving after the strike, he was able to tell him things he had never spoken about with anyone in Local 34. He told Don about his two unhappy marriages, about his youthful ambitions, and about his turning down Gillian's offer. Don listened gravely, his eyes always alert, and his expression sympathetic. He never judged or criticized. One night at the Anchor, Bill admitted that he felt all kinds of fear when he first became involved with Shirley.

"I worried about everything. What would my friends think, what would her friends think, what would her father say, but that was only the surface. What really scared me was whether I could satisfy someone so young and so damn healthy — in bed. I mean, I'm not the stud I used to be. Actually, I never really was, but that's something else. I thought she probably needs someone that can keep it up all night. That's not me anymore. But you know what, it turned out fine. Our sex life is great. I heard her tell Jane Pollard that I'm too energetic for her, that maybe I need a younger woman. I know it's bullshit, but it makes me feel great."

Don laughed. "Hey, who wouldn't feel great when someone like Shirley says something like that? Hell, any man would feel great." Don's enthusiasm tickled Bill and gave him the courage to raise questions about Don's behavior that had been a source of rumor and controversy.

People wondered what gave him pleasure. They knew he wasn't a drinker. He would have an occasional beer when strikers went to a bar, but he would nurse it through the evening, sometimes not even finishing it. His eating habits were spartan, as were his living arrangements. For the first month he stayed at the Twin Pines Motel in a single back room at the edge of the woods. Then, he moved in with the Allairs, sleeping in a small room on an army cot once occupied by their eldest son, now in college.

His curious lifestyle led to gossip about Don's sexuality. When someone asked Gary Sanborn why he was so negative about Don, he replied. "The guy's unreal. He doesn't drink, smoke, or fuck." The line was widely repeated, and more than a few people felt it conveyed something deep, important, and troubling about Don. Not that the strikers considered him homosexual. Despite his peculiarities, there was a toughness about him that didn't gibe with their image of homosexuality. And it was common knowledge that he played football in college, an activity so masculine that it alone established his heterosexuality. Still, everyone knew that he had already turned down several invitations to have affairs. He was a challenge to some of the women in the community: an exotic, attractive male whose lifestyle had elements of mystery, danger, and excitement. But he never came on to them and never indicated his availability.

His discipline and intensity had convinced people that his sex drive was non-existent, or so weak as to be unimportant. Bill himself was confused. How was Don able to resist the lure of sex and focus so intently on the strike? He could think of only one explanation and tried to put it to Don as positively as possible.

"I guess you're one of those guys lucky enough not to have a sex drive so powerful it can take over your life."

Don laughed joylessly. "Billy, you've got it exactly backward. I can't handle sex while I'm organizing because it will become too important. I can't let it take over my life. So, I've learned to live without a woman in strike situations by taking cold showers and masturbating. Hey, it's not so bad. Like Woody Allen says, 'jerking off is sex with someone you love.'"

Bill unconsciously heaved a huge sigh of relief.

Chapter 14

The last week of August, CP announced that it had discharged four strikers for misconduct towards replacement workers. In a press release, issued even before the discharge letters were received, CP stated that it had taken its action because of "our corporate responsibility to protect our recently hired workers from violence, harassment, and intimidation."

Bill's first reaction was amusement. He explained his reasoning to Emil. "Hell, they're already permanently replaced, so who gives a shit." Emil was, as usual, more cautious than Bill and suggested that he check with their lawyer, Jeff Baker. Bill was glad that he agreed. Baker explained that being discharged was worse than being permanently replaced because it meant lost benefits and no future re-hiring rights. He suggested that he and Bill interview the discharged strikers to decide what legal action the union could take on their behalf.

A few days later, Bill put on a shirt, tie, and a grave expression to meet with the angry discharged strikers. Jeff wore his wrinkled gray suit.

Among the first to be interviewed was Tom Blades, who was the union steward for the wood-pulp workers for the past five years. Bill liked him a lot, and he was popular with his co-workers, who knew him to be honest, outspoken, and zealous in representing them. Blades had been discharged because of his conduct at the home of a replacement worker named David McPhail on August 10.

A stocky man, almost totally bald, with short, muscular arms, a thick neck, and a chest like a weightlifter, Blades had a body that seemed to descend in a straight line from his massive chest to the bottom of his formidable stomach. He strode defiantly into Bill's office where the interview was to take place, wearing an old pair of khaki pants and a matching shirt. Bill was not surprised at his aggressive attitude. Blades was a good man and a good worker with a fine family, but he had a notorious temper. After Blades seated himself, Bill read a statement that Jeff Baker had composed. "The purpose of this interview is to determine the facts so that the union can decide what steps to take on your behalf. For us to represent you properly, we must be appraised of the facts in their totality. Please be as frank and complete as your memory will permit."

Bill looked over at Blades.

"Damn it, Billy! You know me well enough to know that I don't lie and I don't need no goddam legal mumbo jumbo to know that I should tell you the truth of what happened."

"I know that, Tom, but Jeff tells me I should read this same statement to everyone. It can help us legally. So, sit your angry ass down and tell us what this is all about."

Blades looked slightly, but only slightly, mollified. "My problem is that this damn scab McPhail has rented a house about 50 yards down the road from me. Landlord is John Kent, who used to be Director of Information for the mill. There ain't a day goes by but what I curse Kent for forcing me to live next to this miserable scumbag."

Blades looked at Bill anxiously, as though wondering what he was thinking. If Shirley and me lived next door to a scab and I had to see him every day, I'd probably go crazy. Bill tried his best not to reveal it. Blades sighed and continued.

"Well, last Tuesday I'm driving down Chamberlain Road on my way home when I seen McPhail and his family out on that smooth front lawn. They're grinning, saying goodbye to some visitors. Everyone is smiling and shaking hands. Chairs are out on the lawn, the barbecue is still smoking, I can smell the burgers. And McPhail is sucking on a green bottle of Heineken. It made me sick — they're having a hell of a good time on the money he's getting from trying to do my job. Here Jean and me are living on macaroni with cheese four times a week, needing charity, and eating beans for Sunday dinner. Now, I got pretty fucking angry, to tell the truth. I drive up to my house and park and walk back to McPhail's. He's still standing there smiling. I run up to him."

Poor guy. He's losing his job and this fucking scab is partying right in front of him, and Don says they're workers just like us. Bullshit!

"Did you have anything in your hands?" Jeff asked.

"No, nothing. I was waving my arms."

"Hands open or fists?"

"Not sure, probably my right hand in a fist."

"What did you say to him, and what did he say to you?"

"I called him something. Scab, maybe Fucking Scab. No, I called him a thieving motherfucker and asked him how he could be so happy living next to people whose job he had stolen. Then I asked his kids if they were proud of their father. They didn't answer. So he steps up next to me, smiling like a gambler who just hit a straight flush. He says, cool as a cucumber, that he likes living in North Bethany and he intends to stay put, and there's not a damn thing I can do about it. I gave him the finger and told him he wouldn't be living here among decent working people for much longer."

"What did you mean by that?"

"That when we won the strike he would be fired and would have to move back to wherever he came from."

"You weren't threatening him?"

Bill knew that if Tom had meant to threaten him, he would have been a lot clearer.

"Shit. Threatening him? I was too busy hating him and feeling sorry for myself. What kind of man wants to earn his money by taking another man's job?" Blades was obviously recalling the emotions of the incident. He turned his distraught face, eyes red with anger, to Bill. "I want my job back, Billy. You're not going to just let them fire me, are you?"

"Hell, no, Tom. I mean to fight it however we can. Jeff tells me we can file a charge with the NLRB, and I mean to do it, but I need to know what happened so we can be ready for anything they say."

Blades was still angry. "I don't understand. How can I be discharged for something that happened ten miles from the damn mill — me that never missed a day's work in ten years?"

Bill and Blades both turned to Jeff Baker, whose normally morose expression had changed to a deeper shade of unhappiness. He swallowed hard. "We can try to overturn the discharge, Tom, but it's far from open and shut. McPhail's going to be dressed real pretty, and he's going to have a story that he worked out with the company lawyers about how you threatened him and he felt frightened. The damn anti-union labor board might just believe him."

Blades shook his head as though to say that the whole business seemed crazy to him — an honest, hard-working victim being treated like a wrongdoer while a scab is protected. Bill knew just how he felt.

Bill sighed and looked down at his shoes. His throat was tight, but he had to make sure that Tom understood the local's policy. "Tom, you can't do stuff like this anymore. It makes us look bad having one of our leaders cursing a man in front of his children. I know how you feel, but, according to Jeff, all kinds of bad things can happen to us if one of us is guilty of violence or ever inciting it. Next time when you get that angry, come to the union hall. You'll be with union brothers and sisters, and we'll give you something useful to do."

"Billy, you have any scabs living near you?"

"No. There are only a few living in town. You just got unlucky."

"Then you don't know how I feel, seeing that bastard driving by every day, knowing that he's taking the food from my family. And then to see him having a good time feasting and not even thinking about the misery him and his like have caused. It really got to me. It would get to anyone. Hell, if it was you, you probably would have punched out the son of a bitch. I only cursed him."

He's telling the truth, I know it and he knows it, but I can't admit it.

"Tom, I know you're a working stiff like me and not a violent person. I don't want to cast the first stone." Bill's voice deepened. "But it's really important that we carry on our struggle peacefully, in a spirit of solidarity, not anger."

"Billy, you're sounding like a damn politician, not like a union leader. I voted for you cause you're a fighter. I need you to fight for me. When this fucking strike is over, I want my job back."

"Tom, I'm learning that union leaders have to be politicians, sometimes. But don't get me wrong. I mean to fight like hell for you."

They rose and shook hands solemnly. Tom Blades walked out looking confused.

The interviews that followed were similar. In each, Bill warned a discharged worker whose behavior he sympathized with that it was important for the union to carry out the struggle (a term he picked up from Don and wished he hadn't) in a spirit of non-violent resistance. In each case, he also promised support by challenging the discharge. None of the discharged workers had done serious harm, but none was innocent of wrongdoing. Albert Stoner had thrown a rock at the car of a replacement worker, kicked it, and cursed at her as she drove home from work. Tom Marlin had been discharged because he harassed various replacement workers by following their cars dangerously close with his red pickup truck. He told Bill that he had drunk too much beer after a frustrating day on the picket line watching scabs enter and leave the mill.

Frank Chicon had pounded on the window of a replacement worker's car, which caused the worker to stop. According to the company, Chicon then "opened the passenger side door, reached in, and tried to grab the replacement worker. He had even said, 'I'll kill you, you bastard.'"

Bill tried to convince each of the discharged employees that his conduct was harmful to the union. In turn, they tried to convince him how angry and aggrieved at the company and the law they were. He had no trouble understanding how they felt. They nodded at his lecture on non-violence, but they made it clear that, in their view, Bill's job was to protect them and not the scabs.

The interviews were more traumatic for Bill than for the discharged workers. He hated being the voice of reason and prudence. Afterwards, when Jeff Baker complimented him by saying that he had behaved responsibly, he had replied irritably, "Fuck responsibility. It's a pain in the ass. These are my union brothers, and I had to act like a damn minister."

That evening at dinner, Shirley noticed that Bill seemed lethargic. "You're looking more tired now than you did when you worked 16-hour shifts at the mill," she told him.

Bill nodded. "It's a different kind of tired than I used to feel when we were working in the mill. Then, my back got tired, or my arms. But now it's like my mind and my heart that's tired, and that's hard to fix. I'm tired of the strike and tired of being president of the damn local. I'm tired being the leader, and I'm sick and tired of telling my members how to behave."

He paused and sighed, took a long swallow, and closed his eyes. Then it all came tumbling out. For the next ten minutes without pausing he described his interviews with the discharged strikers and how miserable it made him. He felt himself on the verge of tears. He could not believe the smile on Shirley's face. What was there to smile about? "What the hell is so funny?"

"Nothing, only I was just realizing why you turned down the management job. You would have been miserable."

Bill had been near tears for a few seconds, then he burst out laughing. He leaned across the table, put his hands on her face, and kissed her tenderly on the cheek.

Chapter 15

Fittingly enough, it was on Labor Day that Local 34 went on the offensive. The weather was clear, crisp, and bright, perfect for the outdoor rally and parade to the state capital in Augusta that Bill and Don Foreman had organized. The outreach committee had done its work well and the number of participants exceeded all expectations. The official police estimate was 10,000, but several of the reporters who covered the event agreed with Bill that many more people took part. When the front ranks reached the capital area, Bill climbed the podium and looked out on the line of marchers, which extended beyond his field of vision. All of the paperworker locals were out in force with hand-crafted signs expressing solidarity with Local 34. He saw banners from teachers, police, firefighters, shipyard workers, carpenters, shoe workers, machinists, and garment workers, and every one of them hailed Local 34 and condemned CP. A number of banners played off his name: "No one is stronger than Samson," proclaimed a sign held by two members of the teachers' union. Another held by high school students reminded Watts of the damage Samson could inflict with the jawbone of an ass. Next to Bill at the head of the parade were labor leaders from all over New England and liberal politicians led by Ted Kennedy and Eddie Brennan. Kris Rondeau of the Harvard Clerical and Technical Union was in the line, and so was Vinnie Sirabella, national head of organizing for the Hotel and Restaurant union. Don Foreman had worked with him in the early days of the anti-war movement.

Bill estimated that more than half the Democrats in the Maine House were there, including the head of the labor committee that was just then considering legislation to outlaw the importing of strike breakers. Bill knew many of the marchers, but most were people he had never seen before. Teenagers and aging hippies marched side by side with patrician-looking housewives. It seemed like half of Maine had turned out.

It was a day of speeches about labor's glorious history and its important future. Lincoln was quoted on the cause of labor, along with Franklin Roosevelt and Martin Luther King. Never before had Bill played a major role in something so important. He imagined that the North Bethany paperworkers would be remembered along with the other heroes of organized labor. It would be a long while before working people in Maine forgot them. What a day!

The ride home was almost as exciting as the rally. Shirley was beaming with pride and Bill, for the first time in months, noticed how sexy she looked wearing dark slacks and a form- fitting pullover jersey. He put his arm around her as soon as they left the city. She snuggled her head against his chest. From time to time he tenderly stroked the back of her neck.

They talked about the strike, about Local 34's new spirit of activism, and about the success of the rally. For once Bill didn't insist that all the credit belonged to Don. "I feel 10 years younger and 20 pounds lighter," he told her. "I'm not lugging around the fear that weighed me down when the strike began."

She bent her head lower, kissed his chest, then bit one of the buttons on his shirt, making a loud gagging noise. He held her head against his chest to protect his button, and they both started to laugh. Bill had almost forgotten how much fun love play with Shirley was. When they got home the first thing Bill did was to take the phone off the hook.

The next morning the coffee tasted especially good and the muffins were delicious. Almost casually, Bill told Shirley, "I'm thinking about making a real speech next Thursday night . . . something with balls. What do you think?"

"You'll do fine. It's time to stop worrying about it."

Of course, Bill worried about it a lot during the next few days. I'm not going to give a great speech, I know my limits. But I can speak from the heart. There's so much anger in my heart, I can't find any room for anything else. Thirty years loyal work for this damn company and now it's my way or the highway, like we're replaceable parts. An obvious thought began to work its way to the forefront of his consciousness. Make CP's lack of humanity the theme of his talk! But how? He thought of and discarded various approaches until he found one that satisfied him. It was fun.

Ten days after the Labor Day rally, lots of people, many first-timers, were at the Thursday night meeting. The crowd was in a festive mood. Before the formal meeting began, Jenny Allair and Robin Lucelli, dressed in bright blouses and short skirts, were boogeying to the union songs recorded by the Almanac Singers almost a half-century earlier. On the right side of a small, overhanging auditorium balcony, a group of high school seniors were moving around excitedly, whispering noisily to each other. When Louise Adams came to the podium to begin playing her guitar, they unfurled a large banner in foot-high red block letters that read DAVID BEAT GOLIATH AND LOCAL 34 HAS A THOUSAND DAVIDS. The crowd noticed it, burst into a loud cheer, and began a call-and-response: "Whatever it takes, for as long as it takes." One side of the room shouted the first phrase and the other side responded with the second.

After a few minutes of chanting, Louise again started strumming her guitar. The crowd cheered and quieted down so she could be heard. She sang

"Take this Job and Shove It" and quickly followed it with "Which Side Are You On?" She was in fine voice. Don had added a verse especially for the meeting:

"They say in North Bethany town no neutrals can there be,
You'll either stand with 34 or crawl for damn CP!"

The crowd laughed and then cheered. Bill Samson, watching from the wings, felt a great surge of affection for plain-looking, no-nonsense, don't-try-flirting-with-me Louise. She was a jewel. She'd be there when the strike ended no matter how it ended. Just goes to show how hard it is to know people. I used to think of her as a hard-bitten bitch. And I never could stand her father when we worked together. Always acted like he was too good for the rest of us. Now she's the soul of the union.

When Louise was hired in 1974, only one other woman worked in the mill, and the union stewards, despite Bill's urging, made a point of ignoring them both. But when management refused to assign her to the forklift, Bill insisted that, in accordance with her seniority, the union file a grievance on her behalf. He even threatened CP with a lawsuit. Management finally gave in, and Louise, shaken and emotional, told Bill solemnly: "I won't forget this." She was proving true to her word.

Bill came on stage to an ovation worthy of a rock star. He began by inviting visiting unionists and legislators to the podium. About fifty people rose from the crowd and, as they walked to the front of the auditorium, the strikers and their families stood and applauded in cadence. The majority of the guests were union people. Each spoke a few words, and most contributed money to the strike fund.

"I'm Jim Tate from Local 100. Here's a check we collected at our last meeting. We are with you all the way. Hang in there."

"I'm Sally Adams from AFT Local 50. Your fight is all of labor's fight. Solidarity forever!"

About fifteen state and local politicians were in the audience. "I'm Democratic representative George Higgins. I represent Brunswick, but right now my heart is here in North Bethany with you."

"I'm Shirley from Camden. Your strike reminds me why my grandfather fought for unions fifty years ago."

When the guests were seated, Bill returned to the microphone. "I want to thank everyone for all the nice things they've said about us, but let's not start believing how wonderful we are."

He paused and looked at the audience. "The truth is, you guys are dumb."

People looked surprised. A few laughed nervously. "You're so dumb, you don't understand the profit system. Some of you were dumb enough to believe that just because you worked hard, took chances with your health, gave your Sundays, your holidays, and your souls to the company, you could expect loyalty from Consolidated Paper Company. Boy, that's real dumb!"

"Damn right!" someone called from the audience to loud applause.

"And you know what? I am dumber than any of you."

Bill paused as the crowd laughed and cheered.

"I really believed that CP management thought of us as flesh and blood people with hearts and minds." Here his voice became almost a whisper. "That they even . . . cared about us."

His voice rose again. "We should have known that all we are to them is a cost factor to be included in calculating profits." He punctuated his remarks by pounding the lectern so hard it started to wobble.

He could see Ray Allair and even Eric, who were usually indifferent to his speeches, listening intently.

"Our ex-friend Tom Gillian told the papers that all they're trying to do is 'reduce costs per unit of output.'

"When M.L. LeBlanc looks at you, what does he see? A man, a woman?" Bill laughed derisively. "Of course not. You are a resource. A cost per unit of output. They used to have a labor-relations section. What they have now is a 'human resources' department. Get it? To the new management of CP, we are no more than resources, just like the wood pulp that we made into paper.

"So what do we have to do to show that we are something more than just costs per unit of paper? It's easy. Hold firm." His voice rose: "Win the damn strike. Become human beings again."

The roar of applause took him by surprise and shook him. Bill could see the teen-age daughter of Joe Richard squirm with delight.

That night he confessed to Shirley, "I feel like I did when I was thirteen and finally learned how to hit a curve ball."

Chapter 16

Bill didn't make any more speeches. They were up to their asses in politicians and professors eager for the microphone. But he became far more confident in presiding at the union's Thursday meetings. He would give a brief rundown of strike developments and respond to company statements each week.

"It's great. I'm speaking for all our brothers and sisters," he told Shirley.

Shirley was the one who first noticed that, as Bill got more comfortable speaking from the podium, he started speaking differently in everyday conversation. Smiling almost shyly, she told him, "Billy, I can't believe it. You're using real words instead of cursing all the time."

Bill grinned. "No shit?"

Shirley laughed and kissed him.

Bill was grateful to Don for teaching him about unions and leadership, but it was Shirley who turned his life around. "It's her I have to thank for changing me," he told Don, "not only now, but since we've been a couple."

In the midst of all the turmoil and battles, he was happy. *I didn't realize I had it in me.* He thought back to his two unhappy marriages and the quick, sordid affairs that followed them. Thank God all that sneaking around, feeling guilty, and worrying about what would happen if he got caught was over. In late September he realized with an insight — so powerful that it brought tears to his eyes — that he wanted to grow old with Shirley. He ran into the kitchen where she was busy adding a simple tomato sauce to a pot of noodles. "Shirley, damn it, you're the best thing that ever happened to me. Let's get married, right now."

She stopped stirring and tilted her head to the side as she evaluated this sudden outburst. Then she shook her head firmly. "It's not the right time, Bill. There's a strike on, and you're on an emotional roller coaster." But she blushed with pleasure. "Let's wait until the strike's over." Her smile was flirtatious. "Who knows? Maybe you'll turn out to be the right man for the job."

"Okay, I'll wait, but I'm not going to change. It took me until I was fifty to really fall in love."

During the next few weeks, the weekly meetings became more raucous and exciting, an emotional catharsis for the community. Bill would start the meetings using an approach copied from UMW Vice President Cecil Roberts. "Welcome to class warfare, New England style!" he would proclaim. The line always brought a roar from the audience. Once he read aloud a newspaper article that referred to him as a "militant troublemaker." He asked the audience in a tone of indignation, "Am I a militant troublemaker?"

The crowd shouted "NO!"

"Well, I damn well am! And I'm damn well proud of it. I'm militant because I mean to do everything I can, use all of my brain and heart to win our struggle. I know the 'suits' at CP are right to think of me as a troublemaker because I'm not going to roll over and let them change this company and this mill to please themselves, when we have put so much into making it what it is."

The audience cheered even louder and, at the next week's meeting, many showed up with newly made buttons proclaiming "Militant Troublemaker."

Laughter soon became part of the meetings, and sometimes played an important part in the expression of community feeling. It was most raucous when Bill read Company officials' statements about the strike, in what became a regular segment of the meetings that was quickly denominated "The Bullshit Hour." The speakers' list was quite diverse: laborers, priests, and professors; union leaders and strikers from around the country. It included several labor radicals who explained why, in their opinion, workers were being short-changed in the name of labor-management cooperation. Most were not good speakers. Even Tony Lucelli, their ideological soul brother, expressed disappointment.

"They don't talk about the strike. They want to lecture about capitalism. That's not what our people want to hear."

Emil Jean was furious. He organized a group of traditionalists, who protested to Bill. "We don't need a bunch of reds horning in on our strike."

Bill listened to them, thought about it, and dismissed their protests. The radicals brought ideas, folk singers, and sometimes hefty contributions.

The program committee developed theme nights as a way of sorting out the speakers. The most successful was on unions and religion. The speakers included a priest from Notre Dame, a rabbi from Yale, and Nelson Thompson, a black preacher who had been active in the civil rights movement. "Best damn speaker I ever heard," Bill later said.

Thompson was a handsome man, coal dark skin and a massive forehead, and built like a football player — broad shoulders and a narrow waist. He dressed elegantly.

Thompson spoke with a deep Southern accent, and his voice at first was almost a whisper. Many in the audience had to strain to hear him as he thanked Bill and Don and told the audience that the beauty of Maine reminded him of his native North Carolina.

His voice, still low and deep, became more audible when he told the audience, "I am proud that you have chosen me — an African-American speaker from the South to address you, a clear signal that what we share as workers is more important than what separates us in terms of color or region.

"A few of the older members of my congregation asked me, 'Reverend Thompson, how come you are going up to Maine to talk to white paperworkers? Don't we have enough troubles here for you to spend your time on?'" Nelson smiled indulgently, and his voice suddenly filled the room. "I told them I'm going to Maine because I got union brothers and sisters there who need my help." He smiled, and the crowd cheered.

"My father named me 'Nelson' after a young South African who went to prison in the fight for human rights. I am proud of my name and honor the struggle that Nelson Mandela took part in. The last time we spoke, Nelson Mandela told me: 'There is no black human rights movement, no African civil rights movement; there is a single human battle for human rights all over the world.'"

Nelson Thompson smiled almost sadly at the audience. "I bet many of you are wondering about why some workers are willing to take other workers' job."

'Damn right!" a husky male voice called out, provoking laughter and a smattering of applause.

"I used to wonder the same thing. What makes people scabs, or strikebreakers, or racists? But I don't wonder about that anymore. I've come to understand that people hurt their fellow human beings because they're scared or needy, sometimes because they're ignorant, and sometimes because they're selfish. I've seen too much of human weakness to wonder about it anymore.

"What I do wonder about today is how can we get people to overcome their weaknesses and fears. What is there in the human heart and spirit that can produce a Martin Luther King or a Nelson Mandela who grows in understanding and love and fights for the rights of his people without hatred? I have talked with Nelson Mandela many times, I have studied his life, discussed it with his friends. His life is built on the three virtues that all human beings must strive to achieve." Nelson Thompson's cadence slowed and his voice grew louder. "COURAGE, COMMITMENT, and SOLIDARITY." He paused as the crowd cheered. "And if you wonder what can win a strike or an organizing drive against a powerful and determined corporate leadership, the answer is the same." He paused and about a quarter of the audience joined in. "COURAGE."

"COMMITMENT." Almost everyone called it out in unison with him.

"SOLIDARITY." The sound was deafening as the audience rose to its feet and passionately shouted the word that had come to stand for their common struggle and mutual dependence.

Bill, who could feel a large lump of emotion growing in his throat, rose to his feet. He could see Arthur Poland fighting back tears, and Louise Adams, her face aglow, shouting her approval. I guess our members are a lot more emotional than I ever realized. I guess I am, too. On the way home, Bill and Shirley talked about Nelson Thompson's speech. He was a fine speaker, all right. But it was his ideas that were so stirring, Bill realized.

"I told Don that for me, this strike was just a local battle between us and CP, but it's not — not anymore. Our strike is part of something big. Reverend Thompson's right. We're part of a worldwide fight for justice. I'll never pass another picket line and think it's somebody else's fight."

Bill blushed. "There I go, making a speech. Don't mind me. I'm just excited."

"It's okay. Bill, you're right. The strike has made you a different person, a better person. I'm a lucky woman."

○

Overriding Don's objection, the committee decided to maintain the picket line. Nobody any longer expected it to keep out the scabs, but as the strike continued, the line came to serve an

important solidarity function. As Eric Miller reported during a mass meeting, "Walking our picket line has become a badge of honor for right-thinking people all over the state."

Among the most active pickets were two groups of wives. Jennifer Schulz, a square-faced, matronly woman in her mid-fifties who wore thick bifocals, was a member of the Wednesday afternoon wives' group that picketed outside the mill's south gate. Her second time on the line, she was stunned when a young replacement worker shouted, "Get out of my way, you old bitch," as he crossed the line. But the next Wednesday she was ready for him, shouting to her friends: "That's the asshole with the loud mouth that cursed at me." He seemed stunned for a moment, and she felt emboldened. "Yes, you, with the dumb, ugly face! We don't want fuckers like you in this community." She couldn't believe that she actually used the "F" word, but as soon as the words came out of her mouth, she felt a remarkable feeling of freedom. The other wives quickly joined in. They began to call themselves the "Garbage Mouth Four," and every one of them looked forward to her time on the picket line.

A group of retired foremen took over the Wednesday evening slot; a group of professors from the University of Massachusetts' labor-history faculty signed up for Saturday mornings, well aware that they were now making labor history as well as teaching it. As a show of solidarity, many pickets wore camouflage fatigues. Ray Allair told Bill, "I never thought I would want to wear these again, but seeing everyone dressed the same makes me proud of myself and our union."

Not everyone in the union was pleased with Bill's new militancy. Several of his old friends saw in his increasingly angry rhetoric an irresponsible playing to the crowd, a desire for applause that overrode the ultimate goal of a settlement with CP. Emil Jean confided to Laurier Lebel, "This is not the Bill I knew and supported."

As Bill got more comfortable with the media, Emil became increasingly annoyed with his style, too bawdy and lacking in dignity. Emil, who even on the picket line wore carefully pressed slacks and Van Heusen shirts, complained that Bill's strike t-shirt, his long hair, and sometimes unshaven face, reinforced the stereotype that many viewers had of union people. "Bill has become a damn hippie."

Bill considered the idea of fashion in strikers' clothes ridiculous. "I look like a worker — so what! That's what I am. My t-shirt is clean. And I don't try to talk like a professor when I'm on TV."

Emil blamed Don for the changes in Bill. Emil never regretted opposing Bill's decision to hire him. "We don't need radicals to help us. They pretend to be your friends, but you can't trust them."

Emil became increasingly open about his deep dislike of Don during the last days of summer. Arthur Poland and Ray Allair argued with him, but Emil remained adamant and converted several of his followers to the view that Don was not to be trusted. Don, a liberal activist, an outsider of Jewish heritage, a college dropout, and an intellectual was an easy target. He was a self-acknowledged radical in a conservative community where radicalism remained a frightening concept. Every time Bill heard Emil rant, he fumed, but Don told him it was just a "part of the endless struggle for worker solidarity."

The group most in a position to attract union hostility was the front-rank supervisors who trained and worked with the scabs and crossed the picket line regularly on their way to work. Some had become targets even before the strike because, based on informational meetings conducted by Professor Eastman, they openly supported CP's bargaining positions. Others became suspect because they defended the work ethic of the scabs, and some, because they wore clothes with the CP logo on them.

Divisions and anger between strikers and supervisors even emerged at Saint Philip's Catholic Church. Once they took communion together in a spirit of mutual caring. Now they. carefully avoided each other's eyes. The aging local priest, Father McInery, had grown up in North Bethany. His father had been a paper worker, and he made no secret of his support for the strike. He attended two of their open meetings, applauded along with everyone else, and even signed a ministerial letter of support drafted by Don. But the strikers were disappointed that he didn't mention the strike in any of his sermons.

Ray Allair, who continued to teach Sunday school, went to see him. "Father, I know that you, as a good man, support our strike."

"I do, Ray, with all my heart. The company's actions lack Christian charity or Moslem or Jewish charity for that matter."

"Then you'll talk about the strike this coming Sunday and speak your mind to everyone like you have to me?"

"I'd love to, Ray. It's a great opportunity to speak about social justice from the pulpit, but I don't think I can do it."

"Why not, Father?" Ray tried to imagine a priest's motivations. It was hard. "Are you worried about the reaction of CP to your sermons?"

"No, that's not it. I have a responsibility as pastor to our members who are supervisors. I feel for them. Several have come to me to discuss the strike. They are in pain, depressed, confused. They feel despised by their neighbors and their own relatives because they are forced to do work that they don't want to do. I know that many friendships have ended, perhaps permanently. I don't want to increase the divisions. The church has to be a place where everyone can find emotional peace during this battle."

"But Father, that makes you neutral between right and wrong. Surely that can't be right."

"It's not neutrality, it's reconciliation. Everyone in town knows that I support the union."

"Thanks, Father, but we need more than that. We're fighting for our lives!"

"I understand how you feel, Ray, but it's the course I feel I must take."

The following Sunday, Father McInery was pleased to see M.L. LeBlanc in church.

"Maxim (Mel's true given name), we must talk about the strike," he said as LeBlanc was leaving. Father Mac had always had pretty good relations with LeBlanc, who agreed to come to his office the following evening.

The next evening at 7:30, LeBlanc showed up as he had promised. After a few polite inquiries about LeBlanc's family, Father Mac got right to the point. "Mel, the strike is tearing the community to pieces. It needs to be settled."

"Father, I would like to be helpful, but there is almost nothing I can do at this point. I know our bargaining positions are tough, but, you must realize, we have a commitment to the replacement workers that it would be dishonorable for us to go back on."

Father McInery waved his hand dismissively. "Maxim, surely that can't be right. Your obligation to the replacement workers does not outweigh your obligation to the people of this community, who have worked so long and so loyally for CP."

LeBlanc reddened slightly. "Father, under the law, when they chose to go on strike, they risked their jobs. The strikers knew what they were doing. After that, my only loyalty is to the company."

Once more Father McInery waved his hand dismissively, this time to show his contempt for LeBlanc's point. "I'm not talking about your legal obligations. I'm not your lawyer — but I am your priest. I do know something about morality, and your moral obligation to the people of this community cannot be ignored so easily. I've talked to some of the replacement workers, and most would be happy to leave this community where they are hated if they were offered similar jobs at other CP mills. They are not Maine people." Father McInery paused. "I don't understand. What happened?"

"Father, strikes set powerful forces in motion."

"I know that, but what has happened to you? Why are you so angry toward your own people?"

LeBlanc's expression suddenly changed, becoming serious, almost grave. His normally shaded eyes were moist.

"Sometimes I don't understand it myself, Father, but I have always felt different from the people here. Even when I was a boy and everyone talked about working in the mill, I vowed to myself that I would not end my life broken by the mill like my father did. I wanted out, somehow, and that made me ambitious. I have always worked harder than anyone else, and that's why I'm now an executive of a major company. You know, Father, even back when I worked at the mill, I couldn't stand all the whining and complaints. Why couldn't they act like men? I thought that then, and I think it now."

LeBlanc's expression became bitter. "They should have been proud of me. But they were jealous and accused me of being a traitor. Traitor to what? So I decided that I owed them no more loyalty than they had given me. We come from the same background, Father, but I don't feel loyal — even related — to these people. I know what they say about me. It used to hurt, but it doesn't any more."

Father McInery was surprised at the depth of feeling. "But Maxim, it isn't healthy for you to carry all this hatred with you for your own people."

"They're not my people, Father. That's the whole point."

Father McInery's smile was sad. "But if you showed some compassion, both you and they would change."

LeBlanc rose to leave. "It's no use, Father. You are a good man, but it's too late. This is a battle, and I'm going to win. They made a mistake treating me like a traitor, and now they can't complain that I don't treat them like family. They're not."

Chapter 17

"It's a different town now," Tony Lucelli said in a tone of satisfaction. "More friendship, more fighting, more flirting, and lots more fucking." The union hall had become a social center. People stopped by at all hours. Sometimes to do strike-related work, but at other times to shoot pool or drink coffee. Ray Allair brought in a small refrigerator. Tony and Bill stocked it with beer, Cokes, and wine coolers. Sometimes in the evening, people two-stepped to the music of the country-music station. Cindy Regan arrived one evening wearing a low-cut blouse, carrying a record/tape player. The next night, several members came with records and tapes; some were union songs, some were country music, and a few were classic dance music. Almost every night wives brought in homemade bread, jello molds, and dips of sour cream and onion soup mix. Despite the hardships, members and spouses realized they were enjoying themselves. Bill often fell asleep at night wondering why it took a devastating strike to loosen Maine people enough to let go and have a little fun.

One night, just before closing, Sharon LeCarne played a tape of Benny Goodman's Greatest Hits. When Gene Krupa's famous drum roll announced the beginning of "Song of India," Sharon, who knew that Bill was a good swing dancer, took hold of his hands and led him to the center of the meeting room. Bill had just finished a few beers and he was feeling mellow, affectionate toward the whole world, and eager to dance. He tried all sorts of intricate moves, and everything worked. He twirled Sharon under his arm and behind his back, changed hands and directions with ease. Several times they danced back to back, rear ends touching, and then quickly twirled to face each other. He ended the dance with his arms around her. When the music ended, she lay her arm around his shoulder and fell back with him in the one easy chair in the hall. She sat on his lap and kissed his neck. Bill's hands roamed over her body.

"Hey, my union president is playing with my tits and I don't mind one bit!" she called out, her voice filled with excitement. Bill suddenly stopped and took his hands from her breasts, as though they had been touched by fire. He looked firmly into her passionate face. "Damn, I can't do this, Sharon. I just asked Shirley to marry me. My playboy days are over. You're a doll — but I'm almost a married man." He gently pushed her away.

Her face fell, but only for a minute. Her smile returned. "Damn, Billy. You're getting a conscience. I never would have believed it!"

"Come here, baby. He don't appreciate what you're offering, but I do." As he said this, Ray Allair, who suspected that his own wife was "playing around," opened his arms wide and Sharon sauntered over to him and pressed against him. "You may be a great president, Bill, but you're only half the man you used to be." Ray sang the last line in a terrible imitation of Willie Nelson.

Bill laughed. "Don't tell anyone."

For Ray and Sharon it was the start of an affair that was to lead to Ray's divorce and their marriage two years after the strike ended.

For a long while, Don remained an exception to the aphrodisiac affect of the strike on the union's activists. Gary Sanborn continued to raise questions about his sexuality. "Maybe he's not queer. Maybe, but if he's not, he's something just as strange — like a neutered rooster."

But Don's solitary life changed dramatically after a troop from Bangor performed a modern dance they had created especially as a tribute to the strikers. The dance, which involved fierce moves to express the strikers' anger, and complex patterns to express solidarity, was a big hit. The female lead, Moira Vitali, was especially well received. A buxom, olive-skinned woman with dark brown hair worn in a ponytail and long, shapely, muscular legs, she danced with such power that the audience was enthralled even when they had no idea what she was portraying. At the end of the performance, she stripped off her leotard, and the crowd gasped. The women were generally relieved — and the men disappointed — to discover she was wearing a strike t-shirt beneath her leotard. Everyone cheered enthusiastically as she came to the microphone.

"I'm here to support this strike because I believe in the cause of labor," she declared. "But I have a more personal reason." She smiled flirtatiously. "Don Foreman was my first boyfriend, and I've never gotten over him."

At this point, Don, wearing sandals, jeans, and a strike T-shirt, visibly pushed from behind by Bill, came out on stage to great applause. They embraced as the crowd cheered. Bill had never seen Don looking so happy. For once the lines of worry around his eyes were not visible, and his odd, semi-guilty smile of pleasure made Bill recall his first visit to a brothel.

That evening Don moved his clothes from Ray Allair's home to the Twin Pines Motel where he and Moira lived till the end of the strike.

"Ain't sex great?" Bill remarked to Shirley a week later. "Don's like a different, nicer person. Smiles more, gets less upset when guys make mistakes."

"It's not sex, Bill, it's love. Everyone's nicer when they feel loved."

"Sure, you're right," Bill agreed. Women! What romantics they are.

Bill's great sex life with Shirley continued, maybe even got better, despite the fact that he was busier than he had ever been in his life. On one typical day in late October 23, he went from the picket line to a radio interview at the union hall. When the interview ended, he raced home, showered, and changed into a suit. A suit! He returned a call from a local reporter while Shirley helped him struggle with his one good tie, then drove for two hours to Boston where he met with representatives of Jesse Jackson and Michael Dukakis. Each agreed to have their "principal" take part in a large parade and rally that Local 34 was planning for January. From this meeting, he went to one involving officials of the Massachusetts building-trades unions, and from there he traveled in the dark to the headquarters of Digital Pathways, Inc., whose young multi-millionaire founder agreed to make a large donation to the strike fund.

Every day presented a new set of challenges. As chair of the executive committee, he mediated disputes, appointed people to head the new committees, and sometimes had the unwanted task of replacing someone whose leadership didn't work out. He came home exhausted, usually sometime after 11. He no longer wondered if he was up the job. "All I can do is my best," he told Shirley, who quickly translated this modest statement as "I can do it!"

One of his toughest challenges arose suddenly in late October when the *Lewiston Free Press*, using material supplied by CP, published an article about Don Foreman's background that was headlined "Former Draft Dodger Now Advises Striking Union." The article described Don's radical background, listing the organizations to which he belonged and mentioned that "fearful of serving in the U.S. Army, he spent the years 1972 to 1980 in Canada."

Bill found out about the article when he came to the union hall and found it posted on the bulletin board. It drew a lot of attention and a lot of comment. He already knew many of the facts disclosed and called a Portland reporter to complain that the article was "a bunch of bullshit that CP's public relations staff has put together to take people's minds off the real issues of the strike."

But there was a lot of buzz within the union, and some veterans, led by Gary Sanborn, declared themselves outraged that a draft dodger should have so critical a role in their union. No doubt about it: the article created its intended crisis. Don suggested that Bill call a meeting of the local's veterans and ask them to vote on whether he should stay. The meeting was held that Sunday in the civic center. Almost 500 strikers, among them roughly 300 Viet Nam-era vets, attended. The discussion went on for about an hour. It began with a series of troubled and confused statements by veterans who expressed their pride in the union and in their military service. All had nice things to say about Don personally, but several were worried about the impact of his presence on public opinion. Most who spoke claimed that it was a red herring that had nothing to do with the strike. Ray Allair, with his long hair and melancholy eyes, seemed on the verge of tears when he said, "The war's over, damn it. And Don Foreman is my friend."

Finally, someone telling it like it is, Bill thought.

The only real attack on Don came from Gary Sanborn, who began by arguing that "This union stands for courage and patriotism — Don Foreman has shown he lacks both."

Bill was outraged. What courage have you ever shown, you grandstanding son of a bitch. You've never even been within 1000 miles of combat.

Gary concluded by saying, "He's a rabble rouser, a troublemaker. Someone who travels from place to place convincing other people to fight for his principles."

Who the hell are you to judge someone's patriotism and sincerity? Bill surprised himself. He was beginning to think like an ACLU-er. Don had really changed him. Gary's statement evoked only a smattering of applause.

Eric Miller, wearing his flight jacket with his Purple Heart and Distinguished Flying Cross prominently displayed, answered him. After describing what Don had contributed to the strike, he concluded, "Don Foreman. He's like us — a man of principle. Hell, he risked his life in Alabama during the civil rights battles getting black voters registered. That took as much courage as fighting in Nam. He left the country to stand by his principles, not because he was afraid. I don't agree with him about everything — but I like him. I trust him. And I'll stand by him just like I'll stand by this union."

Bill could see heads nodding all over the audience. What a relief! The issue was done and unity preserved. He hoped that the meeting would conclude at that point, but Tony Lucelli remained at the aisle mike, seeking to speak. He was angry — that was obvious from the jut of his jaw, the angry gleam in his eyes, and his tightly clenched fists.

Tony began by pointing at Gary. "What have you ever done in your life that gives you the right to question someone else's patriotism?"

Although Tony's rhetoric corresponded to his own thinking, Bill was dismayed. How could a guy like Tony, who preached solidarity, make a personal attack on a guy who, for better or worse, was one of the union's leaders? Didn't he realize that Gary's support was important — critical, in fact?

"Don showed more guts in Alabama than any of us did in Viet Nam. And he knew what we should have: that the war was immoral, an act of cultural imperialism, not a battle against communist aggression."

Some applauded, but many shouted their disagreement. Bill felt it necessary to end the meeting by saying he didn't want any more attacks against any of the members and that included both Don and Gary. This brought a loud roar of approval. The general meeting ended on a note of harmony, but Bill watched Gary stomping out angrily with several of his supporters.

Chapter 18

As the strikers' morale improved, violence against scabs and vandalism of company property decreased. Almost stopped, in fact. Simultaneously, morale inside the mill began to suffer, and productivity fell. Two replacement workers quit and publicly criticized the company. Jason Miller, one of the first crossovers, rejoined the strike at an emotional meeting, stating with religious fervor, "I know I have brought shame on my family for my weakness. I was blind, but now I see that I must stand with my sisters and brothers in Local 34 and never let fear keep me from the path of right."

Union-supporting supervisors reported to a delighted Bill Samson that many of the replacement workers were working less hard and making more mistakes.

In the executive office in Boston, George Watts, learned of the problem, summoned Tom Gillian.

"Tom, I want you to take immediate steps to improve morale and productivity at North Bethany. I hear that some of our new workers are demoralized and fearful that we will sell them out and bring back the strikers. It's ridiculous! Their jobs are safe, but I want you to reassure them." His pale blue eyes sparkled and he spoke with more emotion than Gillian had ever heard from him.

Gillian's bushy eyebrows rose. "Why should they believe we'll be loyal to them — when they know we weren't loyal to the strikers they replaced?"

Watts knew he didn't really have an answer that would satisfy Gillian. Not that it was his job to explain things. He was the CEO. Nevertheless, Gillian had turned out to be loyal and helpful, and Watts wanted him to be satisfied that the company was pursuing an honorable course.

"What you need to make them understand is that we are loyal to those who helped us out at this crucial time."

"I might have trouble being convincing, but I'll do my best. Don't you think M.L. LeBlanc's the best person to handle this problem since he's on the scene?" His question was an indirect, but obvious, way of pointing out that LeBlanc had helped to create the very problem that Gillian was being asked to fix. Gillian sucked in his breath and held it. He felt better than he had in months.

Watts's thin, pale lips twitched in momentary annoyance. "If I had wanted LeBlanc to handle this, I would have called him. I want you to handle this because you're better than LeBlanc in dealing with workers." Watts looked directly into Gillian's eyes. He spoke more slowly. "I'm not as unaware as you may think. I know your sympathies are with the strikers. Your pride in your working-class sensibilities is obvious. I also recognize your abilities far more than you think I do. Otherwise, I would have gotten rid of you and replaced you with someone less conflicted about our program. You have great energy and knowledge, but you are too judgmental of people who approach things differently. Obviously, you consider me ruthless. But you might just consider the possibility that I, too, have principles. I'm not trying to increase my own fortune. I'm working for our shareholders. I learned at the University of Chicago that loyalty to the interests of the stockholders is the highest obligation of corporate officers. I have never lost sight of that message."

Gillian grimaced. For once it didn't sound like bullshit. Watts had a point. He could have fired Gillian at any point. "I wonder if I've been too quick to judge him?" Gillian's tone became more conciliatory. "I'll go down there for a few days and see if I can improve things, but I've never claimed to be a miracle worker."

"I don't need miracles, I need results." Watts' expression was friendly and almost understanding.

Gillian felt a surprising surge of affection. "I'll do my best."

Gillian drove to North Bethany that day and met with Mel LeBlanc in a private meeting room of the Carriage House Restaurant. LeBlanc was already seated when Gillian arrived. He smiled half-heartedly at Gillian but did not get up from his chair.

"Nice to see you, Tom. I'm glad that the powers that be have finally decided to pay some attention to my problems."

"I hope I can help," Gillian said. "We get the sense that morale is down and affecting productivity. I'm worried about losing too many veteran people, which will hurt us with the media, of course, but also seems to hurt productivity."

LeBlanc rubbed his hands slowly back and forth on his thighs, as if he were cold. "Well, there's little I can do about it. The scabs are nervous. They read stories in the local papers about how wonderful the strikers are. Nobody, not the press or anybody high up in the company, seems to recognize how hard it is on the scabs to learn a new job and put up with all this pro-striker crap at the same time. Most of my supervisors are like everyone else in this town and wish the strike and the replacements would go away. We're losing the battle for public opinion somehow, even with all our high-priced public-relations experts."

Stop whining and act like a man, Gillian felt like saying. Instead, he told LeBlanc, "Maybe I can help you. I want to meet with the scabs and with the crossovers."

"Sure, Tommy, it's your show. You're from headquarters. I'm just your man on the ground."

More whining. Gillian mumbled a quick goodbye and left without even offering to shake hands.

The next day, after tying up his steel-toed boots, Gillian arrived at the facility unannounced. He stopped in front of a half-asleep guard who handed him a packaged pair of eye protectors. Gillian put them on and then took out his own padded earphones that he had kept since his days working at the mill. Inside the gigantic machine area, people were scurrying about busily. Someone less knowledgeable might have been positively impressed, but Gillian knew that frantic activity was not a good sign in a paper mill. It indicated that the machines were not properly set or functioning. Watching the earnest, sometimes frantic, efforts of the replacement workers to adjust the machine settings was unnerving. One personnel meeting wasn't going to cure all this. He would have to meet with the supervisors and with the crossovers separately and drive home their responsibility to train the replacement workers.

He wandered, unquestioned, to the pulp mill, where wood was broken down into fiber for the paper machines. Outdoors, surrounded by the familiar stench of sulfur, Gillian found the atmosphere more lackadaisical. A great deal of soft wood was being treated. Increasing the percentage of soft wood was an easy way of producing more paper, but normally the company didn't do it that way because it had too high a cost. He watched as two replacement workers attempted to saw off a wiggling metal pipe without properly securing it. A canister of chlorine dioxide gas, used in bleaching the wood chips, was nearby. For the first time, Gillian understood the strain on the supervisors produced by the replacement workers. If that one metal pipe had dropped on that one valve, the gas released could have killed not only everyone in the mill, but everyone in town. And then Watts wouldn't have a labor dispute on his hands; he'd have a national tragedy.

There were a few pleasant moments. One of the supervisors, watching with Gillian from the breakroom, pointed across to a small unit of workers. "That colored guy Green is a good worker, understands machinery, and doesn't mind getting his hands dirty. The young woman who works with him — Kent, she's good, too, always proving that she can keep up with the guys and outworks most of them. But Young, the punk with the long hair, he's a damn parasite. He pretends to be busy but couldn't learn the job if he tried — which he doesn't." It took only that, the personalizing of a few replacements, for Gillian to feel back at home inside the mill. This experience, plus his now more sympathetic view of Watts, made Gillian feel good, a part of CP again.

After lunch, Gillian met with the supervisors. He let them talk about their jobs and about why productivity was so low. Then he asked what could be done about it. Some of the answers were defensive. "Hey, we're making do with a bunch of untrained workers. Give us some time, and we'll produce as much high-quality paper as ever."

But other answers reflected the opposite view. "We got some people here who will never learn the job and don't care. I can't train a bunch of people who don't know how to work and don't want to."

Gillian assured the supervisors that CP management knew they were working under difficult conditions. He spelled out the official line and then bluntly stated that he knew they were being as loyal to the company as they could.

"You ought to tell that to Mel LeBlanc. He seems to think that we're not treating the scabs nice enough." This remark led to a chorus of approval and a smattering of applause.

Gillian kept his professional demeanor and said that LeBlanc, too, was working under great pressure.

Someone in the rear called out, to general approval, "It's his own damn fault."

Gillian tried but could not suppress a smile.

His last group meeting was with the crossovers. Before going into the small soundproof room next to the cafeteria, Gillian braced himself. He tried to imagine himself in their places. He could not. He was tired, drained by the noise and meetings and his own mixed-up emotions. He had nothing left to offer. Empty, he sat on a small chair facing the crossovers, and intoned, on behalf of the company, gratitude he himself was far from feeling. Then he urged them to help educate the replacement workers. He knew several of the crossovers who sat impassively listening to him. The person he knew best was Jordan Marcon, whom he knew to be a good worker and whom he once thought of as a strong union supporter. When he invited them to return to work, he kicked back his own chair and signaled for Marcon to join him.

By that time, the bright afternoon sun was setting. They walked into the large, almost empty, mill cafeteria for coffee and donuts. When they sat down, Marcon seemed different from the person Gillian once knew: tighter, more fidgety. Marcon's gaze shifted uncomfortably from his coffee cup to a table where a couple of supervisors were sitting. Gillian asked a few perfunctory questions about morale, and about the role of supervisors and crossovers training the replacements. Marcon answered without looking up. As he reached for his coffee cup, Marcon's hand trembled.

"Been tough for you in town?" Gillian asked with genuine concern.

"Worse than I ever thought. Ann's family won't even talk to us. Nobody says hello in the stores. My boys have crap sprayed on their lockers at school."

"I guess people were surprised that you crossed. People used to say you were a strong union man."

Jordan Marcon put his hand to his head. "That was another time, Tommy, before Ann got sick and before my kids got used to living well. I know I did right because the Boston specialist tells me that Ann will recover. I hope you can understand this, Tommy, but I would have stayed with the strike if I hadn't heard the Lord's voice telling me to get up and go to work. I know people in town don't think it's true, but as Jesus is my Savior and Judge, I heard Him, and I'm sure I'm doing His will. I wouldn't lie about something like that."

"No, of course not," Gillian replied. "But sometimes it's hard to tell God's voice from our own fears."

Marcon looked stricken. "You think I'm a coward, Tommy?"

"No more than we all are when jobs are tough to find."

Who was he to criticize someone for fighting to protect his family?

O

The next morning, just before daylight, Jordan Marcon slipped out of bed and into the bathroom in what had become routine stealth. He shaved, dressed, and went into the kitchen where two of his sons were silently shoveling cereal into their mouths. Typical 13- and 15-year olds, their legs and shoes took up most of the walking space, so Jordan stayed near the counter, drinking coffee, watching the white plastic cat's tail move the clock's hands toward 7:30. When it was time, he helped them into their heavy backpacks, murmured encouragement with a short prayer, and sent them down the steps. Since his return to work, they waited at the end of the driveway for the bus instead of joining the other kids, most of whom were the children of strikers, at the neighborhood bus stop. The bus driver, a deacon in the Church of the Redeemer, daily pulled his lumbering bus to the driveway, screeched the brakes as the kids climbed in, and gave a brief wave toward the kitchen window where Jordan stood until the boys were safely aboard.

Jordan was tired, and he hadn't even started his day. As he washed the dishes, he heard Ann return from the bathroom and get into her wheelchair.

The chemo and radiation had taken a toll on her — on all of them, but especially on her. He leaned down and kissed the top of her thin hair when she rolled into the kitchen area, which, with the boys' absence, was large enough for the wheelchair. He handed her a mug of coffee. "Did you sleep okay?"

"Off and on, sure. What's the weather supposed to be?"

They tried not to focus on the cancer, on the pain, on the fear, but it had made a huge shift in their lives and was always at the center now, even more than the strike or his returning to work or the kids being insulted or ignored at school. It changed how they got up each morning, and slept, and organized each day. Today no hospital trips, so today Jordan could get to work on time and stay late to get in his hours, in a workplace he had come to dread.

"I think the sun might stay out all day," he answered, and gently moved her forward, back, and forward to the left until the thin rays of Maine sunlight turned the fragile hairs on her arms into golden threads. "You know, I talked to Tom Gillian yesterday. I don't think he approves of my going back to work. It makes me wonder."

"Jordan, no one had better reason to cross than you. I'm sure Tom Gillian understands. If he doesn't, he was never a true friend."

As Jordan backed down the driveway, Ann again tried to imagine how hard it was to drive through the hatred of 20-30 pickets, screaming insults. Again, she accepted that she couldn't imagine it, just as she couldn't image being 13 and having someone spray-paint insults on her gym locker.

She sat very still and bowed her head in prayer for her boys and Jordan, and for a morning when she'd have enough strength to be a real mother and wife again.

Chapter 19

"We're winning the damn strike," Bill Samson announced before the first meeting of the union's executive committee even began. "Our morale is sky high, and theirs is lower than a snake's belly. Only one asshole, Bob Kinney, crossed the line last month, and two of our people saw the light and came back out. And the media! Remember the editorials telling people how we are no different from the Mafia, Now they write about what good, hard-working veterans, fathers, and all-American guys we are!"

Cindy Regan looked doubtful. Men! They all believed what they wanted to. Bill, too. "Billy, it's time to grow up and face facts. We have a long way to go before CP will even start thinking about settling. Production is down, probably even way down, but we all know they can meet their contracts by shifting work to other mills."

Don Foreman put down his coffee cup and nodded his head vigorously to show his agreement with Cindy. As an invited guest he rarely spoke at Executive meetings, but Bill could almost always tell from his expressions how he felt about issues. Both Eric Miller and Emil Jean added their own doubts about Bill's rosy estimates.

 Bill was shaken. I guess I'm listening too much to my own speeches, he thought.

"OK," he said. "Everyone seems to agree we need to do more. But what?"

When no one on the committee volunteered, Don Foreman raised his hand, and Bill quickly recognized him. "We need to spread the strike to other CP locals. If we can get another primary mill to join us, we'll have a real chance. If we can get two, we'll win for sure. Local 55 in Machias is the key. Their contract expires on November 30th. "

Bill rolled his eyes. "I wish we could get them to join the strike, but it's not gonna happen. CP has been sending them love letters for a month, and their contract offer is a lot better than ours. They give up Sunday premium pay, but that's the only concession CP is asking for. And they get real signing bonuses — about $2,000 a person. Tom Jordan, their president, says their guys are real grateful to us for putting up such a great fight because they're getting a much better contract than those pricks would have given them otherwise. But he tells me he's pretty sure that his people will take it. They know what happened with us, and they're scared. They don't want to lose their jobs anymore than we did. They know that Watts plays hardball."

Don remained standing. "We need them, Billy, need them bad. Let's use a full-court press."

"Meaning what?"

"Meaning, first of all, member to member contact. We've got to convince them that if they join us they won't have to make *any* concessions. Not Sunday, not anything, and if they sit back and we lose, they will have to give up jobs and seniority sooner or later. Let's get our people into it. Send a personal letter to everyone in Local 55 from someone in North Bethany. Tell them how we've learned the true meaning of solidarity and how every damn local in the country will do better if we join together and win the strike."

Bill looked dubious. "Solidarity is great but doesn't make up for losing your job to a scab. Besides, we don't even have their addresses. If I ask Tommy, he'll want to know how I'm going to use them, and he may get pissed that we are making an end-run around their leadership."

Emil Jean looked at Don with profound contempt. "If you think letters from us are going to win them over, Don, you just don't know as much about paperworkers as you think you do. You say 'we,' but it's not. You're not a member of this local and your job isn't at stake."

Now it was Bill's turn to look angry. "Look, Emil, I don't agree with Don, at least not now, but he's a union brother same as anyone here, and he's working his heart out for the strike. He's part of this local and if he wants to say 'we,' damn it, he can say it, and I'm proud to hear it."

Bill turned back to Don, his expression far from pleased. "As for you, Don, use your head instead of your radical ideas. I know you've got balls, but we'd really piss Tommy off if we wrote letters to his members and didn't even clear it with him."

Don looked thoughtful. "OK, then. You need to contact John Elder and ask him to set up a meeting where some of our key people — maybe you, Emil, Arthur, Cindy — meet with their members and talk about the strike and ask them to turn down CP's demands and join us."

Bill's face had lost the radiant happiness it had during the first part of the meeting. "It won't work. It will hurt. I can't ask for a meeting with his members without going to Tommy first. And it won't do us any good to try to convince the members to strike and risk their jobs even if the leadership of Local 55 supports it, which I very much doubt they will do. They and their people want to get a contract signed and go on with their lives. I'll talk to them. But I'm not going to push them to join the strike.

"I know how they feel. Before the strike, I would have told whoever called me from a striking mill that I would be glad to help but that I was not going to have my members risk their jobs. I don't know what I'd do even now. Not everybody, even in Local 34, feels the joy of solidarity. Lots of our people are scared. Some are depressed, some have trouble getting out of bed in the morning, and let's face it, some are pissed at us. This is a democratic national union. Nobody can tell another local to strike."

Don kicked at the ground. "A labor movement means that we take care of each other. One local's strike is every local's strike. You know the motto, 'United we stand, divided we fall. An injury to one is an injury to all.' At least the decision to strike or not should be made on a grass-roots level, not at a leadership meeting between you and Tommy."

Bill was adamant. "Right now most of our active members are high as a kite. And more people are becoming active every week. They're giving their hearts and souls to the strike, and everyone thinks we're winning. If we give them the idea that we need Local 55, and Local 55 doesn't join us, it will be a real downer.

"Another thing. John Elder won't like us making contact without his approval. He'll see it as an end-run. National union presidents don't like end-runs."

"That's exactly what's wrong with the labor movement." Don spoke in his lecturing voice that Bill had come to hate, despite his affection for Don. "Decisions that should be made by the workers are made by union leaders who are always more frightened than the rank and file members. What you're saying is, one local has to beat a huge, multinational corporation all by itself."

"Damn it, Don, we're not fighting by ourselves, and I don't need a speech on labor solidarity. If we lose, I lose my job, and all the members that now love me will be out for my ass. Don't you think I'd like to have every damn local in the whole fucking union striking with us?" He put his right hand on Don's left elbow. "I'd take a lot of chances to win this strike, but I feel in my bones that we can do this only if Tommy Jordan is behind us."

Bill was sick of the discussion. It made him think about his original suspicion of Don. He was so sure of being right, and he wanted everyone to take the same kind of chances that he took. But other people had families to support and a way of life to defend.

Don may have sensed Bill's reaction because his expression changed to express submission. "It's your call, Bill. I'm just here to work for you." The issue was tabled until Bill could talk with Tommy Jordan. Don's pissed at me, thinks I'm acting like a frightened union politician. He wants me to act like a kamikazi, but what good would it do anyone?

When the meeting ended, Emil Jean made it a point to walk out with Bill. "You gotta watch him, Bill. He's a troublemaker who shouldn't have any say about what goes on in this union."

Bill felt a momentary twinge and lowered his head. Emil had a point. But almost immediately he felt ashamed of himself. Don was always thinking of ways to make the union stronger. That's what Bill needed him for. He turned more confidently to face Emil. "He's my friend. We're lucky to have him — so fuck off." Emil said nothing, and Bill did not see Emil's hooded eyes narrow.

The next day Bill followed through with a call to Tommy Jordan. He asked whether Jordan would be willing to publicly urge his members to refuse an agreement with CP until the company promised that North Bethany strikers would be rehired.

He could hear Jordan sighing on the other end of the line. "Billy, I can't promise that. My people are scared. They don't want to strike. They want to keep their jobs. As far as I'm concerned, my primary job is to protect my members. They wouldn't listen to me on this anyway."

"How would you feel about us sending your members letters explaining why it would be in their interest to join the strike?"

"It wouldn't work, and it would put me on the spot with them. If you want, I'll give you their names and addresses. But when they ask, I'll have to tell them that our leadership is not urging them to strike. In the end, it would mean that we'd do less to support you guys. I'm ready to collect money, hold rallies, send letters. Hell, I'll spread the word every way I can to our people that now is not the time to set any production records. But that's the most I can do, and I can only do it if you don't interfere with our own negotiations. If it were the other way around, your people wouldn't strike for Local 55. I believe that, and so do our members."

The next day Bill described the phone conversation to the union's executive committee, which voted nine to Tony's one not to follow Don's advice and not to seek a meeting with the membership of Local 55. For the next several days, Don and Bill were less easy with each other. Each thought himself unfairly judged. Bill felt that Don now thought of him as a union bureaucrat, while Don was sure that Bill now saw him as a theorist with little understanding of reality.

Each was partly right.

Bill remained convinced that he had handled the matter properly, but the discussion had eroded his confident feeling that the strike was being won. "Don and Cindy are right," he told Shirley the next evening. "We've got to hit CP harder."

"How? I thought you were doing everything you can now."

Bill suddenly had an idea. "I've been reading about corporate campaigns. If we had one going, CP wouldn't be so busy ignoring us. They'd be on the phone asking for negotiations. I'll have to talk to John Elder."

Chapter 20

Snow began falling early on the morning of November 15th, and it did not let up till the afternoon of the 16th. By then, the branches of the spruce and elm trees that framed the elegant Victorian homes on State Street were bent into graceful, sparkling, snow-laced arcs. The snow-covered town looked unusually lovely and peaceful, but Gary Sanborn's mood was anything but peaceful. At breakfast he argued with his wife and yelled at his kids to stop playing around with their food. Even as he growled and fumed, he knew was using his family unfairly.

 Gary was scheduled to picket at the south gate, but, after starting out for the line, he stowed his picket sign in back of his pickup truck and drove instead to the West End Café.

It wasn't the weather that was bothering him. Gary was used to dealing with snow. And it wasn't Consolidated Paper. It wasn't even the veterans' meeting, although he could never be friends with Tony Lucelli again. The problem was Bill Samson, who managed to get himself quoted daily in the newspapers. Bill was playing politics to improve his reputation and using Don to attack Gary. He pretended to defend Gary at the meeting, but Gary suspected that he had secretly encouraged Tony. All the publicity focused on Bill and none on him, although he had been the one who warned the members before the election and who afterward never said I told you so, but just pitched in. What an ungrateful self-promoter Bill had turned out to be. Worse than Bill was Don Foreman. Just last week Foreman had the effrontery to chew him out publicly in the union hall in front of lots of people for telling a reporter that Negro scabs were setting back race relations in the state. Everyone knows it's true! He had gone right to Bill's office to protest, and Bill had told him he was acting like a child. But it was Bill himself who was being childish playing at being a radical. It was bound to backfire. It was Red Don's influence that created Bill's new style — his stir-the-crowd speeches, his opening the union meetings to all sorts of outsiders. Don was a typical Jewish radical. Not that he had anything against Jews generally. It was just that radicals with New York roots did not understand Maine and its code. Most infuriating of all, Don had fooled almost everyone. Even Gary's friends, like Eric Miller and Joe Grant, were now kissing Don's ass, telling Gary how wonderful he was and what a good job he had done in mobilizing people. When Gary pointed out Don's flaws, his radicalism, and his inappropriate attitude of command, they just rolled their eyes and exchanged smiles as though Gary was being jealous. Gary told them that if they had to deal with

Don regularly, like he did, they'd know what an arrogant son-of-a-bitch he was — a show-off, a know-it-all with no humility, an outsider, a traveling radical who had little at stake in the strike's outcome. If they lost, Don would move on like a shining knight to some other fight. His friends pretended to listen, but he sensed that he was getting the reputation for being a crank, and this made him even angrier.

Gary entered the restaurant, stomped the snow off his boots, and started towards the counter when he noticed Emil Jean and Lucille Caron sitting at one of the booths in the rear, talking earnestly to one another. Gary had a soft spot for Lucille. He liked her womanly appearance — round, ruddy cheeks, wide hips, and a well-formed bosom. Before she hooked up with Emil, he used to flirt with her all the time. His spirits lifted when Emil signaled for him to join them. Gary was well aware that the alliance between Bill and Emil was frayed, because Emil didn't like Don any better than he did.

As Gary approached their table, Lucille, wearing a bright blouse with imitation pearl buttons open at the throat, her hair loose, smiled pleasantly at him. "Nice to be indoors, isn't it? I hope the snow scares away some of the scabs."

"They'd just hire a new batch," Gary said in a hopeless tone.

Lucille looked up at him questioningly. "Don't you think we have them on the run with our great solidarity and Bill's brilliant leadership?" As Lucille spoke, Emil smiled as though amused by a private joke.

They want to join up with me, Gary thought. It was appealing.

"Maybe it's me that's confused," he said, seating himself next to Emil in the small booth and directing his remarks to Lucille, "but I think Bill's living in a fantasy world. All he hears are the cheers, and all he reads are his own press clippings."

Lucille leaned forward and smiled engagingly, speaking in a low, breathy voice that was not quite a whisper. "You want to know what I think?" Her eyelashes fluttered. "In my opinion Bill is confusing being a union president with being a rock star. He just soaks up the applause and the limelight. He's got women practically swooning over him, and you know Billy has always been a ladies' man. He loves all the attention. That's why he and Don have cut Emil out of the leadership picture. And if Emil was president, he wouldn't have let Tony keep his position after attacking you and practically saying that everyone who fought in Viet Nam was a fool."

Emil took a deep drag from his cigarette. "Damn right, I wouldn't! And to think how many times I discouraged people who wanted me to run for president so Bill could keep the job."

Gary nodded emphatically. "I'm glad that I'm not the only one pissed off at Bill's show-off ways. And he's beginning to think of himself as a radical and the strike as part of a damn revolution."

"Exactly. There's a lot of us who feel that way," Emil said in a low voice. He took another deep drag and mashed his cigarette in the ashtray. He looked around to make sure they would not be heard. "I used to really like Billy, but not now. I can't feel comfortable with all these radicals and left-wing politicians giving speeches at our meetings."

"Bill isn't even running things. He thinks he is, but he's just a dupe," Gary said. "Don is the guy in charge of things. Makes decisions and doesn't even check with the elected officers about policy. And he's always giving lectures about his days in the civil rights movement. I'm sick of hearing about it."

Lucille became more animated. "He took it on himself to appoint Louise Adams head of the food bank. Gave her credit for all my ideas. Emil says I should have been made head of the committee, but Don knows I'm close to Emil, and he wants to keep him from having power."

Emil spoke bitterly, "Billy is having such a good time thinking of himself as a union hero that he's missed chance after chance to restart the negotiations. I heard from an international rep who services locals in New Hampshire that Dunsford had called Billy a couple of times to suggest informal meetings, but Billy just blew him off."

"He doesn't know what he's doing," Gary said. "We can't beat CP the way things are going, no matter how high people get and how much they enjoy singing 'Solidarity Forever!' Don is so sure that what worked for the civil rights movement will work for us, but in my humble opinion, he doesn't know what he's talking about. He's sure convinced Bill, though."

Once again, Emil nodded. "Another thing I hear is Bill is trying to get Don appointed International Rep to take George Connerton's place now that George has retired. I can't imagine anything worse."

Gary was genuinely shocked. In his fantasies, the job was his. Bill's support for Don was another betrayal of the membership to an outsider. "John Elder is the guy who makes those appointments, and we need to let him know that Don Foreman just wouldn't be acceptable to us."

"That's a good idea," Lucille said.

"Another thing. Let's organize the people in the local who share our views and plan to take it back. Maybe Billy will find out in the next election that he isn't as popular as he thinks."

"Fucking A," Gary said. He turned his gaze to Lucille. "Excuse my language." She nodded graciously.

Two days later, Bill Samson called John Elder to discuss the appointment of Connerton's replacement. He began enthusiastically. "Our guys are working hard, picketing, traveling, telling people about the strike. Our solidarity is unbelievable, and we're opening new fronts all the time."

"Great, Billy. Everyone knows you're doing a great job leading the strike."

"Don't give me the credit. The guy who deserves credit is Don Foreman. He's probably the best damn organizer in the world. He's the guy to replace George Connerton."

Elder was silent for a few seconds. "To tell you the truth, I have been thinking about appointing you to the National staff, Billy. It would make no sense right now 'cause you're doing such a good job as local president. But we'll have a place for you when it's over. Whoever I appoint now, though, it won't be Foreman. What I'm hearing is a lot different from what you're saying. Lots of people say he's arrogant, too radical, and doesn't appreciate that he's supposed to be a soldier, not commander-in-chief of the strike."

"John, that's bullshit. He's the hardest worker and the best organizer I have ever had the privilege of working with." Bill paused, and then, raising his voice in exasperation, added. "And he follows directions a hell of a lot better than the assholes you've been talking to. It's Gary Sanborn that acts like he's in charge, not Don."

"That may be, Billy, but if I were to appoint Don, there's executive committee members in the local who'd be pissed, and the last thing I need is officers of Local 34 pissed at the national union. You may not know it, but right now you people are heroes to the members." When Bill did not respond, he added, "You're the guy that members all over the country are telling me we should nominate for national office."

For a moment, the thought of national office grabbed hold. Being national president of a major union would be like fulfilling old fantasies. But his flight of ambition was short-lived. Hey, I could be president for 20 years and never do anything more important than this strike. He realized that Elder was waiting for him to say something. "John, I don't give a damn about my political career in the union. What I want to do more than anything is win this damn strike, and appointing Don would help a lot. Your giving in to Gary and his friends won't help me or you in the long run."

Now it was John Elder's turn to be angry. He understood that he was being accused of cowardice. "I'm the president of this damn union, and I'm going to do what I think will help make the union stronger. We're not a radical union, and I'm not going to appoint a well-known radical just to please you.

Like it or not, I'm going to appoint Tommy Izzotti, a solid guy who has 10 years as a paperworker in New York."

Bill hung up in disgust, infuriated with Elder's tone and furious that some of his members, undoubtedly led by Gary Sanborn, were selfish enough to oppose Don by going behind his back to lobby John Elder about union politics.

Chapter 21

The national union hired Sidney Rubin of the Herman Publicists group to make pro-Local 34 commercials for Maine's local TV stations. Most weren't very good, and they were expensive. The union could only afford occasional showings. In air time and quality, they were overwhelmed by CP's slickly made "Let's get back to work" commercials, made with professional actors. Rubin, a professorial-looking man — with a thick mustache, high-domed forehead, and soft brown eyes magnified by thick, wire-framed glasses — decided to change direction and focus on celebrity endorsements. He arrived at the union hall in October proudly bearing a videotape that he assured Bill would "play a key role in the battle for the hearts and minds of the people of Maine."

As Rubin set up his equipment to show the video, Don Foreman, sitting beside Bill, scowled visibly to express his impatience at the entire effort. "If that's a way to win a strike, I'm an astronaut. Even if the videos are good, they're not what we need. Whoever hired these incompetents is wasting union money."

Rubin returned holding a video in each hand. "I've got one by Susan Sarandon and one by Emma Taylor."

"Who's Emma Taylor?" Bill asked

"A wonderful British actress — very persuasive, adds class and dignity to the strike."

Rubin, busy inserting the video into the cassette player, did not see Bill's look of disgust or hear Don's sarcastic "Class and dignity? What does he think this is, a Miss Universe pageant?"

The video began with a close up of Emma Taylor, a middle-aged British actress, looking grave and important.

Hi, I'm Emma Taylor. Normally when you see me I am playing a part, but today I want to speak from the heart and talk about an issue I really care about, the struggle being waged by decent, hard-working union people in North Bethany, Maine. They are employed by Consolidated Paper, and most of them have worked at the paper mill there for many years. Because of their hard work and the hard work of other unionized paper makers around the country, Consolidated Paper made record profits last year — almost two hundred million dollars. Enough to give generous bonuses to their top executives.

But when it came time to acknowledge the workers, who made the profits possible, they couldn't find it in their hearts to offer them anything. In fact, they demanded that the workers take cutbacks, and they insisted on the right to subcontract union jobs. If the union agreed, hundreds of people could be put out of work. That is why your neighbors and friends in Local 34 are striking and why they need your support.

Don't believe the CP ads. They are not telling you the truth about this strike. Support Local 34. With the Thanksgiving and Christmas holidays coming on, they need help. Give generously to the strike fund. Do what I just did — write out a check for as much as you can afford and send it to Paperworkers Local 34, North Bethany, Maine 04523.

When the cassette finished, Rubin's normally nervous expression relaxed a little. I guess he means well, Bill thought. It shows work. Might do a little good. Not much, though. He could imagine Maine people laughing at her accent. Bill put a friendly hand on Rubin's shoulder. "I can see where this might work in a political campaign, but it's not what we need to win the strike. Our own people can tell our story better than an actress reading from a script. Particularly one with an English accent."

Don nodded approvingly.

"I don't think you're in a position to know. We've tested these spots on focus groups, and they always get a positive response."

Bill's benign expression changed quickly to a look of impatience.

"I don't care about your focus groups. What we need is to get people aroused and involved. Statements by high-class actresses won't do that for us."

Rubin insisted that Emma Taylor's regal appearance and accent made her support for the cause of labor especially effective. Bill somehow refrained from saying bullshit. Instead he said, "Well, that makes sense from a business-union point of view, but we're a rank-and-file union and this is a rank-and-file strike."

Don, in delight, almost swallowed the gum he was chewing. How changed Bill was, how differently he thought and spoke.

After Rubin collected his papers and videotapes and returned to the motel room office that the Herman group had rented for him, Bill placed a call to John Elder at union headquarters in Nashville. "John, you're wasting a lot of union money on a high-class ad campaign that has done us no good and won't do us any damn good. I just sat through a tape of the Queen Mother sobbing for the poor common people on strike. Give me a break! We need a campaign that'll shake CP up, not one that'll make them laugh. Forget the Herman Group. If you want to provide us with outside help, hire somebody tough like Ray Rogers."

"Billy." He could hear Elder sigh. "Billy, You know enough to know I can't hire Ray. Too many union leaders wouldn't work with us if we did. Forget it."

Bill was not surprised. He had his response ready. "Then give us the money you've been paying the Herman Group, and we'll run our own grassroots campaign."

Elder was quiet for a long thirty seconds. "Well, I guess I owe you one," he said finally. "I can afford you guys as easily as the Herman Group. You won't do worse," he laughed mirthlessly, "and maybe, just maybe, you'll do better. I'll fire Herman, and I'll foot the bill for a Local 34 campaign up to $3000 a month. How's that sound?"

"Better, John, a whole lot better. You're a good man — most of the time!"

Bill relayed his conversation to Don and quickly added, "It's your baby. Make it work." Don was jubilant. He had a lot of ideas he was eager to try out.

Bill appointed two strikers, Dennis Marceau and Jill Carter, to work with Don . Dennis, cherubic-looking with a pleasant smile, was a stubborn fighter. Well before the strike, he had argued to anyone who would listen that the chemicals created by the paper production process were a danger both to the workers and to the environment. At first, other papermakers laughed and called him a sissy and a crank. But after three boiler room workers were hospitalized because of the discharge of V-Bright gas in the pulp mill, Dennis Marceau's reputation quickly changed from crank to prophet.

The third committee member, Jill Carter, was one of the large group of paperworkers who had never been active in the union prior to the strike. When she first started working in the mill during the fall of 1985, she grumbled about paying dues and couldn't understand why she was governed by something labeled a collective bargaining agreement that she had never read and had no voice in negotiating. But, once the strike began, by virtue of her course in creative writing at a junior college, she was recruited into the media committee where Don soon realized that she had a fine way with words and had the ability to make friends quickly. She was not conventionally pretty. Her face was too narrow and her lips too thin. Her small face and large, soulful eyes were her dominant feature. Her deep-set brown eyes gave her a waif-like appearance most of the time and made guys want to protect her. But when she dressed up to show off her woman's figure, put mascara under her eyes, and let her lustrous hair hang down her back, the waif could turn sexy. Despite being a working mother, she had a lively social life.

Dennis concentrated on environmental issues. He organized a watchdog committee consisting mainly of strikers who had worked in wastewater disposal. They were soon able to demonstrate that, because of errors made by the replacement workers, the Swampscott River and several nearby streams and ponds had become dangerously polluted. Dennis gave the press specific pollutant names and numbers, which the reporters used for dramatic exposes. He got a lot of publicity. Environmental issues were big in Maine. Right after the exposes appeared, both OSHA and the Maine Environmental Protection Agency made unannounced visits to inspect the mill.

The new publicity made the strike far more visible to the state's many environmentalists, who showed up in increasing numbers at the union's weekly meetings. Assisted by a professional cameraman hired by the union, Marceau made a video showing toxic gases bubbling at the mill's exposed waste dump. Bill took the video to key Democratic legislators, who brought it to the attention of liberal media personalities — Roger Moore, Molly Ivins, and Jim Hightower — all of whom gleefully agreed to publicize it.

The outreach and corporate campaign committees were able to get an impressive list of signatures on a statement condemning CP's lack of concern for the environmental degradation caused by its hiring of permanent replacements. Prominent clergymen, including the archbishop of Portland, signed. So did academics from Bowdoin, Bates, Colby, and the University of Maine, labor experts from Harvard, Yale, and Cornell, and a few well-known politicians, including Edward Kennedy and former Maine congressman Joe Brennan.

Then, Don and Dennis pulled off a spectacular political coup. They used the funds provided by the national union to hire an ex-Sierra Club lawyer who drafted a local environmental-protection ordinance. The ordinance established an EPA-like commission with regulatory authority over local environmental emissions. The commission was given the power to issue fines or revoke the operating license of any corporation whose toxic emissions went beyond legal limits. A town meeting vote was scheduled on the ordinance. CP, fearful that a commission established by North Bethany voters would be eager to find fault with its operations, brought in lawyers and scientists who argued that the ordinances were not needed because it duplicated existing state and federal law. But Local 34 hired its own environmental experts, who pointed out that both the state environmental protection commission and the federal EPA were notoriously soft on the paper companies, Maine's largest industry. The North Bethany Commission was not likely to be hampered by a pro-industry bias.

Don also engaged a University of Maine law professor to draft a second ordinance, this one authorizing the town to hire about 500 people during the next six months for "public works projects." The expectation was that almost all those hired would be strikers. Both plans would be funded by raising property taxes, which ironically meant that Consolidated Paper Company would supply most of the money. CP, even with its property significantly undervalued, currently paid seventy-five percent of the town's property tax. By reappraising CP's property to a realistic level, North Bethany would add enough money — money to fund new community projects. Both ordinances passed by large majorities at a town meeting held early in November.

Gary, who had good contacts around the state, was given the job of getting other mill communities to consider adopting similar ordinances, a move that sent shock waves through the executive suites of Georgia Pacific, Boise Cascade, and Scott Paper Companies, all of whom began to pressure CP to settle as quickly as possible.

Bill was jubilant. Not even the fierce November frost that swept through the area could dampen his spirits. "We've got those bastards on the run, I can feel it," he told Don.

Don's eyes were expressionless. "We're doing fine, but we need more pressure. We need a knockout punch. Watts probably knows he's in a tougher fight than he ever expected, but he still feels it's worth all the trouble to scare the other locals, the ones that are giving us money and coming to meetings, but not joining the strike. I think we're at a make-or-break point, and a well-thought-out civil-disobedience campaign can bring us over the top. I mean a civil-disobedience campaign that'll make news from here to Washington — Washington State. We need to get lots of people arrested for trespassing on mill property. If we can do that, we can generate publicity nationwide, great pictures that will lead to spontaneous boycotts, more publicity, more people admiring the courage of the strikers, and more people seeing CP as the embodiment of corporate greed. It may be the final step to victory."

Bill took a deep drag on his cigarette and slowly exhaled the smoke. "It could be the final step to victory," he said, "or it could wipe out all our gains. Maine people are conservative. Civil disobedience is so risky. I learned that from the books you gave me to read. It means jail time, injunctions, editorials attacking us. Some of our people will refuse to break the law. Others will get angry at us and feel the union is becoming radical." He laughed mirthlessly. "Some of them will blame me, and say it's your way of taking over the union."

As Bill raised his objections, Don looked surprisingly cheerful.

"What makes you so fucking cheerful? I thought I just shot holes in your plan for final victory."

"I'm smiling because everything you said is right on. You've become a damn sophisticated labor leader. Lord knows, civil disobedience is risky for us. Anyone who doesn't see that isn't worthy of leading a strike. Still, I think it will cause them more trouble than us. It'll increase the pressure on them to settle. It will bring in other groups. Watts will worry about it spreading to other mills."

"I've been reading about Watts. He's no fool. He's been listening to Eastman up to now, who thinks he knows everything, but Eastman has never dealt with anything like this, and Watts may be learning that Eastman's so-called expertise is worthless in this situation."

Bill could feel his hand tremble as he raised his cigarette to his lips. He signaled for quiet. "I want to think more about it. I need to talk with Shirley. She doesn't know shit about civil disobedience, but she's got great instincts."

Don decided to let the matter drop for the moment. He didn't want to get crosswise with Bill again. "It's up to you. Think about it some more. Anyway, maybe just before Thanksgiving is not the best time to get people thinking about going to jail."

○

It was after dinner — the third straight spaghetti dish — sitting together on the rollaway bed couch that Bill explained the proposal to Shirley and outlined his worries. She asked a lot of questions, then put her arm around him. "You're like a father whose kid wants to do something risky — it's scary. If the strike fails, you're gonna feel like you failed, but I kinda, sorta, somehow think Don is right."

They talked some more. Bill remained worried, but he couldn't hold out with Don and Shirley on the other side. He woke up excited the next morning. I guess we've got to roll the dice one more time. When he got to the hall around 7:30, Don was already there. He presented Bill a copy of his civil-disobedience plan.

Bill studied it carefully. It called for an escalating series of acts of civil disobedience, starting with strikers and families and culminating in mass arrests of strikers, clergy, and as many nationally known figures like Jesse Jackson, Joe Kennedy, Joan Baez, and Tim Robbins that the union could enlist.

He clapped Don's shoulder. "It's good, Don. It still scares the shit out of me, but it's damn good! If we're going down, this is the plan to go down with."

The executive committee meeting to discuss the civil-disobedience proposal was contentious. Although Don was not present, both Gary and Emil referred to the plan sneeringly as "Don's plan for making the union go bankrupt." Gary Sanborn, Emil Jean, and Cindy Regan opposed the plan. A few others, including Dennis Marceau, were uncertain.

Gary argued that Don confused the labor and civil rights movements. Bill was prepared. "I guess that Cecil Roberts didn't appreciate the difference either. He was stupid enough to expect civil disobedience to work for the miners during the Pittston strike. Of course, it was the biggest labor victory in about twenty years, but I guess that was just dumb luck."

"You're not making a speech to the membership," Emil said angrily. "We're not Mineworkers, Bill, and the government forced a settlement at Pittston, which they won't do for us. A coal strike is a big deal. Nobody's going to be worried about a strike by a few paperworkers."

"Hey, paper is the heart of the whole government. If IP stops producing paper, the country comes to a standstill." The ensuing laugh diffused the tension. "The key was that the coal company wanted a settlement. Non-violent resistance is the best way to make CP want a settlement."

Cindy Regan argued that once law-breaking began, it would be difficult to keep it non-violent.

"Wrong," Tony Lucelli announced. "Taking real action, hitting CP hard, will keep people from wanting to take things into their own hands."

Eric nodded.

"If the union breaks the law, CP will be able to sue us. I mean all the officers and members of the executive committee. I don't want to lose my house and car, and I don't want to see anyone else lose everything," Gary argued.

In response, Jeff Baker explained why individual liability was legally impossible and why bringing a suit would be dumb tactically for CP.

After three hours of debate, the executive committee solemnly voted six-to-three, with one abstention, in favor of civil disobedience.

Chapter 22

I don't give a flip. Why should I care what a bunch of deluded fools think about me, M.L. LeBlanc kept telling himself, as he struggled to fall asleep on a cold night in November. But the *Lewiston Sun's* sympathetic report of the previous night's union meeting, with an accompanying picture of a smiling Bill Samson, tormented him The union and the newspapers have everyone convinced how great Bill is and what a terrible person I am. My own sister, for God's sake, acts like I've got the plague. My nephews who used to come ask my advice about girls hardly say hello. They were such good kids once.

I have to change things, he thought. I can do it. But how? The damn media are whores. They kiss Bill Samson's ass, quote every dumb thing he says, ignore the fact that my life is threatened — that I got so many crank calls that I had to change to an unlisted phone number. I guess I'd have to get shot for them to realize that these strikers aren't really the touchy-feely heroes that the reporters have fallen for. Idiot reporters! They really believe this non-violent line that Bill Samson has been peddling. Maybe I could force him to show his true colors…I wonder how hard it would be…I bet the security people could help me. The next morning, M.L showed up at The Bottomless Cup, a coffee shop where Black Hawk security guards regularly met for breakfast before the eight o'clock shift. About five guards were seated at the shop's large round table, and he went over to join them. M.L. found their appearance — muscular, with military bearing — comforting. Most had close-cropped hair. Their eyes were alert, and their pistols dangled nonchalantly from their tightly cinched belts. They were as alike as marching soldiers in a newsreel.

"How's it going, guys?"

"O.K., Mr. LeBlanc. No problems that we can't handle."

M.L. knew that the guards and the local police did not get along. The guards were convinced that the police favored the strikers; the local police thought the black-shirted security guards were interlopers who were interested in showing off their toughness.

"I just came by to tell you that I appreciate the job you are doing. If we had to depend on the local police force, the damn strikers could burn down the mill, and nothing would happen."

"That's for shit sure," a guard named Lopes said matter-of-factly.

"Well, you're our security force, not the cops. We're counting on you to show the strikers who's boss. Don't be afraid to get tough with them when they throw things or call you names." He could see the looks of confusion in the eyes studying him.

"We were told to ignore what they said," Lopes reminded him. "Mainly, as far as I can tell, they're just blowing off steam. What they say don't usually bother me that much."

"Well, I don't like strikers, and I don't like unions, and I know what they're saying. Stupid name-calling like 'gestapo' and yelling 'Heil Hitler,'" a young blond man interjected. "When they shoot off their mouth about what they're gonna do when they catch me alone in town, I wanna bust them right in the mouth."

M.L. nodded approvingly. He looked at the speaker's name tag. Anderson. My kind of guy. "Listen, guys, if you agree with me and Brother Anderson, we can do something about it. What we have here is guerilla warfare. Jack rocks, drive-bys, pickets threatening people, throwing stones. And you have my permission to use whatever force is necessary to stamp it out. I want you to do your duty. Understand? Do your duty, whatever it takes. I want to get rid of every damn law-breaking, violence-preaching, loud-mouth striker son of a bitch out there."

His voice changed to a confidential whisper. "If you can get pictures of the strikers breaking the law and bring the film to my office, I'll make it worth your while. I'll pay $400 for every striker I can get rid of."

"Why do you have to fire them? Aren't they already permanently re-placed?" a tough- looking, long-nosed young guard named Schwantz asked in a high-pitched, almost feminine voice.

"My lawyer tells me that if I catch them breaking the law, CP can be rid of them once and for all. Believe me, that is just what I want. I'm ready to reward any of you that can help me. And guys, no mention of this to the damn reporters, understand?"

The guards laughed. "Don't worry," Anderson said. "We get your point. We'll deliver for you."

"That's what I hoped you'd say," M.L. replied, picking up the check and signing for it. "I'm counting on you guys. I hope you drop by my office real soon." With that, M.L. walked from the restaurant.

"What the hell was that about?" Lopes asked.

"Simple," Anderson said. "He wants us to egg the strikers on. If we can get them to break the law, he can fire them. That's what he wants. If it works, I might actually start to enjoy the gig."

"That's playing with fire. It makes us worse than scabs," Lopes answered.

"Who cares? As long as he pays up, it's no skin off my ass."

McPhail, who had been quietly observing things, added, "Makes sense to me." And on that note of understanding, they returned to their posts.

After this meeting, angry confrontations between guards and strikers became more common. The guards taunted and threw stones and when the strikers responded in kind, they captured it on film and turned the film over to LeBlanc. Five more strikers were formally discharged during the next week.

The main point of contact between the strikers and Black Hawks was not at the well-guarded mill entrance but at a picket shack on the dirt road leading to State Highway 3. Two carloads of striker replacements came down this road daily past the hurriedly built picket shack that Eric Miller used as his headquarters. On most days, neither local nor state police was near.

Almost daily, the guards taunted and the pickets cursed and threatened. Some days it was half-hearted. Other days, something in the news—or even the air—ignited both sides into rage. The confrontations grew angrier after LeBlanc's meeting with the guards.

On a cold day in mid-November, the Black Hawk guards drove by a group of pickets playing basketball, having installed a wooden backboard and an inexpensive hoop on a nearby paved surface. Angry insults were exchanged. About twenty minutes later, five of the security guards returned and parked their car by the side of the road and walked shoulder to shoulder toward the picketers, who were too engrossed in their game to pay much attention. Leroy Baker, a Black Hawk sergeant with large, cupped ears, called out, "Hey, you. You with the long hair and stupid smile."

"You talking to me, Dumbo?"

The pickets laughed.

Baker flushed red. "Yes, you dumb Yankee asshole. You're trespassing on CP land."

"Bullshit! This land is public property. It's part of the national forest."

"Yeah, well, it's owned by CP, and they want you off it right now."

"Show me the deed."

Anderson, who was in command of the guard group, drew his gun. "Here it is, I'll show it to you up front so you can read the fine print."

Instantly, as if on cue, the other guards drew guns and advanced on the strikers. Two of them leaned against the basket and tore the backboard apart, eyes never wavering from the strikers. The scene resembled a prison movie: guards in uniform formed a half-circle and narrowed it, forcing the strikers to retreat backwards. Only Eric Miller stood still, waiting until the strikers were all behind him before he also took a first step back, then another. Their basketball, forgotten, rolled between his legs. The scene was eerily quiet now.

The strikers — some in rage and some in fear — piled into Eric's van and slammed the doors. When Eric finally broke eye-contact with the closest guard and got in, they took off, peeling and skidding down the hill. When the strikers finally spoke, it was all at once.

"Holy shit! They would have killed us!"

"They can't do that! This is America, for God's sake!"

"Maybe we should go by the union hall for reinforcements. Our guys have guns, too," Eric said.

"Bill would have a shit-fit if we started using guns. Drop me at the Anchor."

No one knew what to do, but Eric headed straight for the Anchor Pub's parking lot, where he pulled up against the back wall. They all hurried in.

The shaken strikers gathered near the bar, some sheepish, some defiant, and all shaken. As they drank and exchanged stories, during which time their heroism and the guards' viciousness both increased dramatically.

This was big. It was even bigger the next morning at the union hall when the pickets told and retold the story of the confrontation. Like men forced off their land anywhere, the strikers vowed revenge on the outsiders who were destroying their community.

Chapter 23

When Don asked Jill Carter to concentrate on building alliances with student groups, she was not happy. "I took a few courses, but that's all. I don't even know any college students," she said, her normally lustrous eyes clouded with fear.

"Don't worry," he told her, "you'll get to like it. A dynamite guy has volunteered to work with you. He's a graduate student at Bowdoin, named Jeffrey Levin."

She pursed her lips in a half-hearted effort to look critical, as though she doubted that a graduate student was up to the job. "I'm sure he's just brilliant, but does he know anything about real unions and the real world?"

"Don't worry. I wouldn't link you up with an empty-headed theorist. This guy knows a lot. He comes from New York, but he's not your typical Jewish intellectual. He was a student at Yale when their clerical workers struck. He got everyone in his dorm to pledge not to attend classes unless they were held off campus. And he found meeting spots in churches, in restaurants, even in a pool hall. He was so effective that John Wilhelm, probably the world's hippest union official, offered him a job as a full-time organizer. He turned it down to work on the Harvard- staff organizing drive and then he came to Bowdoin to work on a Ph.D in American studies. Get this. His topic is union music. He's also the founder of *Radical Choices*, a damn good left-wing newspaper." Don smiled reassuringly.

Jill froze. Was Don kidding? What would she have in common with a half-Yale, half-Harvard, all-Jewish intellectual? Someone who had all the experience she lacked? Don seemed to have forgotten that she was just a worker whose pre-strike job was to make sure that the paper came out evenly coated. It was an interesting job sometimes, but hardly one that required great brain power. No one thought they should give Ph.D's in that.

"What's he look like?"

"Huh? I don't know — sort of wiry, a little like a distance runner, medium height, curly hair, slim, long nose. He usually wears a 'proud to be union' sweat shirt."

It was going to be humiliating. He would know stuff about unions that she didn't and use words she couldn't understand. He'd probably talk about books that she had never heard of. It took two days before she summoned up the courage to call Jeffrey Levin, and when she did, she was so nervous that she was practically tongue-tied.

When Jeffrey finally realized that she was one of the Local 34 strikers, he became excited. "Wow! You're with Local 34! I'm glad you called me. I've been to two of your open meetings. Inspiring! Sent chills up my back. You guys are the greatest thing to hit the labor movement in this state since the paper strike of 1921.”

The strike of ‘21? She remained silent and felt like a coward.

He asked her if she wanted to meet at the Chuck Wagon the following Monday.

She was waiting nervously when he arrived. Lean and intense-looking, with curly black hair, a prominent nose and mobile dark eyes, he would have been easy to pick out, even without the *Proud to be Union* t-shirt. Standing still he looked much as she imagined he would. What she did not expect was the vitality, the sense of bottled up energy conveyed by the quick darting of his eyes and the constant movement of his hands, an impression that was later emphasized by his rapid speech and quick flowing ideas.

They ordered coffee. She watched him bring the cup to his mouth. His hand is shaking. He’s as nervous as I am. What does he have to be nervous about?

“I’m really flattered that you guys took me up on my offer,” he said. “I would love to help you win your strike. You’re fighting for the future of unions in this state. What can I do?”

He really wants to help, and he’s not too sure of himself. Maybe he really is a nice guy. He’s not too young. Nice eyes, kind of dreamy — staring at me like I’m the blue-plate special. A faint blush added color to her cheeks, but she quickly regained her composure. She tried to sound like an official union organizer.

“Don says that there are three steps to progress — educate, organize, and act. I think we’re still at the first step. We need you to help us educate students. Then we can organize them, and then together we can act.”

“Educate, organize, act. That’s good. Should we try for a state-wide student support group?” He looked up at her eagerly. He exuded sympathetic understanding. Not at all what she imagined? She stroked the sides of her cup without realizing it.

“I’m sure I can get at least fifty people together by next week. But you need to be there to explain why you went on strike and what CP is like. Then we can decide how to help. Of course, we’ll walk the picket line, post notices about the strike, get the college radio stations to invite strikers to speak, get the student papers to write pro-union editorials, and ask our professors to discuss the strike in class. But you’ll have to tell us what else.”

She laughed, delighted by the rapidity of his thinking and by his boyish enthusiasm that reminded her of her ten-year-old son. She could see the eager child behind his eyes. He’s the kind of guy women want to mother. That must be what I'm feeling now. She put her hand on his. "I can see that Don got me the right person. You organize the meeting and I'll be there."

They talked about the strike for a while. He told her that he admired the union's ability to restrain violence when anyone could see that CP was blatantly provoking the strikers. He asked her how long she had worked at the mill. When he found out that she was a single mother and worked over fifty-six hours in a typical week, he whistled with admiration. "Did you enjoy working at the mill?"

"Sometimes. Making sure that the color is right on a roll of paper can be real demanding. It's exciting to see a roll of paper coming out of a machine all clean and colored exactly right. I was happy with my life before the strike, even though doing my work and trying to be a good mother was a lot harder than I ever thought it would be. Now I wonder if my life will ever be the same again. I wish I had your education."

"Ever think about going back to school?"

The question caught her by surprise. She looked down, stirring her empty coffee cup. "Oh, I think about it sometimes, but it's just a daydream. I don't have what it takes to be a student. I barely made it through high school."

"That doesn't mean anything. I hated high school, too, but now I'm a damn good student."

She smiled but waved her hand dismissively. "That's nice of you to say, but I know my limitations."

He almost leaped at her. "You don't know your limitations. Nobody does." He blushed and leaned back, assuming a more relaxed pose. "I don't want to be too presumptuous, but one thing I learned working with the clerical-technical workers at Yale was that they thought that it takes far more brains to go to college than it does. Hell, Lucille Dickess, a clerical worker who never went to college, outsmarted and out argued the great A. Bartlett Giamatti, the president of Yale, in a debate on the Phil Donahue show. He was supposed to be a genius. Till then nobody including Lucille knew how smart she is. Do you have kids?"

"A boy ten and a girl of six."

"Husband?"

"Not anymore. I got rid of that womanizing, boozing, male chauvinist pig five years ago."

"How would your kids feel if you told them you were going back to school?"

"They'd be shocked, especially Roland. He'd have trouble believing that anyone would actually want to go to school. Jennifer wouldn't understand, but she's at the age when anything Mommy does is automatically great." She thought for a few seconds. "Roland might be a little proud if he thought I were going to be a doctor or a lawyer like he sees on TV." She seemed lost in thought for a few seconds.

Then, to change the flow of discussion, she said, "Is it true that you write union songs?"

Now it was his turn to study an empty cup. "Sort of, in an amateurish way. I try, but I suck at it. My voice isn't very good and my words come out so damn stilted. I wish I could be like Woody Guthrie and Bob Dylan and write lyrics that sound like people talking."

She hesitated. "I like Dylan a lot, but who's the other guy?"

He tried to stifle a look of surprise. "Did you ever hear 'This Land is Your Land' and 'So Long, It's Been Good to Know You'?"

She thought for a minute. "Oh sure, I know 'This Land is Your Land.' I just didn't know who wrote it."

"Woody Guthrie wrote it. He was one of the greatest folk-song writers ever. Lots of singers today have covered his songs. He was a radical who traveled the country and told the workers' story, wrote about unions, wrote about work, wrote about injustice. And sometimes he wrote just for fun. He was the guy Dylan tried to sound like when he first began. I have every recording he ever made. …There I go, lecturing again. I need to learn to keep quiet sometimes. But I love union music. I'd love to play some for you sometime."

She could see herself wearing jeans, sprawled on the floor of his student apartment, drinking wine, maybe munching on a piece of imported cheese while listening to union music. Not too bad a picture.

"That might be nice," she said matter-of-factly, hoping that her feeling of excitement at the idea was not conveyed.

They talked for about an hour. When Jeffrey said he had to get back for class, Jill was surprised at how quickly the time had passed. She walked him to his car, a beat-up old Chevy. She extended her hand. Actually, she felt more like hugging him. But that's because he reminds me of my kid, she decided. He took her hand eagerly, pumped it up and down enthusiastically, and assured her that he would call soon about the student-organizing meeting.

On December 4th, Jeffrey called to invite her to a meeting at Bowdoin College the following Monday. "I'll pick you up around 7. We can talk strategy on the way down and back."

"Thanks, Jeffrey. You're sweet to drive all the way here."

"I hate it when women tell me I'm sweet."

She laughed. "You're sweet, but in a sexy way."

"Much better." He, too, laughed. "See you Monday."

When Jill returned to the union hall, Dennis was there. He noticed that she was more lively than usual and that she spoke emotionally when she told him about the upcoming meeting.

After listening to her wind down, he suggested that she seemed more contented than she had in awhile.

"For the first time since I was a little girl, I feel connected," she told him. "The union is my family now along with my kids, the people I care about. I want to show Bill and Don — and you, of course — that you were right to pick me for the committee."

"I knew you would be good for the committee once you got started, but you got started faster than I thought. But then everything happens fast with you, doesn't it?"

She wondered what he was driving at. They walked out the back door as usual, and before they parted to go to their separate cars, she was able to answer. "I sure haven't been fast to discover what and who I care about or even what I want to do with my life after the strike. But I guess you mean I made up my mind quickly when we started messing around together."

"Messing around? I don't think of our relationship as 'messing around.' I think of it as loving. I really care about you."

"I know you do, Dennis." She paused and took a deep breath. "But as you've told me repeatedly, you're a married man who loves his wife and kids, so there's no real future to our relationship."

Dennis started to say something and then stopped. "You know, Jill, it's very hard on me. Gloria's been a good wife and mother. I don't want to hurt her, and I don't want to hurt our kids, but you are the most exciting thing in my life."

Some compliment. She could feel her anger rise. "I hate being the other woman. I hate it when I call you and she answers, and I hate it when I see you and her looking so right for each other at church."

Dennis moved forward and put his arms around Jill and kissed her on the lips. He could feel her breasts against his chest, and he was surprised at how unyielding she felt. "What's wrong?"

"You know what's wrong. That's what we've been talking about."

"I guess. You're telling me that our romance is over?"

"I am. But not our friendship."

For about ten seconds, he looked like he was about to cry, but then his face stiffened like someone getting ready to move into a swift wind. He moved forward again and kissed her, this time tenderly on the cheek. It was a sweet farewell kiss, and her face brightened. It seemed to him that they were acting out parts from a corny old movie he had recently seen on television. Jill smiled at him. He thought he noticed tears in her eyes, felt comforted, and smiled back.

It was easier than Jill had imagined. She had decided weeks earlier that she needed to end their affair. He was a good person. She liked him, but she was not in love with him. I worried that he'd be devastated, but he's far from it. Maybe he felt relieved, the same as me.

The next day she was to go with Jeffrey Levin to Bowdoin for a meeting. Why am I so excited? Is it Jeffrey, or is it the meeting? Must be the meeting. It can't be him, he's just a kid. But waiting for him to pick her up, she changed clothes three times before settling on a conservative, dark-colored cotton blouse and nice slacks. She looked at herself in the mirror, thought about it, and opened one more button. Then she sprayed perfume on her wrists and neck.

The trip to Bowdoin was pleasant but business-like. Jeffrey used the time to tell her about the students who would be at the meeting and which groups they represented. The amount of information was bewildering. The groups at the meeting would include liberals, Young Democrats, Democratic Socialists, Revolutionary Socialists, members of the Portland commune, the Lewiston collective, and the Bangor People's Collective. Most were graduate students. Many came from old New England families. One was the daughter of a former governor and one, the son of a distinguished writer. These students were, she knew, future lawyers, doctors, and politicians — more intellectual, better read, and certainly wealthier than the people she knew and worked with.

She would speak as soon as Jeffrey started the meeting and then take questions. She agreed, wondering how to convey the spirit of the strikers, and the issues involved. She tried to scribble notes for a speech, but everything she wrote seemed stupid and childish. She scratched out idea after idea, and finally, in a moment of total madness, decided to speak spontaneously.

Over fifty people were waiting when she and Jeffrey arrived, and, while they waited, at least twenty more came in. At 7:30, Jeffrey led her to the front of the crowded room, called for attention, and began speaking in a loud, clear voice with his New York accent. "Brudders and Sisters, we are honored by the presence of Jill Carter, one of the striking paperworkers from Local 34 and a real cool lady. She's going to say a few words. You'll get to ask some questions and den we will figure out how to help the strike." The students jumped to their feet, applauded, and shouted their welcome.

Jill was shocked. She almost burst into tears but caught herself. "It's great to be among friends. I'm a newcomer to the ranks of labor. Before the strike, I just wanted to be left alone, do my work, and raise my kids. I never went to union meetings. The union was 'them.' But now I realize, the union is us, all of us. Being active and part of the union is as important as going to church. It's something you owe the people you work with."

She was surprised by cheers and by the looks of admiration coming from the audience, especially the women. She went on. "Another thing I now realize, looking out at you and seeing how enthusiastic you are, is that we need each other. Unions need friends, and those of you who want to change the world should know that you're not going to do it without the support of working people like me." The audience broke into enthusiastic applause. I can do this, she thought, and the realization surprised her. She leaned forward and rested her elbow on the podium.

"We are in a fight against a ruthless enemy. Some of my friends say the enemy is corporate greed. I say it is corporate arrogance. Our CEO, the famous George Watts, thinks that the company is making money only because its management is up there in their fancy offices thinking great thoughts. I think that we, the paperworkers, are the heart of the company. The top management is giving itself bonuses and stock options and they're insisting that we take pay cuts. They expect us to be so grateful for our jobs and their generosity that we ignore their unfairness. Ha! We are fighting for a way of life that has lasted for over half a century. Mr. Watts is in for the fight of his life." She stopped and the audience again rose to its feet and cheered.

"I'll be happy to answer your questions." She smiled with pleasure, her fear a thing of the past.

Several hands were up, and Jeffrey called on a young woman with long, straight blond hair, wearing granny glasses. "I understand that you are striking to protect the seniority system, but isn't seniority the enemy of women and minorities — a way of keeping white males in power?"

Jill noticed several of the women in the audience nodding their heads in agreement. She thought about her job and the people she worked with.

"No, seniority is not the enemy. Seniority is my protection against being discriminated against by management. If I apply for a job and have seniority on my side, management knows that if I don't get the job the union will file a grievance on my behalf." She noticed looks of curiosity and surprise. How young they seemed, how naïve, how eager to learn. I guess no one has ever taught them about unions.

A chubby young man with thick glasses was recognized next. "CP claims that wages at the mill averaged $35,000 per year. Is that true?"

The question brought an audible undercurrent of hissing.

She raised her hand to quiet the murmurs. "It's OK," she said. "If you people don't ask about what's bothering you, you won't learn the answers. It's true we have high incomes for workers in Maine, but what the company PR people don't tell you is that we work almost sixty hours a week. The average paperworker works thirty-six Sundays a year. It was the union that got us high wages. It didn't come easy. That's why we are fighting so hard. And," she said proudly, to a great cheer from the audience, "we are great paperworkers."

An older woman sitting demurely in pearls was recognized.

"Do the male workers harass you?"

"When I first started working at the mill, it was terrible. They made it a point to use the worst language. They made comments about my body, my eyes, my legs. They kept groping me like fifth-grade school boys. But when they realized that they weren't going to chase me out and that I was a good worker, things got much better. Not perfect, but better. A lot of flirting went on. Didn't bother me. After a while I could join in. I enjoy flirting sometimes." This brought a laugh of empathy from many of the women.

"What I never enjoyed was the damn foremen. They acted like they were doing me a favor when they touched me — oough!" The audience erupted in laughter. "And, since the strike, the union guys have been great, as if they suddenly realized that women paperworkers have brains and hearts. Now they are family. I feel like a little girl with a thousand big brothers."

The questioning went on for over an hour. Jill was amazed at how easily she handled it. "They're nice kids, but I know so much more than they do about the way the world works."

A very thin man, with a long beard, Jill thought he resembled the Jesus of a painting that hung above her mothers fireplace, waved his hand, frantically seeking recognition. "I just learned that CP will be coming to Bowdoin in two weeks to interview people for management-trainee jobs. What do you think we should do?"

"Of course, that's your decision to make, not mine, but we would be very happy if you could let them know and let the media know that CP is not welcome and won't be until they agree to get rid of the scabs and return union papermakers to their jobs." Loud applause. Several in the audience raised their fists to the sky.

Someone moved that they form *Students in Support of Local 34* and plan a reception for CP whenever it arrived on any campus in the state. The rest of the meeting was devoted to organizing the new group and planning its activities — marches, meetings, and publicity.

After the meeting, she and Jeffrey went with the newly elected leaders of the group for coffee. At the coffee shop, the conversation changed focus. They talked about books, movies (they called it film), and politics.

Jill listened, spellbound. What interesting lives they had. During the conversation, Jeffrey had his arm draped lightly on her shoulder. She leaned back and felt his arm against the back of her neck. It felt good.

The trip back was enjoyable and exciting. He drove with one hand and stroked her neck with the other. She cuddled against him. When they got back a little after midnight, she told him, "I'm sorry I can't invite you in. My mother is sitting with the kids, and I promised to be back by 12."

"That's all right," he said, smiling. "There will be other chances." They kissed gently for a few seconds, then suddenly passionately.

Over the next two weeks, she and Jeffrey set up student support groups at all of the colleges in Maine, made love at motels from Bangor to Portland, and spent hours listening to each other's music. She played Roy Orbison, the Platters, and Elvis, and he introduced her to the Weavers and Woody Guthrie.

Working with the students was challenging, exciting, sometimes bewildering, and often inspiring. She was surprised at how deferential they were to her and how they simply assumed that her tentative ideas and intuitions constituted working-class wisdom and understanding. She tried hard to resist the temptation to pretend to greater understanding than she had. And when students asked her about how the workers stood on political issues, she often had to resist an impulse to laugh. She was frequently tempted to say, "How the fuck should I know?" but she held herself in check and admitted her lack of certainty more politely. But she loved them, their earnestness, their innocence, their brightness, and their passion for justice.

The students that she and Jeff recruited showed up to picket and ask hostile questions whenever someone from CP made a public appearance. Their greatest success — the action that got the most attention from the media — took place in Boston.

A Bates student learned from an MIT student that George Watts was scheduled to give a talk on "The Social Utility of Corporate Profits" to a group of young executives on December 20th at the Harvard Club in Boston, which was housed on the top floor of the Bank of Boston Building.

When Jeffrey heard, he told Jill, "It's an organizer's dream. Watts doesn't know it, but he's gonna wish he never agreed to give this talk, and we're going to get a million dollars worth of publicity."

An elaborate plan was developed by Jeff, Don, and Jill, who made three trips to Boston the week before Watts's talk to spread the word to supporters and alert the press.

Watts treasured the Harvard Club. His great-grandfather had been its president, and his father, head of the finance committee. They were a group he liked. When other senior executives railed against the younger MBA's, Watts regularly defended them. As he told his younger brother, "They're better educated and tougher minded than we were. They're not apologetic about their ambitions, and they're willing to work a damn-sight harder than we were."

Giving the lecture was, for Watts, a labor of love, although his normal fee for speaking was $5,000 for an hour presentation. He agreed to talk at the Harvard Club for free; he was flattered when he learned that his talk had to be moved to a room that could hold a larger audience. And even at that, the lecture hall was nearly full.

During his opening remarks, he explained why corporate entrepreneurs were the people most directly responsible for the "production of goods and services at the heart of our economy." As Watts spoke, he would look up from time to time to observe the audience's reaction. Less enthusiastic than he expected. Some even appeared to be staring at him angrily. Once, after making what he thought was a particularly strong point, he noticed two members of the audience exchanging contemptuous smiles. Something seemed wrong. Watts became uncharacteristically nervous and stumbled over some words. When he finished, the moderator thanked him and asked for questions.

Immediately, a dozen hands shot up. The first person the moderator recognized was a well-dressed young man, wearing an elegant bow tie.

"Mr. Watts, can you tell us how someone who is in the process of ruining the lives of over a thousand loyal workers and destroying an entire community has the temerity to lecture about morality?" This was followed by a huge burst of applause and some cheers.

Watts felt trapped. "Oh my god! They've got the place packed!"

"I won't dignify that slur by treating it as a question," he announced in a firm, clear voice.

His announcement drew a smattering of applause, but the applause was quickly drowned out by shouts of "Answer the question! Answer the question!"

The moderator tried to call on someone else, but a new chant drowned out the moderator. "Frauds out, union in! Frauds out, union in!"

Finally, Watts shouted, "I will not let myself be humiliated! The lecture is over!"

This provoked another cheer and more chanting. Watts and his small entourage hurriedly left. When they walked out the front door of the building, a crowd of several hundred people, which included strikers, students, and union supporters, met them. Signs denouncing Watts and Consolidated Paper were everywhere.

The press was out in force recording the scene as the crowd chanted, "Settle the strike! Settle the strike! Settle the strike!"

When Watts started to walk through the crowd, the protesters dropped to the ground and stopped chanting. No one moved. Not a sound was heard other than Watts's murmured "Damn radicals!" as he carefully stepped over and around them on his way to the garage. It was the most unsettling experience he had ever had.

Watts's troubles were front-page news in Boston and all over Maine. The crowd's reaction was reported in both the *LA Times* and the *New York Times* and was a featured news story on CBS and ABC. Most of the stories emphasized how imaginative and united the union was.

The next week an investigator and a cameraman from *Sixty Minutes* showed up at the union hall, taking pictures and interviewing strikers. Everyone was excited and whispered to everyone else that they should just be themselves. They all agreed and then tried to look as photogenic as possible. The producer told Bill that the segment was "a natural" and would be shown early in 1990.

The Harvard Club incident and its press coverage increased the numbers of students in the support group. They hoped to repeat their media success through the civil-disobedience campaign. Not only did they overwhelmingly volunteer to get arrested, but they used their influence and contacts to line up celebrities like Barbra Streisand, Jesse Jackson, Mike Dukakis, and former U.S. labor secretary Ray Marshall.

They were rolling.

Chapter 24

Things were never better. Jill's life had purpose, excitement, and romance. And to think — it all came out of a strike that threatened to leave her on the brink of bankruptcy. She didn't know before this that people could be happy facing impending disaster. When she wasn't traveling for the union, she was at the hall, writing press releases and answering the phone. She could not remember another period in her adult life when she behaved so like a teenager. She wore colorful blouses and short skirts and found herself singing excerpts from "Pretty Woman" and "Unchained Melody," songs that she remembered from high school. She was surrounded by people she felt like hugging. Jeffrey came to the hall at least three times a week, and when she saw him coming through the door her heart beat faster. Everyone seemed to know that they were lovers. Once, when Cindy Regan asked what she found so wonderful about Jeffrey, Jill replied, "He makes me think, he makes me laugh — he makes me hot."

Cindy laughed. "Wow! That's as good as it gets. I'd settle for any two."

Even Jill's kids noticed how happy she was, that she hummed in the driver's seat on the way to their school. She found herself saying foolish things like "Doesn't the air taste delicious?" and then wondering why. When she told them that she was getting stronger and stronger, they didn't understand why, but they knew it was true.

She was writing a letter about the strike to the *Camden Press*, carefully editing her first draft, making it shorter, stronger, and more personal, when seemingly out of nowhere she felt a sudden surge of anxiety. She wondered what was happening, counted slowly to ten, and thought about the last evening she and Jeffrey had been together. She had trouble visualizing him, and when she finally saw him in her mind's eye, he was pointing to a large, cathedral-like building. Her anxiety returned. My God, she thought. I don't ever want to go back to the mill. I want to go to college and learn to use my mind, become a writer or teacher. It was a thought that she had been pushing to the back of her mind ever since Jeffrey had first told her that she should consider going back to college.

That afternoon she called the University of Maine Community College and asked to speak to the admissions office. A woman, who sounded very young, with a very cheery and professional voice answered the phone.

"Are you thinking of applying for the spring semester?"

"No, yeah ... maybe ... I don't know."

"I'll send you the application, and you can decide."

"Sure, that's fine." She gave her name and address and, when she hung up, she felt another rush of fear. Could she go to school and still work for the union? Would she be betraying the strike and risking the friendships that had come to mean so much to her? Perhaps the strike would be over by then. But what if it wasn't? Would people see her as a turncoat? Someone putting on airs because she was having an affair with a graduate student?

When the application came, she carefully filled it out, indicating she wanted to be admitted as a part-time student taking three courses—two English and one labor history — starting on January 21. The next week, she got a letter from the university admitting her to a special program for working mothers. It was a simple letter written in formal academic prose, but she posted it on the refrigerator with great care and read it over and over as though it were a secret message that contained a map to a long-buried treasure. She spent the next two days fantasizing about life as a student. She visualized herself at one of the coffee shops passionately discussing important issues with fellow students or staying up late listening to music and writing papers. How wonderful it seemed. For the first time in her life, she could shape her future the way she wanted. Let's get started!

After she mailed the material back to U-Maine, every day, every hour, she would change her mind. How could she really be committed to the union if she were busy seeking a new life elsewhere? Each morning, as though to demonstrate her continuing commitment to the strike, she arrived at the union hall at 8:00 and worked straight through to lunch, preparing faxes, making phone calls, and consulting with Bill and Don about strategy. One day, Bill — working across from her — shouted in exasperation: "Jill, will you stop with the humming? It was hard enough to put up with Don mooning around when his sexy dancer moved in, but now it's even worse with you and this graduate student. This is a strike, damn it, not a dating service," he concluded, barely avoiding the book hurled by Don and the copy of the union constitution that Jill aimed at his head. And then all three started to laugh. Each one's amusement fueled the others till Jill was wiping tears from her eyes and Don was sucking in his breath. It seemed like a long time before they got back to work.

Around 11:30, Lucille Caron arrived with Emil, who came for an executive committee meeting. Jill asked Lucille to join her for lunch. Lucille was always saying that the women in the local were undervalued, and Jill wondered how Lucille would react to her plan to return to school.

Lucille gave her the opportunity to raise the issue by being openly nosy about Jeffrey. "How's it going with that nice Jewish guy from Bowdoin?"

Jill smiled happily. "Great, and it's getting better. He keeps telling me I should go to college. Says I'd make a great teacher."

Lucille's mouth tightened for a few seconds before returning to a sympathetic smile. "Emil always tells me I'd have been a good lawyer, but I never take that too seriously."

"I'm serious about going back to school," Jill said. "I can't think of anything I'd rather do."

"I feel I need to stay here and help Emil and the strike," Lucille said sharply.

One part of Jill felt like it'd been slapped. Another part felt sorry for Lucille. She was a big mouth who lived in a small world. Jill changed the subject.

The next day, on an impulse, she called Dennis and asked him to meet her for coffee at the Lakeside Cafe. He was waiting, and she thought he looked irked when she arrived. She felt sure he would feel put down by her desire to go to school. It would be the same as her choosing Jeffrey over him – proof that she thought herself too good for the other strikers. I should have called Bill Samson, not a former lover, she thought.

He stood up to greet her and gave her a kiss on the cheek. "Hey, Jill, you're looking great. What's up?"

Her throat knotted up. "I've decided to go back to school. I want to change my life."

He looked surprised. "To do what?" He added, half jokingly, "What could be better than making paper?"

"Only about a million things, but what I want to do is teach and write stories."

Again he looked surprised, but not at all upset. "Wow, Jill, you sure have guts. Good for you."

"But the thing is, I'm going to begin in January."

He didn't seem to understand what was worrying her.

"It bothers me that if the strike is still going on, people will think that I ran away from the struggle."

He was silent just long enough to scare her. "If they say that, fuck 'em. You're a great union sister, and you deserve your own life. And I know that, if the union needs you, you will be there."

"Dennis, have I told you that I almost love you?"

He looked confused for a moment. "Does that mean no more fucking?"

"Men," she said, and broke into a happy laugh. She *was* happy.

Chapter 25

The replacement workers knew that they were unwelcome at most of the bars, restaurants, and stores in North Bethany where their very presence was likely to lead to name-calling and possibly a fight. But Bethany was different. Some great eating places and everyone was welcome. Among the best of the affordable restaurants was the Maine Sail, a seafood restaurant located on a wharf overlooking the water. You could get fresh lobster, newly caught blue fish, great crab cakes served with specially prepared coleslaw, and soft, warm rolls. Its prices were reasonable. Travis Green and Edith Kent decided to go there for lunch on December 15, the first sunny day after a week of cold winter weather, mixing snow and chilling rain. They traveled in Travis' green 1982 Chevy Nova, which was dented in the back from a rock thrown during the drive-by riot.

They were both silent for a few minutes. Edith, holding her right hand against her cheek as though it might otherwise collapse, seemed lost in thought, not even glancing at the Shawmut hills, covered with slowly melting ice and glistening snow. It was not like Edith to be preoccupied on the way to lunch, and Travis unconsciously turned his eyes away from the road and looked at her questioningly. Her normally pleasant features were twisted as though she were in pain.

"Edie, if your face gets any longer, it's gonna drop through the floorboard. That's not like you," he said.

"You're right," she admitted. "I'm worried. It makes me sick to go into work every day and hear all those hateful things the pickets yell."

Travis smiled almost apologetically. "I've got pretty good at ignoring it. Being a scab is tough for people who can't deal with other people not liking them. But I'm black. In some ways, that's kinda like being a scab. People who don't know you hate you. We learn to live with that."

"It's not me I'm worried about," she responded, smiling shyly. "It's the baby."

"The baby?"

"Yeah. I'm scared that all the hate and the yelling will hurt him in some way."

"Edie, if it don't affect you, it won't affect him."

"But it's hard for me to ignore them. It's like they're putting a curse on Doug, Jr." Travis could see the fear pour from her eyes like tears. At that moment, in some way he could not have explained, she reminded him of his mother.

"You know, I hate taking someone else's job. Sometimes, I think about the strikers' wives, and wonder if one of them is pregnant. It must be terrible to be expecting a child and have your husband without a job."

"I try not to think of them," Travis said. "Still, I believe it's wrong that strikers can lose their jobs." He spoke almost in a whisper. "But someone was going to get these jobs, and I decided it might as well be me."

She made no response.

They entered the restaurant and asked for a seat in the back room, overlooking the ocean. As soon as the hostess showed them to their seats, Travis recognized Bill Samson at the next table. A chunky, tough-looking guy with sloping shoulders, wearing a shirt and an open combat jacket, sat across from Samson. Travis had seen him several times shouting angrily when he crossed the picket line on his way to and from work. The third guy at the strikers' table with the dark beard and curly hair was new to him. Travis wondered whether they would recognize him. He wasn't long in doubt. Eric Miller looked over at Travis and Edith, and his eyes narrowed menacingly.

"Let's get out of here, the place has started to smell like a dung heap," he said to Bill in a voice loud enough to attract the attention of the waiter.

A man in a gray suit and striped tie (Travis thought he looked like a lawyer) nudged his companion and whispered something into his ear. They both turned their heads to stare at Travis and Edith, who picked up their plates and headed for the buffet table in the main part of the dining room.

"Did you ever notice that scabs have a special smell?" Eric asked rhetorically and loudly.

Edith tugged at Travis' arm, "Let's change our seats. I don't want trouble."

"Yeah, let's go," Travis said, "but I want to tell this guy something first."

He was now only a few feet from Eric. He spoke in a low voice, almost apologetically. "I'm sorry that you guys have lost your jobs. I really am. But I wanted to be a papermaker since I was a kid, and this was my chance. I'm not there to bust your union. We should be friends, not insulting each other. Your shoulder patch tells me that you were in Nam. So was I. I'm just a working man, same as you. And if your union had stood up for black people, I wouldn't have to think about being a scab."

Across the room, someone applauded.

Eric's face was now mostly pale as though it had been drained of blood, but the pupils of his eyes were a fiery red. "Look, you dumb asshole, just because you were in Viet Nam doesn't make you my friend. Being a scab makes you the enemy just the same as if you were Viet Cong. So don't think you and your friends can go places around here and be welcome."

A large, overweight man in a bright blue blazer had risen from a nearby table. He walked over and clapped Eric on the back. "That's telling him. These damn black scabs come up here, date our women, and spend their scab money in our restaurants. Somebody needs to tell them that we don't want there here."

Eric pivoted to face the man, his body hunched as though he were still playing linebacker and was about to make a tackle. His fists were clenched and his eyes glazed with anger. "Look, fat ass, this isn't about race. Charles Hicks, my best friend and my door gunner in Viet Nam, was black just like this damn scab here." Eric's expression turned from anger to one of great sadness. "He's still in country, caught in a crossfire when we were picking up a group of grunts, and I crashed. Man, how I miss him. Him and I were a team — always together — so don't talk any more racist bullshit near me if you want to keep those round soft cheeks in one piece." Eric seemed to lunge forward and the man quickly retreated to his table, mumbling something that no one could make out under his breath.

Travis, who had unconsciously grabbed Edith's hand, let go of it.

"I appreciate that, man." He stuck out his hand.

Eric ignored it. "I didn't say that for you. It was for Charlie Hicks."

Chapter 26

George Watts pointed angrily to the *Springfield Gazette*. "Have you seen the article in last Tuesday's paper, Professor Eastman? It details my fiasco at the Harvard Club. Then it describes, in excruciating detail, how a student sit-in forced our representative to leave MIT under guard. It says, and I quote." Watts lifted two elegantly shaped and manicured fingers over his head. "'Over half of the Sloan School at MIT's senior and junior classes have pledged not to interview or accept employment from Consolidated Paper Company because of its labor policies.' And then it quotes a Professor named William McCormick, who says 'Consolidated Paper used to have the most enlightened policies of any company in the paper industry. But that was before Mr. Watts became CEO. I don't know if their new approach is his idea or if his self-styled labor expert — 'Damn the Unions Eastman' — has sold him a bill of goods. But what they are doing now makes no sense.'"

Watts lowered his hands. "If you prefer Wednesday's paper, which I also have right here, the headline is 'OSHA Seeks Record Fines Against Consolidated Paper.' Thursday, all we have to worry about is an editorial hailing the solidarity of those heroic strikers and referring to us as 'a relic of another, less enlightened period in American labor relations.' Friday's paper is the one with the article about teacher groups urging spontaneous boycotts against us. Professor McCormick shows up there too — saying he's not seen such support for a union in twenty-five years."

"Nobody listens to senile old Bill McCormick," Eastman said disgustedly. "He's the last of the New Deal labor relations professors. Being insulted by him is practically a compliment."

"We don't need such compliments!" Watts's normally calm voice rose almost an octave. "We have had too many of them in the last month, and it looks like more are on the way. Do you know what my secretary does all day? She takes calls from angry people. Angry investors. Angry plant workers. Angry college students from everywhere. And guess what — she's angry too. Did you see yesterday's paper?"

"Are you talking about the civil-disobedience announcement?" M. L. LeBlanc asked uncomfortably.

"Yes, of course. It's a long, detailed article, lots of news, none of it good for us. We have priests, rabbis, the Western New England Ministerial Alliance, a host of Democrat politicians, enough professors to staff a university, and they're all threatening to take part in demonstrations at the North Bethany mill and to get arrested if necessary. Reverend Jesse Jackson says he will take part. You remember him? The guy who got over 10 million votes for president and appears regularly on TV, commenting on the news. And he won't be alone. Oh, no. Ossie Davis, Bruce Springsteen, two members of the Boston Patriots, and three cowboy singers from Austin, Texas all announced yesterday that they will join him. Leading the entire program will be some minister — Reverend Nelson Thompson. A hero, I'm told, to civil rights and human rights groups. Isn't this the strike that you and Professor Eastman assured me would be over within two months at the latest?"

Both Eastman and LeBlanc simultaneously started to explain why their projections turned out wrong despite being sensible and well informed.

Watts interrupted. His expression was cold as ice. "I don't want excuses! And I don't want to be remembered as the CEO who arrested more clergymen and professors than the whole damn South African government."

Watts turned to Gillian. "Tom, you tried to warn me, and I now realize that I should have listened to you. You know Bill Samson. What do you suggest?"

Gillian had listened to the tirade with a mixture of pleasure and contempt. With all his talk about loyalty, he's not showing much to his bumbling advisors. Maybe I should let them all sink together in one glorious splash. Watts is smart, no doubt of it. Maybe he's even learned something, and maybe we can salvage something from this mess.

"The solution is simple. We should offer to enter into real negotiations if they will stop their corporate campaign, including the planned civil disobedience."

"Will they do it?"

"I think so. I need to call the union. They know they can trust me. At least they used to know that. I probably have just enough credibility left to convince them that we are serious about negotiating an agreement that will not be a surrender. Our lawyers say that there is enough wiggle room in the contracts with the sca... replacement workers that we can let them go or place them behind the strikers based on seniority with the company. But, out of decency, to preserve what's left of our reputation, we have to come up with a plan that doesn't totally abandon the people we convinced to come up here to change their lives."

Both Eastman and LeBlanc raised objections. Each insisted that the company was in fact winning the strike, but Watts ostentatiously ignored them. The meeting ended with Gillian directed to contact the union and offer negotiations in return for an end to the corporate campaign, including the planned civil disobedience.

Gillian was not sure whom to call. Negotiations could have begun by his contacting Bill Samson or George Connerton's replacement, but he finally decided that his best bet was national union president John Elder, whose frantic calls to Gillian, filled with complex settlement offers, made clear that ending the strike on any terms that could be called a victory or even a draw was acceptable. Elder had also indirectly approached the company through two prominent mediators and John Dunlop, a former secretary of labor. The cost of the Maine strike to the national union had to be enormous. Gillian guessed that its strike fund was probably almost depleted.

On January 16, Gillian made his call. Elder, although obviously pleased, was initially non-committal. "I won't nix it, Tommy, but I won't order Bill Samson to accept. You're not offering anything except negotiations that might lead nowhere. I've got a lot of angry members in North Bethany who are sure that they're winning the strike. They may see this as a trick to take away the momentum we all know they have right now."

Gillian assumed that Elder was exaggerating the problem, but he kept his suspicions to himself. "I appreciate your problems, Jack, but I hope that you can convince your people that it's in everyone's interest for us to negotiate an honorable settlement of the strike. You know me well enough to know I wouldn't call if I wasn't in a position to offer a fair compromise. I'm expecting to make proposals that your people will like. And I know returning to their old jobs is the key to any settlement."

"I trust you, Tommy, and I just hope that the local leaders will see it the same way. When strikers put their blood and guts into a battle and feel that they're winning, they're unpredictable. If they think they're being tricked, they will refuse the best damn deal the good lord ever persuaded a company to offer." He sighed audibly.

"Good luck. For the sake of everyone, I hope you convince them."

"Thanks, Tommy. I trust you. I'll give it my best. It's nice to know that the good guys are back in power at CP."

As soon as he hung up with Gillian, Elder called Bill Samson and told him the news. "CP wants to resume the negotiations. They'll meet with us, and Tom Gillian says they have new serious proposals to make. But we have to call a halt, at least temporarily, to our corporate campaign and civil disobedience."

"Jack, what terms are they offering?"

"I talked to Tom Gillian. No specific offer, but he as much as told me they're ready to get rid of the scabs, and they're ready to talk realistically about a new contract."

What did it mean, Bill wondered. Elder sounded excited. But they didn't even have an offer on the table. If we called off the corporate campaign, it would be hard to start up again. Elder was putting his faith in Tom Gillian, but why should they trust him now? The guy is a big part of a rotten structure. He's an untrustworthy son of a bitch, and I'd like to tell him to fuck off, but who am I kidding? We need to end the strike.

"What do you think, John?"

"I think you should grab it. Tommy Gillian wouldn't call like this unless they were ready to settle."

"First — and it won't be an easy sell — I'll have to meet with our executive committee."

"Sure, I understand, but do it right away. I don't know how much time we have."

Bill hung up, paced back and forth outside to the hall, and then called an emergency meeting of the executive committee for the next day. Dare he follow his instinct for revenge and turn it down? That would be stupid. The union's momentum was weakening. Morale was not as high as the favorable media accounts suggested. Some of his members were depressed by the thought that they would never return to the mill. Others were questioning the policy of non-violence. Many had personal problems either brought on, or exacerbated, by the strike. Ray Allair and his wife had separated. Ed Freschette and Tony Cornello, both recovering alcoholics, had gone back to drinking. He sighed. And Gary Sanborn and Emil seemed to be plotting against him and Don. It would be difficult to maintain solidarity over Gary and Emil's opposition. I gotta give Gillian a chance.

Eric Miller was one of the union's depressed members, but for a unique reason. His relationship with Sherry Meserve had ended. Her father Maurice had been tipped off by someone who saw them coming out of Tony's cottage holding hands. When he questioned her about it, she confessed that they were lovers, and Maurice, outraged, had demanded that they stop seeing each other. Bill was not sure about the details, but, according to local gossip, Eric wanted to run off with her, but she said she would hate herself if he abandoned his fellow strikers for her. It was another leadership headache. Had he done right in urging Eric to end the relationship? Don didn't think so. "This wasn't just about getting laid, Billy. He really cared for her. He's going to be filled with anger, and that's never good for a strike." Shirley had agreed with Don, which added to Bill's discomfort. It was another reason why the strike needed to end soon.

And Jill, who had played a key role in the corporate campaign, was now back in school and, according to rumors, was facing the end of her affair with

Jeffrey, who had just received an offer from somewhere in California. Would she join the already too full ranks of the depressed?

After telling Shirley about the offer, Bill went to the tiny tub in their tiny bathroom and let the water flow over him. How nice it would be to wash away so easily all the worry, the responsibility, the fear of making a catastrophic mistake. He would become clean again.

Beyond all the practical reasons for wanting the strike to end quickly, Bill realized that he was tired of being the focus of so much emotion. Everything he did or said was analyzed, appraised, and evaluated. Emil Jean and Gary Sanborn were busy second-guessing him and blaming everything that went wrong on Don Foreman. Bill was even tired of the people who declared him to be the greatest union leader since Joe Hill. He was far more aware of his weaknesses than he had ever been.

If the strike ended now, with everyone going back to work, he could go back to being a normal person. That would be wonderful. Of course, it would take some getting used to. Never in his life would he do anything so important and noble. He would someday tell his grandchildren about the strike and how it helped working people all over the country. He wanted desperately for his efforts to achieve a memorable victory for his members — for the cause of unions for workers.

Bill wondered how Don Foreman would feel about giving up the civil disobedience action that had been so carefully planned and that had enlisted such unexpected support from members, celebrities, and ordinary citizens. How would Eric Miller and the radicals feel? He hoped they would not feel betrayed. They were the people he most admired, the ones he knew would never cut and run under pressure.

He called both Eric and Don and invited them for an 8:00 am breakfast. He wanted to hear their views before the executive committee meeting. They arrived together in Eric's jeep a little before 8, having carefully navigated the icy dirt road that led to Bill's small, ramshackle house. Shirley was there to greet them, but the table was set for only three. Don and Eric seated themselves on either side of Bill. Shirley quickly served them eggs, bacon, and coffee along with homemade bread and then quietly left for work.

They could tell something important was in the offing.

They listened intently while Bill described John Elder's version of Gillian's offer. "Jack is sure that Gillian wants to end this strike by bringing us back. He said he can tell Gillian now has the authority to do it. He says it's turning out to be a big victory, and he says it's up to us whether to accept."

Eric's eyes clouded. His neck muscles tensed visibly. "Did Gillian make any promises about what he is willing to offer us about anything?"

"No, not really, but he said enough to convince John that the deal is there."

"What deal? I don't know what deal we're talking about. All these months, Gillian has been announcing to the press that they have to have all these fucking concessions, and suddenly we are supposed to trust him and give up the tactics that are winning the strike for us. It stinks, Billy, stinks like day-old shit. It reminds me of Nam. To prove what good guys we were to get the North Vietnamese to the bargaining table, we didn't use our power. And when they got there, they didn't give us the sweat from their little yellow nuts. What makes you think CP is any more trustworthy than the Viet Cong?"

Bill had expected Eric to react suspiciously. He responded calmly, speaking with greater confidence than he felt. "We've been dealing with Tommy Gillian for years. Everyone knows he's as straight as they come. John says he lost power with the new administration of CP, but now they realize they should have listened to him and bargained in good faith with us. That's what Jack Elder thinks."

"And what do you think?"

"I believe him. Jack's a straight guy, and you know I always liked Tom Gillian, at least before the strike. We always got. ..."

Eric interrupted him before he could complete his thought. "It's a matter of negotiating power. We had it then, and we've just gotten it back. Let him put something definite on the table. Then maybe I'll vote to suspend the campaign."

Eric's position was difficult to reject. It would have plenty of supporters. The issue of accepting Gillian's offer could easily split the membership and leave the union weaker if the negotiations failed.

Eric and Bill each looked over at Don, who had been unusually quiet, listening to both of them intently.

For once, Don was unsure of himself. He needed time to sort things out. Eric's arguments appealed to him, but he wasn't sure why. "Right now I agree with Eric, but I need to think about it."

Bill was surprised. "Hey, aren't you the guy who taught me about leadership and compromise?"

Don smiled sheepishly. "It's tough for me, Bill. Why should we trust a corporate VP, someone whose career was built on putting profits ahead of people?"

But as he listed to himself the reasons to be suspicious of the proposal, Don realized that he was straining to put the worst possible light on it. The truth was that he was not emotionally ready for the strike to end. For the first time in many years, he was feeling fulfilled, exhilarated by the weekly meetings, and delighted with the emergence of a new group of local activists. He was doing good work, the cause was just, and the North Bethany strikers were overwhelmingly decent and likeable. Working with Bill, observing his courage, his intelligence, and his daily growth as a leader, could not have been more satisfying. And his love affair with Moira Vitale was going great. Just sharing breakfast with her was a reminder that life offered pleasures not connected to combat. He didn't think their relationship would continue after the strike. He'd be back where he was before, wasting his time arguing with union leaders who resisted change and thought him a radical fool. It was an absurd, frustrating life.

When he removed his own needs from the equation, he could not justify opposing the negotiations. *I've been talking the talk. It's time to walk the walk.*

The executive committee meeting was stormy. But when it ended, the powerful desire to end the strike and go back to work won out. Only Eric voted no.

On January 18, CP and the union held a joint press conference to announce that negotiations would resume on January 21 in Boston and that both sides were hopeful of an agreement. The parties stipulated that the union was free to maintain its picket line, but that its corporate campaign would be suspended. Most strikers were delighted by the announcement. The New Year was starting off better than they could have hoped.

Chapter 27

Bill was eager to get started. George Connerton, God bless him, had come through again, returning from retirement to handle the negotiations. Bill's role would be to sit at the table and look tough. He was relieved. If CP wanted an agreement, and it looked like they did, George would get the best possible terms for the union. Right now he could relax and enjoy a leisurely breakfast. He watched contentedly while Shirley filled his plate with fried eggs, potatoes, and ham. It had been a while since the kitchen smelled so good. She placed the plate in front of him and poured a cup of coffee.

While he ate, she stood behind him and stroked his shoulder tenderly. "I'm so proud of you," she said. "Everyone knows now what a great leader you are."

Bill tried, without success, to look modest. "There's a lot of folks who get some of the credit, and we ain't finished yet. But I believe down deep that it's gonna happen. Will it ever feel good to go back to a real job making a real product and not to worry about who gets credit and how it will play in the papers and whether it will please the national union."

During the trip from North Bethany to Boston, Connerton cautioned Bill that it would take time, probably a few weeks before they could finish. Nevertheless, he, too, was optimistic. "Tom Gillian is back in control. That's the best news we could have. I haven't told you this before, but I had a few confidential talks with him during the strike. He hates the new Eastman policies and fought them just as hard as he could. With him leading the negotiations, this sucker should be history pretty soon."

No wonder George never agreed when I called Gillian a union buster. He sure sounded like he meant what he was saying to the news people. Well, in a strike, we all do things we're not proud of.

Marc Lowell, an experienced mediator, was dispatched by the Federal Mediation and Conciliation Service to help the parties reach agreement. Lowell sighed with relief when he realized that the principal negotiators trusted each other and were eager to reach agreement. Not that he thought a settlement would be easy. They had to figure out a way of satisfying both the strikers and the replacement workers and then had to settle the issues that led to the strike in the first place.

Gillian and Connerton plunged into the task before them with intensity. Each understood that the period given to them to settle the dispute was limited. If there was no settlement in a month, the union's membership would feel manipulated and insist on restarting the corporate campaign. Eastman and LeBlanc would be in a position to argue that the effort was a waste of time.

They reached their first agreement, Operation Teamwork, after two days of continuous negotiation. It gave to management some of the flexibility that it was seeking to go beyond traditional job classifications, but it permitted the union to challenge departures from seniority. Hardliners on both sides objected to the vagueness of the agreed-to formulation, but after a series of phone calls, both Elder and Watts gave the plan their approval.

It took three days to come up with a new wage scheme partly tied to productivity, and two more days to negotiate an agreement giving management a limited right to subcontract maintenance work if existing jobs were not lost. They needed only half a day to agree on a voluntary scheme based on generous bonuses for avoiding a cold shutdown on Christmas.

Thus, after a little more than a week, they were ready to tackle the future of the replacement workers, an emotional issue that required both negotiators to posture a little. Connerton needed to report to the members that he had demanded the immediate firing of all replacement workers. To maintain his credibility at CP, Gillian felt it necessary to argue that all the replacement workers be given the option of remaining at North Bethany. By Friday, January 29th, they had agreed on a formula that permitted the strikers to exercise seniority over a 90-day period to reclaim their jobs. The replacement workers were given the right to transfer to other company facilities without giving up the seniority they had accrued.

The mood of the negotiations had become so pleasant that Lowell was able to assure his superior that an overall agreement was imminent. "Just a matter of crossing some 'T's and dotting some 'I's, and I'll be ready to pose for the pictures with everyone smiling and shaking hands." He knew from past experience that negotiations were near completion when the chief negotiators began telling funny stories of past negotiations.

Like almost all collective bargaining, the Boston negotiations were conducted under a pledge of mutual confidentiality. Keeping the details of negotiations secret ensures that the parties will direct their attention to convincing each other and not to the press or wavering supporters. But the cost of secrecy is the spread of rumors. The North Bethany paperworkers traded what were supposed to be inside stories as they waited for the negotiations to end.

Eric Miller, his eyes bleary from lack of sleep, his face puffy with unhappiness, his mind constantly replaying his breakup with Sherry Meserve, remained opposed to the negotiations. He insisted to anyone who would listen, "It's a trap to get us to accept the damn scabs and to kill off the corporate campaign!" He vowed that picket-line activity would continue, in full force, until the strike officially ended. Those who continued to walk the line shared Eric's view. They were a tough, angry group — mostly the guys who had confronted the Black Hawk guards and vowed revenge. The majority of them were veterans. All were long-time employees.

Their hatred for the replacement workers was not reduced by the negotiations. If anything, it was increased by the fear that desire for an agreement might cause the national union to make concessions, giving jobs to the replacement workers at the expense of the strikers. Almost daily, angry verbal battles between pickets and guards took place at the picket shack on the road leading to the mill. Anderson, the most pugnacious of the guards, found a way to alter guard vehicles so that they backfired with a loud, sharp, gunfire-like crack when moving very slowly. He would do it at least once a day, laughing uproariously at the fear it caused.

Before the first morning shift of the Friday on which the Boston negotiations moved to the point of basic agreement, the guards driving replacements to the mill in two four-wheel-drive vehicles were met by a line of strikers spread across the road, wearing camouflage fatigues. This had happened before, and the guards had easily broken the line by driving their cars slowly forward. But this time the lead vehicle stopped and guard William Ortiz, with spit-polished boots and sharply creased trousers, got out and ostentatiously drew his gun. Several other guards followed his lead. Most of the pickets backed away, but Eric Miller, looking like the sheriff in a Western movie, legs spread wide and his hands on his hips, walked forward toward the leader of the guards, a man who from a distance might be mistaken for his twin.

They stood belly to belly, trading angry insults and threats. Another of the security guards interrupted the shouting match and announced that it was time for the replacement workers to be at work and for the guards to get back in their cars. "You damn well better be gone from this road when we get back," the guard leader finally said.

"If you value your ass, don't try scaring me!" Miller responded.

After this exchange of pleasantries, the strikers opened a small pathway, and the guards gunned their vehicles through it.

When the guard cars left, the strikers returned to the shack, hearts pumping furiously. They drank coffee, puffed furiously at their cigarettes, and passionately cursed the guards and their ancestors and vowed revenge. About 45 minutes later, they left the shack and drove to the union hall. The story of the incident was retold several times, growing more dramatic with each retelling. Several outraged strikers agreed to return to the line with the original pickets slightly before 5 that afternoon when the shift ended. About fifteen pickets were at the shack at the appointed time.

Right after 5:00 p.m., the cars bearing replacements and security guards came down the road, driving slowly. The angry pickets directed a volley of insults towards the guards. "Fucking bullies," "miserable cowards." Several raised their hands stiffly in front. "Heil Watts!" they shouted. The vehicles slowed down and backfired in quick succession. Some of the strikers jumped back involuntarily, raucous laughter from the guards. Eric angrily motioned for the guards to come out of their cars and fight. As though in response, the trucks stopped, and several Black Hawk guards left their vehicles. Eric thought he saw two of the guards draw weapons. Not since Viet Nam had he faced hostile men in uniform pointing guns in his direction. Feelings of anger and mortal danger, long suppressed, enveloped him. He was back in Viet Nam, surrounded by enemy snipers. He raced in serpentine style to a clump of bushes, searched the ground for something to use as a weapon, found a stone, and hurled it with all his power at the guard vehicle. It struck just before the windshield and bounced harmlessly to the ground. Several more of the picketers also ran for the bushes, searching for rocks that they started tossing as fast as they could find them.

The guards were excited. Memories of past battles also filled their minds. They got back in their vehicles and drew guns. Shouting curses, they drove deliberately and slowly in the direction of the strikers. Another backfire. Amidst the confusion and noise, many of the scared replacement workers pleaded with the guards to get the hell out of there, to take them down to their cars so they could get out of the line of battle. The guards ignored them. More guns were drawn, more stones were thrown.

"They're going to fire at us!" one of the pickets shouted. A shot rang out — then, two more. The side window in one of the guard vehicles shattered, pieces of glass flying in different directions. Shouts, curses, and screaming from guards and pickets. More shots were fired. One struck the union banner hanging from the picket shack, and one flattened a tire on one of the guard vehicles. The scattered guard vehicles, driving in front of the strikers, suddenly came to complete stops. A man with some sort of insignia on his shoulder jumped from the lead vehicle, waving a shirt like a flag. He pointed to the strikers, shouting loudly, "You stupid bastards have shot a woman! She's hurt bad. You better give yourselves up and surrender your weapons. You're all under arrest."

The strikers did not move. They stood frozen in place until police cars and an ambulance arrived, sirens wailing. Two ambulance attendants raced to the guard vehicle and quickly emerged, carrying a stretcher. On it was a woman, her face colorless and devoid of any expression. They placed her on a stretcher. The strikers looked ashen as the medical personnel frantically attended to the fallen woman.

Eric, his expression one of horror, silently prayed that she recover. His fear grew stronger as he noticed the worried looks on the faces of the emergency crew.

David Farrigot, the local police chief, talked to the medics, shook his head sadly, and walked over to where the strikers were standing in a shocked huddle. "She's dead," he said. "You'll have to come with me."

The victim was Edith Kent, now seven months pregnant. The police quickly determined that the fatal shot had been fired by a striker named Rocky Louis. He was a thirty-seven-year-old paperworker, a veteran, and the father of two children. He had never been in trouble with the law before. He was arrested, charged with criminal homicide, and held on $50,000 bail. The other strikers were given field citations for disorderly conduct and released.

Bill Samson returned from the Boston negotiations that evening a little after 7, convinced that the strike was about to end on terms favorable to the union. He headed for the union hall, thinking about the victory party he meant to throw. When he got there, he was surprised at the number of cars in front of the hall. *I don't like it. Something's wrong. What could it be?* He entered the hall quickly, his heart pounding. Arthur Poland was sitting by the table in front of the hall, crying. When Bill asked what had happened, Arthur could barely control himself long enough to describe the basic details of the confrontation.

"Son of a bitch," Bill kept repeating, unconsciously rubbing his hands together as he listened to Arthur's version of the confrontation. Bill felt sick to his stomach and quickly became conscious of a sharp pain behind his right eye. *Why on earth had he left angry, seething Eric Miller in charge of the picket line? Any fool would have realized what a threat Eric posed!* Bill quietly stepped out of the union hall into the cold Maine air to try and regain his composure. His head swam, the pain in his side was intense. He felt nauseated, ran to the side of the building, and threw up.

All the hard work, all the sacrifice, all the time, all the emotion that had gone into winning the strike might now be wasted because of a stupid incident that never should have happened. He drove to the Twin Pines Motel, where Don and Moira were staying.

Don, who had spent the day in Augusta talking with Ed Makum while Moira performed at a Unitarian Church, had not yet heard the news. He was sitting in the room's only easy chair, reading, when Bill came in.

Bill told him directly, "Rocky Louis shot a scab crossing the line, Don. She's dead." Bill's voice suddenly choked.

Foreman sat on the edge of his chair, facing Bill silently. When Bill could speak again, he said: "Her name was Edith Kent. She was seven months pregnant, too. She's dead!" His face disappeared into his hands, and he rocked back and forth on the stiff chair. "We killed someone. We shot a woman. I can't fucking believe it."

Don sat uncharacteristically still for a long time. Finally, he spoke, his voice sad as a funeral procession. "This will change things, Bill. It'll probably mean the agreement's as dead as Edith Kent, and the strike will never be the same. We can both be sorry as hell, and we both are, and will be. But we're going to pay a big price."

Bill Samson sighed. "Damn, damn, damn," was all he said. He didn't move his head. The only thought that gave him any consolation, and even that not much, was that he was going home to Shirley, who would understand how he felt.

Chapter 28

The Gillians had just finished a pleasant dinner of strong red wine, roast beef, salad, and potatoes. They had clinked their glasses to celebrate the successful termination of the negotiations. They were talking, sipping wine, and half watching the news on television, when the face of Edith Kent flashed on the screen. It was a close-up of a smiling studio portrait, probably a wedding picture, and as soon as Gillian saw it a deep sense of foreboding overwhelmed him. Pictures like that are what they show when someone dies. When he heard that she had been shot crossing the picket line, and that she was pregnant, Gillian put his glass down and wept. "She was a fine woman, a good papermaker," he told Laura between sobs. "She was a worker."

Laura said nothing for a while. Then, "Maybe Watts and Eastman will realize that you have to settle the strike quickly so no one else will be seriously hurt."

Gillian shook his head while his tears continued to flow. "Eastman will look at this tragedy and see an opportunity. I don't know about Watts, but my guess is he'll be persuaded to blame it on the union and want revenge. He doesn't like unions, and he hates Local 34. That's why George and I worked so hard to finish the negotiations before he could change his mind."

The killing was the top story in the local news throughout the weekend. Pictures of Edith Kent and features on her husband's grief appeared in all of the papers and were broadcast on TV and radio. Travis Green was interviewed twice by local TV reporters. The first time, just after he learned of Edith's death, he was so stunned that he was barely coherent. He was able to control his emotions long enough to pay tribute to his friend.

"She never hated the strikers. She always said that they were workers just like us. But she worried about the hatred, was afraid it would hurt her baby. Poor woman!"

On Sunday, an in-depth analysis of the circumstances leading up to the tragedy included a segment about Jordan Marcon. He told in detail about the attacks on him and his family following his decision to cross the line. "There has been no peace in the valley since the strike began," he told one of the reporters; the quote became the lead and headline for an article the next day in the *Boston Globe*.

When he returned to work on Monday, January 27, Gillian's fears were quickly borne out. Watts instructed him to postpone further negotiations for a week while he reconsidered the agreement that had been negotiated. Watts, Eastman, and LeBlanc were constantly huddling. Eastman's look of righteous self-satisfaction became more pronounced. Gillian feared, with good reason, that their whispered discussions spelled the end of any chance to settle the strike honorably. By the end of the week, Watts summoned Gillian to his office. "Tom, you've done a good job, but we can't give in to a union that is ready to violate the law by civil disobedience or by violence against innocent people. I'm not going to force the replacement workers to leave. We told them they were permanent and permanent they will be. We owe it to Edith Kent."

"It wasn't the union," Gillian said firmly. "It was a couple of stupid, scared strikers. What we owe Edith Kent is a decent settlement, jobs for the replacement workers, and peace. We owe that to everyone. Bill Samson and George Connerton are as upset as we are by what happened. They are decent people, not murderers, and they know this tragedy hurts their cause."

"The last thing I feel is sympathy for Samson — he's a radical hypocrite! If the shoe were on the other foot, he wouldn't feel sorry for me. He proved that by their little game at the Harvard Club. Thought they had beaten me by rowdyism and ridicule. But they've done themselves in. We're not going to return the strikers to their old jobs. We can't trust them. This strike has ended their loyalty to the company. We don't know how many more Rocky Louises and Eric Millers there are. I've talked to Eastman and LeBlanc, and they..."

"With all due respect, you shouldn't be taking advice from Eastman and LeBlanc. They got you into trouble with their earlier advice, and they haven't gotten any smarter because someone got killed in a strike — a strike that would have long been history if you had listened to me and not to them."

"They tell me that the union is on the ropes and that the strike will end soon. Common sense tells me that they are right. The union will never again get the public and media support it was getting earlier"

"That's true, but we have a chance right now for an honorable settlement and a long period of industrial peace. We'll get cooperation and productivity until we do something else that angers them, like subcontracting out work or introducing new machines that require fewer workers. They're not right — they're wrong — profoundly, horribly wrong. If you listen to them, we'll never get what we need — industrial peace and productive workers."

"Eastman tells me that, if we hold firm, the strike will collapse. Then the replacement workers will decertify the union. Is he wrong?"

"We won't be rid of the union. It will be decertified, but it won't go away. Our mill will remain a battlefield. By law, the strikers will be entitled to future openings whenever a replacement worker leaves. And they'll come back hating the company."

176

"We'll just make sure that the replacement workers don't quit. And if some strikers come back the union won't be in control. They'll have no option but obedience. It will send a message to other mills. This is the last time they'll take us on.

"I know this is hard for you. You did a fine job as our spokesman and negotiator, but the best thing that can come from this horrible tragedy is for the strike to end on our terms."

Gillian started to speak, swallowed hard, and said nothing. Almost unconsciously he lowered his head till it almost touched his chest. The argument was over.

Once again Gillian thought about resigning, and once more he realized nothing would be gained. But as he decided to remain, the image of Jordan Marcon asking whether he was a coward flashed through his mind. He nodded grimly. " I'll try to complete the negotiations with as much dignity and decency as I can."

Watts knew that Gillian would follow instructions. And he did not want him to quit. He patted him on the back "You can handle the details in your own way."

That afternoon Gillian placed a call to George Connerton and broke the news to him directly.

"George, I feel sick. I've got to tell you that our chances of reaching an agreement are about nil. It's a case of tragedy breeding extremism. The only thing I could even think of offering you would be a chance for your members to get first crack at job openings at other mills. The scabs stay. Those strikers that we suspect of acts of violence are out. And I'd have to argue to get you that."

Connerton responded as Gillian expected. "We won't ask our people to move elsewhere. Most have lived here all their lives. Their ancestors are buried in the town cemetery. I don't envy your job, Tommy."

"We had our chance, George. I sure wish we had grabbed hold of it sooner."

"Me too, Tommy. Hindsight's wonderful. And it's useless."

○

When Travis Green returned to the mill the Monday after Edith's death, he almost didn't recognize the Number One machine. Everything looked different. The machine might as well have been covered in black crepe. All during the day he kept expecting to see Edith. He was in the men's room washing his hands when, for the first time, he understood that he would never see her again. He started to cry and wept for a long time. He mourned for Edith, her baby, and for himself. He had trouble sleeping that night. In his dreams he was being chased in a large empty lot by a furiously barking dog. Behind the dog were men in strange military uniforms.

The next morning, he felt a general, undifferentiated rage that included Eric Miller, the Black Hawk guards, and Mel LeBlanc. He could not stay at the damn mill in this damn town. He negotiated a payoff of his future rent, called his old friend and boss Charles Dyson, who quickly rehired him, and resigned from his mill job.

Bill Samson remained furious with everyone involved in the tragedy. He had always hated the Black Hawk guards who strutted, marched, shouted, orders, and taunted the strikers. His anger grew when he heard the strikers' version of how they were lured into a confrontation. But he was angrier with Eric Miller for being "a stupid, hot-headed asshole" and angriest at himself for not recognizing the danger involved in the breakup with Sherry Meserve. Don saw it, Shirley saw it. I was a damn, stupid fool for not paying more attention.

The strikers' spirit plummeted. All of the union's activities were affected. The pickets were almost silent, the weekly meetings poorly attended and dispirited. When Louise Adams sang "Solidarity Forever," it sounded like a dirge.

Eric Miller, his head down and shoulders drooping, told Bill that he was resigning as picket captain and Executive Committee member. Bill's first thought was, "You should have done that last week!" Then, as he looked at Eric's eyes, red from lack of sleep, and his contrite, hopeless expression, he realized that nothing he could say could make Eric feel any worse than he already felt. Without being quite conscious of what he was doing, Bill put his arm around Eric's ample waist and patted his stomach affectionately.

"Eric, I know what you've given to the strike and the union. I'm not going to accept your resignation. So grab hold of your balls. You're in for the long haul."

Eric appreciated Bill's support, but it made him feel worse rather than better. He continued to mope around the striker hangouts for the next couple of days. On Friday of that week he was in the union hall, watching a pool game on the local's beat-up old table, when he was told that he had a phone call. He picked up the phone and spoke listlessly.

"Hi, this is Eric."

"You're a murderer and we're going to get you." It was a male voice, chillingly calm. "We know where you live and don't think you can get away from us by moving."

Eric felt his anger stir. All of the abuse he had taken and the guilt he had felt was transformed into a feeling of rage. "Well, you have an advantage on me. You know where I live, and I don't know where you live. But if you tell me where you live, you won't have to come get me, I'll be waiting for you right beside your red pickup truck, and we can have at it." Silence.

"I don't hear you." Eric's voice grew colder. "I heard you before, you miserable, cowardly bastard. I thought you wanted blood!" I must have guessed right about the red pickup truck, he thought. The asshole is scared. Good!

He heard the phone click.

Bill recognized Eric's familiar aggressive tone of voice at the end of the conversation and felt thankful to whoever called for stirring the fires that Edith Kent's death had banked. Ironically, the crank call did what the understanding and sympathy of his friends could not. It restored Eric to his old fighting self, but nothing could revive the momentum of the strike.

On Thursday, February 14, the union's executive committee met in an atmosphere of gloom to discuss the future of the strike. Some urged an immediate decision to end the strike. That would spare the union the humiliation of a race by its members to return.

Bill rejected the plan. "We have to vote. The only thing we can do is to send around a letter telling our people the truth, urging them to stand tough, and telling them what Jeff told me, that they probably won't get an advantage going back a few days early anyway."

The committee voted to follow his suggestion.

They spent the next three hours composing a short letter to the membership.

Brothers and Sisters,

The time has come to consider ending our strike. The tragedy that led to the death of Edith Kent has hurt us badly. Our members are tired, and many have expressed the need to go on with their lives. At next Wednesday's meeting we will vote whether to continue our struggle and, if so, how to regain the momentum lost by the tragedy.

Please do not cross over till we vote. As far as we know, there are no jobs right now, so nothing would be gained. We have inspired union people all over the country by our solidarity. Remember our slogan, "No one goes back till everyone goes back."

If we vote to end the strike and announce our readiness to return as a group, we can retain the most precious thing in the world — our self-respect. And our community will not be torn apart any more than it already has.

In Solidarity,

Bill Samson
Emil Jean

The meeting was held on February 14. Don and Bill were surprised that only five people crossed over and applied for reinstatement beforehand. It was the only semi-bright spot in an otherwise dismal week for the union, which continued to get hammered in the press while its membership argued with each other over everything. A small but determined group of militants, who called themselves the "union zealots," campaigned against ending the strike. They wore t-shirts that read "Proud to Be Union," buttons that said "Continue the Fight," and sent letters to all the members urging them to vote against ending the strike.

Bill Samson chaired the meeting, his mind in turmoil. We've got to end the strike, he thought. People have to get on with their lives. I can't believe it, we came so close. Just before the vote, he went to the microphone. "My gut tells me to keep on fighting," he announced to loud applause, "but my brain tells me it's time to end it." He understood the groans. "What I care most about is protecting our members and making sure the union lives to fight another day. The strike may end, but the struggle continues. Whatever it takes for as long as it takes."

The line that once drew tumultuous applause was received in near silence. In the end, the strikers voted overwhelmingly to end the strike. Bill Samson returned home, sent a telegram to the company ending the strike, and then, with Shirley standing by his side, put his head down on the kitchen table and wept.

The bitter ending of the strike was only one of the emotional blows that Bill took during the next three months. At the beginning of March, Don Foreman, his job with the union over, privately told Bill that he was leaving North Bethany. He and Moira were heading north to Machais, where he purchased two acres of land overlooking the awesome beauty of Lake Wapahuche close by a cottage owned by Tony Lucelli. They would live rent-free in Tony's place while they constructed a cottage of their own.

Their conversation was short. They looked solemnly at each other for a long time, but neither was able to say how much he would miss the other. They talked a little about what they had accomplished during the strike, shook hands, and then pulled each other forward and embraced. Bill felt his throat tighten as sadness overwhelmed him. "You're a hell of a guy, Don. I'll never think of radicals the way I used to." He seemed on the verge of tears, but quickly caught himself. He smiled his gap-toothed smile. "But don't try and get me to join one of your commie organizations." It was Don who, for once, had nothing to say.

During the next weeks, Don's absence became a central fact in Bill's life, confronted each time he wanted to talk with someone about union strategy or the strike or his reactions to the rush of unpleasant events that seemed to engulf his life. If it had not been for Shirley's steadfast presence, he would have been overwhelmed by the depression that he fought against every day.

Early in February, Bill learned that Gary Sanborn and Emil Jean were campaigning to oust him as president of Local 34. If he sought re-election, the battle would be bitter. He had become the object of intense recrimination. Some argued that he capitulated too soon, others that he should never have accepted the offer to negotiate. Using hindsight, many members now claimed to have been opposed to striking from the beginning. "We should have just rejected their demands and stayed on the job." And some even claimed that Bill had sold out the local in some mysterious, devious way for personal gain.

Bill wasn't sure what to do. If I don't run, those self-important fools will think I'm afraid of them, but I'm sick of fighting. I don't ever want to be president of anything any more. Fuck 'em. Let Emil or Gary be president — of what? It's all over anyway. He sent a letter to the executive board, announcing that he would not be a candidate for re-election. The most exhilarating period of his life had ended with the thud of failure.

A week later, Bob Ouellette swallowed half a bottle of aspirin in an effort to kill himself. The whole town seemed locked in a massive depression — a mix of anger, hopelessness, and poverty. Restaurants and stores that catered to union people were doing terribly. No one had money to spend. Ugly confrontations between former strikers and scabs were now a part of the daily rhythm of life. New reports of former strikers being ill, drinking too much, or having marital problems came to Bill almost daily. It was difficult getting out of bed most mornings, and some days almost impossible to go to the union hall and attend to the petty details left over from the strike.

In April, Bill got a phone call from mill personnel informing him that, under the law, he was eligible to return to the mill as a helper on the Number

One Machine. His first thought was to tell the caller, a pleasant woman named Barbara Williams, with whom he had once had a brief affair, to "take this job and shove it!" But the words never passed his lips. He needed the job. The strike had depleted his savings, and he had no prospects for any kind of decent job elsewhere. So he thanked the caller and dutifully wrote down when and where he was to report.

He was one of fifteen strikers recalled on that Monday in accordance with the Laidlaw Doctrine that gives former strikers a preference for future job openings. When he reported for work, he was reassigned to the Number One Machine, the only former striker on his crew of twenty. During the next month he spent each day working alongside the people he had fought so hard to oust. He still despised the replacements as a group, and whenever one spoke to him, he was reminded of the co-workers, neighbors, and fellow strikers with whom he once worked. He also had the humiliation of working as an assistant to replacement workers who had never, before the strike, seen a paper machine.

Downtimes were the worst. Some of the scabs he worked with tried to make small talk. Bob Thomas, a slim young guy from Alabama, was the hardest to avoid, always asking Bill questions and trying to start conversations. *Fuck him and all of them. I've got brothers and sisters who'll never get their jobs back because of these lowlifes. He's a good worker, can't deny that. Friendly type. If he wasn't a scab, we could be friends. But not now, not ever. It was hell!*

Bill tried to keep his misery from Shirley, but she noticed the slow, sometimes hesitant walk that had largely replaced his earlier bouncy, determined stride. She heard his new, unconscious habit of sighing. And she missed his silly, toothy grin.

"It must be terrible to work with people and not let yourself like them or even be friendly," she remarked one day over breakfast.

"More than I could have guessed," he replied, his voice trembling with emotion.

On April 14th he was sitting at home trying, without success, to watch a baseball game on TV while Shirley prepared supper. He was miserable. *I can't take it. I feel like I'm living in a town that's been invaded and occupied by the enemy. If it wasn't for Shirley, I could take my 22 and end it all. One shot and no more misery.* It was a comforting thought. *Wonder who'd come to my funeral? Probably Gary would want to make a speech. That miserable fuck! How many of those hypocrites who were cheering me a few months ago would come?* He could visualize a few dispirited friends at his graveside, Don, Tony, and Ray comforting Shirley, who was crying bitterly. *What a sad* scene! How unjust. Suddenly, as though it came from outside himself, he was conscious of a voice kind of like his father's, only deeper, filled with disgust. "Stop whining and act like a man. You lost the strike, dumb shit, but you're still alive and healthy and you're living with a woman you love." For the first time in a month he felt like laughing.

"Shirley!" His voice was insistent.

"Wait a minute Bill, I'm making soup."

"I can't wait. I've got something important to tell you. Hurry!"

She rushed from the kitchen, wiping her hands on her jeans.

"What is it?"

"Start packing. We're going to Las Vegas to get married and have a honeymoon."

"Bill, that's silly. We can't afford it." But her face flushed with pleasure.

They were gone for eight days, and when they returned Bill was several hundred dollars poorer, but after a week of gambling, watching shows, and making love, their mood had changed. They smiled at each other as they entered their home. Bill whispered, "I love you," then picked Shirley up, slung her over his shoulder, and carried her over the threshold of their rented home.

Chapter 29

The district attorney for Panscott County, Tom Tierney, a well-regarded Republican, came under intense political pressure to bring murder charges against Rocky Louis. Party leaders told him the trial would help his career and weaken organized labor, but he was the kind of prosecutor who made up his own mind, based on the evidence. Early in March of 1990, Tierney announced that the only person to be charged with criminal conduct was Rocky Louis, who would be indicted for involuntary manslaughter.

His conclusion was greeted by considerable editorial outrage. Conservative newspapers throughout the state declared his actions a sellout and a betrayal of Edith Kent's memory. Liberal papers praised his judiciousness. Most of the people in North Bethany were pleased. To them, he was, like Edith Kent, a victim of the strike.

Local 34 collected enough money to hire Frank Powe, a well-known Boston criminal defense lawyer, to represent Louis. Bill Samson contributed $100 to the defense fund. Powe thought it barely possible that a self-defense plea would work if he could convince a jury that the security guards initiated the confrontation and that Louis reasonably felt in danger of great bodily harm. Louis's status as a family man and an honorably discharged war veteran with a clean record might create sympathy among the jurors. When investigators reported that the strikers might have felt threatened because of deliberately caused backfires, Tierney himself thought that Louis had a chance to be acquitted if they went to trial.

Powe and Tierney plea-bargained seriously. They argued about the strength of the case against Louis and about the need for jail time. In the end, they agreed on a two-year sentence; four months in prison and the remainder suspended. Another round of criticism. Douglas Kent bitterly denounced the settlement as a sellout, and various replacement workers were quoted to the same effect. But the settlement had its defenders, including law professors, former prosecutors, and defense lawyers. Public outrage was limited, and after a week, the story seemed over.

Its demise was short-lived. The killing of Edith Kent and the mild sentence given to Rocky Louis was somehow picked up by anti-labor groups around the country. It became a regular topic of outrage, fanned by radio talk shows and right-wing political journals. Reed Carson, President of the Workers' Freedom Foundation, started the barrage with an article in the *National Conservative Review* titled "Why We Need to Curb the Power of Labor." Carson used the Kent killing as his major evidence of the need for tougher laws to punish union-instigated violence. "Can unions get away with murder? Until Congress amends the law to make strike violence a federal crime, there is little to deter union militants from thinking they can get away with murder. They have done so — literally. Ask the Kent family of Damariscotta, Maine."

Professor Eastman appeared on the Liberty Forum, a televised discussion show, to discuss the implications of the killing, which he blamed on the need of union bosses to control both workers and employers. He was asked by moderator Jim Lee to explain why unions used violence even though it was often self-defeating.

"That's a good question, Jim. What you have to understand is that the relationship between unions and unionized employers is a feudal one. The employers own the castles. The union bosses sweep down on the castles from time to time, using their members as troops seeking spoils. Fear is their chief weapon. The union bosses know that, if their troops don't see them as tough enough, new leaders will push them aside. Consequently, an incentive exists for the union boss to use violence. Violence sends a message not only to the employer; it sends a message to rivals that the union boss is not someone to mess around with."

In early April, Armand Bradley, the U.S. Attorney for the Western District of Maine, announced that he was launching his own investigation into the facts of the killing. Looking directly at the TV cameras he stated firmly "I am prepared to bring to justice those who did not fire the shots but who bear responsibility for this heinous crime."

Bradley was a Democrat with a reputation as a maverick. He was sometimes mentioned as a possible nominee for higher office. He thought of himself as mildly pro-labor. But he insisted that organized labor needed to rid itself of its reputation for violence and corruption. He had, in the past, brought charges under the RICO (Racketeer Influenced and Corrupt Organizations) Act against locals of the Teamsters and Laborers unions. Both cases had ended in settlements that provided for the ousting of mob influence and for a public review panel. Bradley's handling of these cases had brought him a lot of favorable publicity. He was frequently described as the Maine Giuliani. He had no doubt that he had done something that was of benefit to the pubic, to himself, and even to the labor movement.

Bradley was sure that the RICO statute, which he had utilized in the past, was the best vehicle for bringing criminal charges against those responsible for the violence that led to Edith Kent's death. He would be fair. He was not out to convict the innocent, but he would be tough. He would show the public that labor violence would not be tolerated.

As part of his investigation, Bradley and his assistant Anthony Pigotti interviewed strikers, company security officials, replacement workers (among them Travis Green), management, and union leaders. He also subpoenaed tape recordings that the union had made of its regular weekly meetings.

On May 10 of 1990, almost exactly a year after the strike began, Bradley announced the indictment of Bill Samson, Don Foreman, and Eric Miller under the RICO statute. They were charged with conspiracy to conduct the activities of the union through a pattern of criminal activity.

The former strikers, still struggling to live with the consequences of their defeat, were outraged by the indictments. "It's bullshit," Ray Allair told a reporter for the *Boston Globe*, "union-busting, labor-baiting, worker-hating bullshit. Everybody in the union and everyone in North Bethany knows that Bill Samson fought his heart out to make sure that our strike was honorable and non-violent. 'Violence is our enemy.' That's what he said at our public meetings, and that's what he told people in private. And now he's supposed to be corrupt and a racketeer. No way."

In the days immediately following the indictments, the Letters to the Editor columns of the local papers were filled with expressions of outrage from Local 34 members and their families. Some of the letters, like Arthur Grant's, were heartfelt but inarticulate: "Nobody nowhere has less commitment to violence to help overcome powerful forces in what some of us feel is a battle between David and Goliath." Other letters, like Jill Carter's, were equally heartfelt and more literate. "During this strike, Bill Samson has become our own Martin Luther King, a person who understands the necessary link between righteous struggle and non-violence. Don Foreman is a person of implacable honor who has devoted his life to helping the poor, the oppressed, and the downtrodden."

The letters of support were answered by contrary letters applauding the indictment: some by replacement workers, some by supervisors, and some anonymous. The indictees themselves reacted differently. Eric, who showed both his anger and his toughness to his friends and supporters, nevertheless felt both guilt and foreboding. He urged Don, who had returned to North Bethany, and Bill to disassociate themselves from him and to get their own lawyers. "I'm the guy who has fucked things up, and if anybody has to go to prison, it should be me. I let you guys and the union down."

Don laughed mirthlessly. "Eric, if I go down, I want to go down with the war hero who defended me."

Bill waved his hand dismissively. His expression was firm. "You wouldn't cut me loose if the situation was reversed, and we're not cutting you loose. Besides, nobody's going to prison. It's a phony indictment, and no jury in

Maine is going to convict us." He spoke with genuine assurance. His belief in the American system of justice was too strong for him to even consider the possibility of conviction, and his sense of loyalty to his friends made the possibility of separating himself from Don and Eric unthinkable. "We were together during the strike, and we are going to stand together during the trial. We're going to show people what union solidarity is all about."

Don was less optimistic. He knew from his days in the civil rights movement that law could be used as an instrument of repression. During the '60s and '70s, he had seen friends unfairly convicted of vague crimes like conspiracy and disorderly conduct. An old girlfriend, who had barely escaped from an angry mob in Montgomery, Alabama, had been subsequently convicted for inciting a riot. But the idea of worker solidarity — a common front — was what he stood for.

None of the defendants had enough money to pay for an attorney, but a defense fund was established by contributions from the strikers, from the national union, and from sympathizers. The national union hired Frank Powe to represent all three defendants. After reviewing the facts, he too urged Don and Eric to hire their own lawyers. As he told them, "Bill's defense and yours might actually conflict, and no good lawyer wants to give up a good defense for his client because it might hurt another client."

Bill quickly vetoed the idea. "We're in this together, and we are going to sink or swim together," he declared, while Don nodded vigorously in agreement and Eric stared at his feet.

Chapter 30

Travis Green left the mill, determined to leave everything about Maine behind him. He was sick of telling himself that he was different from Springer and Young — the replacement workers who seemed to enjoy making their living off other people's misery. He was sick of living in a white world where his co-workers walked white, ate white food, listened to white music, and laughed at white jokes. He had had his fill of it and was eager to be surrounded by soul brothers, soul food, and soul music. He told himself he was glad to be back at Dyson Auto Repair. He parked his car in the back of the repair shop and found an apartment on Convent Avenue similar to the apartment he had left a year before. He rarely saw a white person now—on the streets, in the stores, everyone was dark-skinned like him, dressed cool, and walked with a strut, the combination of rhythm and self-expression that he had missed while in Maine. Now, even people he didn't know seemed familiar in accent and expression. He was back home.

But it still wasn't that easy to leave his Maine experiences behind. It took two weeks before the neighbors' loud voices quit bothering him and longer for all the people walking so closely on the streets to seem normal. Sometimes he found himself thinking longingly of the open road between his little apartment and the Panscott mill. But it was Edith, their friendship (his first with a white woman), and her death that most often brought his thoughts back to Maine. Whenever he saw a pregnant woman, he thought of poor Edith Kent, who would never have her child.

Usually, he ate lunch while working on a car—a customer's or his own, if business was slow. Today, he and Charlie decided to take a break and go together to the family-run corner diner where they could buy fried egg rolls, egg tacos, or a slice of pizza. It was a far cry from the Maine Sail.

"Hey, Charlie, did I ever tell you that when I was in Maine I ate fresh fish every week? Not just crusted and fried, either. Baked, grilled—you name it. Man, was it fresh. Once we all had lobster. You buy it by the pound, while it's swimming in a tank looking at you. 'Course, you pay for all that shell and stuff, but man, is it worth it. All that white, delicious meat."

Charlie had heard this tale before. It always made him feel defensive for New York, a city that he loved. "White meat, huh, mahn? You still had to drive your black ass the hell out of there before you got it shot off!" When Travis laughed in agreement, George teased, "Besides, we got real seafood in New York. We got Island food, Korean food, and Indian food. Not that old-fashioned stuff you got in Maine. What is your choice of coo-zeen today? Chinese, Mexican, Eye-talian or good old soul food?"

Travis bought two egg tacos, which he quickly finished. As they walked companionably back to the shop, they could hear the shop's loud phone ring. Charles picked it up with his spare hand.

He looked back at Travis and whispered: "It's some attorney from Maine."

It was Armand Bradley asking if he could meet with Travis the following Tuesday when he would be in New York

Travis agreed, but he did not look forward to their meeting. He had heard something about the indictment, and it reminded him of everything he hated about being a replacement worker.

They met at a small coffee shop and delicatessen — four tiny tables covered by oil cloth on the corner of Convent Avenue and 138th St., not far from the CCNY campus. Bradley was there, seated in a corner booth when Travis arrived at the appointed time.

Bradley's smile of greeting was broad and almost sincere. "Mr. Green, I'm delighted to meet you. My assistant, Mr. Pignotti, told me that he found his interview with you most rewarding."

They shook hands and Travis smiled as if to show how pleased he was at the compliment. But the smile merely concealed his suspicion. *This dude is trying to snow me for some reason. He must think I'm pretty dumb not to notice it.*

Bradley began by asking him about Edith Kent. What was she like? How did she feel about the strikers? How did she feel about the job? Was she a good worker? All were questions that Travis had already answered in his interview with Pignotti.

Bradley next inquired about the riot that followed the drive-by. Had Travis heard any racial epithets? Was Travis, whom he knew to be a decorated Viet Nam veteran, frightened? Bradley directed most of his questions to the incident at Charley's restaurant. He examined Travis in great detail about what was said, especially by Eric Miller. After Travis described it all as faithfully as he could, Bradley had looked directly at him, his eyes grave and troubled. "Do you think he would have behaved the same way if you were white?

"Well, not exactly. You see…."

Bradley almost pounced. "So you think that, perhaps unconsciously, he was exhibiting racist feelings."

Travis did not reply. He could see in his thoughts Eric's tortured features as he described the death of his door gunner. Then he turned his eyes on Bradley, who seemed like a fisherman waiting for a bite. It made Travis angry. *The sneaky motherfucker is trying to use me like a black puppet.* Travis remained silent. Bradley's expression changed to one of entreaty. "Mr. Green, I think your testimony could prove enormously valuable to the state in seeking justice for those responsible for the death of your friend."

"What are they charged with exactly?" Travis asked.

"Conspiracy under the RICO statute."

"I knew it," Travis laugh hollowly — the laugh of a man whose suspicion of skullduggery has just been proven correct. "Con-spiracy." He said it like two words, heavily stressing the first syllable. "I know about Con-spiracy." He could see Bradley eyeing him in confusion.

"My uncle Delbert, he was charged twice with conspiracy back in Alabama, once for being at a meeting with Dr. King. My cousin Roxanne was charged with conspiracy for going on a freedom march. 'Conspiracy to be free,' that's what we called it."

Bradley was now obviously offended. "This has nothing to do with the charges of conspiracy during the civil rights days. This is about protecting federal rights for replacement workers like yourself."

"Bullshit!" Travis shouted loudly enough to cause people in nearby booths to turn around. "Conspiracy to fight for their jobs. That's what they were guilty of. You think you're different from the prosecutors in Alabama but . . . ."

"Mr. Green, I did not come here to be insulted." Bradley's expression was icy.

"Then go. Leave. You're not doing this for Edith. You're doing it for yourself. Get yourself another boy."

Bradley left, his face red with rage. He didn't even remember to pay for his coffee.

Travis felt totally vindicated when he heard from a former co-worker that slimy Charles Springer was going to testify for the prosecution.

Chapter 31

The racketeering trial began on the morning of June 16 at the Federal Courthouse in Portland. Bill entered the courtroom in something of a daze just before 8:30 a.m. and was surprised to find it packed. He was grateful that the majority of the seats were taken by paperworkers. In the first row of spectators, he saw Ray Allair and Cindy Reagan. Arthur Poland sat behind them in a suit too tight for his strike-expanded waistline. His massive head was turning and twisting to see everything going on, and he was holding hands with his wife, Laurie.

I think they're more nervous than me, Bill thought, and the idea both pleased and amused him. No reason to be frightened. I'm innocent and the whole stupid case is just politics. No jury is going to convict us — I mean, if they did it would be so unfair and so unjust. The jurors are going to be decent Maine people, not a bunch of anti-union morons.

Over in the corner near the back, trying unsuccessfully to look inconspicuous, was Sherry Meserve, her lovely, troubled, dark eyes fixed on Eric Miller.

To his left, Bill could see Jill Carter, a notebook opened in front of her, wearing a press badge on her suit jacket. She turned towards Bill and flashed a thumbs-up sign. Bill waved and smiled confidently in response. Bill had never even seen a real trial before, but he had an optimistic view of the legal system that came from watching shows like *LA Law*, *The Defenders*, and *Perry Mason*. The trials were dramas of justice. The good, law-abiding guys who were innocent and the bad guys who sought to convict them battled for the minds of the jurors. The bad guys relied on technicalities, confusing objections, and misleading statements. The good guys relied on truth and fairness. The good guys almost always won. An element of Bill's patriotism was the conviction that the American legal system — relying on the good sense of ordinary people serving as jurors — had a foolproof way of revealing truth. It was reassuring.

He knew that Shirley was worried sick. I guess any wife would be. She's a worrier anyway. They had spent the night before the trial at Portland's towering Holiday Inn, overlooking the harbor. Downstairs, in the largely deserted bar, they had each had two drinks, and Bill signaled for his third before Shirley had motioned that it was time to leave. Back upstairs in their room with the lights out, Bill lay down gently beside Shirley's curled back. He was excited — a pre-battle rush of feeling made him high and eager to make love, something he always enjoyed, particularly in hotel rooms. He ran his hand across her top hip slowly, their private signal for the start of lovemaking. He awaited her customary yielding response. But Shirley had rebuffed him and scooted slightly away.

"What's the matter, baby?"

"Bill, I'm scared. What's going to happen tomorrow? Do you realize that you could be put in jail? You'll be 56 soon. I don't want you to spend your birthday in prison!"

Bill felt her shoulders tense. I guess she has a right to be worried. Her life is on the line, same as mine. Whatever happens, we've had a great run together. He patted her on the back.

"I'm not going to jail. I'm going to trial. You haven't been in the practice sessions our lawyers have put us all through. I know what I'm doing. I've answered everything the other side could ever dream up." He added somewhat proudly: "You know, I've gotten pretty good with words."

But his rush was over, replaced by a feeling of emptiness. He felt tired. Patting Shirley affectionately on the rump, he turned over, and fell instantly asleep. He woke up sometime after three, thinking, I got a lot at stake here. If we're convicted, my happy life is over. He felt Shirley move. She had buried her head in the pillow. What a wonderful, loving wife she is. It's a horrible business, but we're going through it together. When it was all over, he would take her dancing, buy her a big bouquet of roses, and find a card that told her how wonderful she was. He could imagine her delight. Feeling good, he closed his eyes and fell fast asleep.

○

The trial began slowly. Nothing happened during the first fifteen minutes except for the lawyers walking around importantly and holding whispered conferences with Judge Alcott, a distinguished-looking man with a hawk nose and small, forceful-looking eyes that looked out sternly from behind his wire-rimmed glasses. Bill recalled Alcott from his days as Maine's Lieutenant Governor. Not a friend of labor, but not a bad guy, he thought. The only real action came from the press, including cameras for *Court TV* scurrying about frantically. The trial would be seen all over America. Good thing! Maybe people would learn from it, understand how hard he and Don had fought to make the non-violent policy work. They'd done a damn good job of it, too. Sure guys were angry and hated the scabs, but it was a non-violent strike. Everyone in the labor movement knew that. Edith Kent's death was a crazy, stupid accident, not something that anyone in the union had sought.

The first order of business was the questioning of potential jurors. Judge Alcott told the lawyers that, given the nature of the charges, he would give them lots of leeway in their questioning. Bill thought it only fair.

The question period gave Bill an opportunity to study the prosecutor. No doubt about it, silver-haired, sharp-featured Armand Bradley was a distinguished-looking man. His looks were accentuated by a wide, friendly smile, and a rich deep voice. He exuded fairness. Hollywood might have cast him as the Good Rancher in a Western movie. Seems like a good man, Bill thought pleasantly as Bradley got ready to question the potential jurors.

Bradley - "Juror One, have you ever been a member of a union?"

Juror One (a heavy-set, middle-aged man) "For about a year when I worked for Rockport Shoe Company, I was a member of the Teamsters."

Bradley: "Ever been on strike?"

Juror: "No."

Bradley: "Have you ever heard the term 'scab'?"

Juror: "Sure."

Bradley: "What does the term mean to you?"

Juror: "Someone who breaks strikes by crossing a picket line during a strike."

Bradley: "What do you think of such people?"

Juror: "It's their right to do it if they want."

Bradley: "If you were working at a unionized facility, would you consider working during a strike?"

Juror: "Never."

Bradley: "Thank you, you are excused."

Juror Four was a black woman who had been on strike and loyally supported the union. She, too, was dismissed. Bill was surprised at this turn of events. It made no sense. Union members could understand the pressures on him during the strike. But how could students, small business people, rich people, professionals, housewives or anyone else who had never faced what he had to deal with every day during the strike?

After another potential juror who had been a union officer was dismissed, this time by the judge, Bill was deflated. The trial could be lost if they ended up with the wrong jurors. Bradley was trying to make that happen. And I thought he was trying to be fair. Another dishonest politician, that's what he was.

Thank goodness that Frank Powe, after initially declaring that the defense would take any fair-minded jurors, asked a lot of questions to make sure that those prejudiced against unions were also disqualified.

The group finally selected was mainly ignorant of unions and strikes. It included seven women and five men. One woman and one man had once been union members, but that was awhile ago and they'd never had to go on strike.

Bill's optimism returned. "They're regular people. I can take my chances with them. They're smart enough to realize that the whole case is a bunch of bullshit."

Armand Bradley began his opening statement in a conversational tone, devoid of anger.

"Ladies and Gentlemen of the jury. This is a difficult case for the people to bring. The defendants are not the sort of people it gives me any pleasure to convict of a serious crime. Yet, in their desire for victory in a strike against a powerful adversary, they engaged in a pattern of criminal conduct that had tragic consequences for an innocent woman and her unborn child; for Douglas Kent, who lost the people who gave his life meaning; for the community of North Bethany, which has not yet been able to purge itself of hatred and bitterness; and for the union and its members, who were also innocent victims of the defendants' behavior."

Somehow Bradley's statement touched Bill and made him feel sorry for all the pain of the strike, especially for Douglas Kent. Bradley had a job to do and he was doing it.

He whispered to Don, "Bradley looks sad."

"Yeah, sad," Don said disgustedly, "like a jackal looks sad before feasting on a carcass." Bill laughed softly. Don was probably right. What a shame it was.

Bradley's voice grew stronger. "The conspiracy for which the defendants are charged grew out of a strike. The right to strike is an important right of American citizens that has been used honorably by working people for generations. I would never seek to weaken this right in any way. Nor would I appeal to any prejudice that anyone might have against unions and their leaders. This case is not about the right to join unions or conduct strikes. Those are rights protected by the law and respected by those of us sworn to uphold it. But the right to strike does not give union members the right to conduct their affairs through a pattern of racketeering or from conspiring to do so. And that is what the defendants are charged with. To find the defendants guilty, you must find beyond reasonable doubt that they conspired to participate, directly or indirectly, in the conduct of the union's affairs through a pattern of racketeering activity. The death of Edith Kent is part of the illegal activity, but only part, as we will show. The defendant encouraged, participated in, and ratified a large number of criminal acts. These criminal acts constitute racketeering under the law."

Racketeering, for God's sake. What did racketeering have to do with the strike or Edith Kent's death? Why would anyone who believed in unions try Local 34's leaders on such charges, especially since they hadn't any idea that Edith Kent was going to be killed?

Bradley went on. "Now, as His Honor will later instruct you in greater detail, a pattern of racketeering activity can be shown by at least two of what are called 'predicate offenses,' mainly acts of violence or attempted acts of violence that are made illegal by federal law.

"The concept of conspiracy under the law has sometimes confused even learned commentators, but the basic idea is simple. A conspiracy exists whenever two or more people band together to commit or support illegal acts. If you are a member of the conspiracy, you can be found guilty for all of the illegal acts committed or planned by it.

"It is clear that a RICO conspiracy does not require that all defendants participate in all racketeering acts or that all of them know of the entire conspiratorial sweep or even that all of them must be acquainted with all other defendants. Instead, the law requires that the component parts be linked together so that we can conclude that an agreement existed. We can prove the existence of the necessary agreement, or conspiracy, to violate RICO by proving that a defendant agreed to the overall objectives of conspiracy."

Bill grew irate. This is ridiculous. What in God's name is Bradley talking about? It sounded like he could be guilty of things he hadn't planned or didn't know about. Surely that couldn't be right. Maybe the other lawyers understand what he's saying." Bill was not even sure of that. He whispered to Powe, "What the hell does that bullshit mean?" Powe patted Bill on the back. He had earlier tried, without success, to explain some of the ramifications of conspiracy law to Bill, who had dismissed it as confusing and stupid. It seemed unfair, even un-American for the law to find people who agree to one thing guilty of something else. No jury would convict him on that basis — would they?

Bradley wound up his introduction, his voice now strong and commanding, his face firm, almost angry: "Our evidence will prove beyond reasonable doubt that the defendants were bound together in an effort to commit criminal acts to prevent people like Edith Kent from exercising their rights under the law. And the results were tragic."

Once again, Bradley's expression changed to suggest a man performing an unwelcome but necessary task. He stood still for a moment, his eyes raised upward, as though to pray for justice or reflect on the solemnity of the moment.

Damn. The guy was full of shit, but he's good. Bill was beginning to feel just a trace of fear. I guess someone who doesn't know about strikes could be confused. He hoped Powe had good answers, but Powe chose not to give an opening argument.

Bradley called his first witness, a company security guard who testified about the attack on Jordan Marcon. Then, other guards and replacement workers wearing suits took the stand and testified about other "criminal" acts, including attacks on vehicles, jack rocks, physical assaults on replacement workers, and threats issued on the picket line. Powe's constant objection to the relevance was overruled by the judge after Bradley pointed out that Eric Miller was picket captain and that Bill Samson exercised overall control of strike activity.

Now Bill was getting more worried. Piled up like that, one incident after another, it looks like violence and law breaking was all the union did. Powe, in response, was able to demonstrate that much of the criminal conduct was conducted by "persons unknown." Where one of the witnesses could link the action to one specific striker, like the near riot that followed the August drive-by, Powe's questions focused on the shakiness of the witnesses' recollection. Or he pointed out the witnesses' inability to connect the criminal conduct to the defendants. All helpful, but still the image of a violent strike hovered over all the questions. The jurors, Bill could tell, were troubled.

Bradley spent a lot of time with John Dickerson, a replacement worker who had his nose broken during the riot. Looks like the guy Eric tackled. Bill wasn't sure until Dickerson pointed Eric out as one of the people who tackled him.

Bill sent a note to Powe. "I saved the son of a bitch's life." On cross examination, Dickerson claimed not to recognize Bill as the person who came to his aid.

The final witness, another security guard, testified that Eric Miller had the leading role in several confrontations between guards and pickets in the mini-riot that led to Edith Kent's death.

When the trial adjourned, Bill was surrounded by supporters who patted him on the back and assured him that the state's case was nonsense that no self-respecting juror would believe. But despite their cheery words, he could tell that they were worried and confused.

Powe announced that he needed to return to his office to prepare some motions and write out questions to ask the state's expert. Bill and Shirley decided to walk to the waterfront for a drink and possibly a lobster dinner.

Neither Don nor Eric wanted to join them. Bill suspected that Eric meant to find Sherry Meserve. He had no idea what Don meant to do.

As Bill and Shirley left the courtroom, they ran into Jill Carter, who looked trim and professional in her business suit and smart summer hat, so different from the person they once knew.

They exchanged small talk for a while, agreed that Bradley was smart and totally dishonorable and that the whole trial was political. She told them that she was living in Bangor and that her children were fine. Then Bill asked the question that both he and Shirley most wondered about: "What happened to Jeffrey? You guys seemed to be the hottest romance in Maine?"

"He got a post-doc at Berkeley, and I got a job as a reporter. I decided that I couldn't go with him. Hardest decision I ever made. I'm seeing this TV producer now. Nice guy, but he's got a tough act to follow. I'm not ready for another love affair. I need peace in my life."

"Amen," Shirley said with such great fervor that Bill was once more reminded of how tough the whole business of the indictment and trial had been on her.

They hugged, and then Bill and Shirley headed for the waterfront.

It was a warm evening, with a pleasant breeze coming from the ocean, along with the cries of seagulls, as Bill and Shirley headed for the pier. They decided to have their drink on the outside deck of the "Nancy," a restaurant converted from an old Schooner. They agreed not to talk about the trial, and as a result, since they could think of nothing else, they sat sipping their drinks in silence and looking out sadly at the fishing ships, dinghies, and gulls swooping gracefully over the water in search of food.

When they had paid their check and headed for the hotel, they noticed a large crowd of mostly young people on a nearby pier. At the front of the pier, standing on a makeshift platform, was Don Foreman.

"I should have known why he didn't want to have dinner with us," Bill said as they headed over to join the crowd. Bill knew that Don had not mentioned the rally to him because Powe had insisted that they not make public statements.

Don's face seemed to glow with purpose and determination. "They may convict us — probably will. Lying prosecutors, unsympathetic juries, and conservative judges have been making martyrs for the labor movement since the '20s. But the struggle won't end. It's time that we got together — students and workers and everyone who cares about justice." The crowd cheered and whooped. When the applause ended, an older person in the audience, obviously a reporter, shouted at Don.

"Are you saying that Bradley is a liar and that Judge Alcott is biased?"

"Make your own decision but don't tell me that what's going on is justice. It's not justice to put the best labor leader in the state on trial, and it's not justice to try and convict a war hero just because he fights for his union brothers and sisters."

The crowd cheered again. Don had been so absorbed he never noticed Bill and Shirley. As they left to return to their hotel, Bill smiled. "Don will never change."

Bill spent the rest of the evening watching TV looking for reports of the trial. Shirley refused to join him. "I hate it. The whole thing is unfair, just like Don said."

But she watched intently when *Court TV* came on and featured their case. The legal experts who commented on the day's proceedings agreed that more than enough criminal conduct had already been shown to establish "a pattern of racketeering activity" as required by the RICO statute. As Professor Kennedy of the Harvard Law School told an interviewer: "The key to the case will be the ability of the prosecutor to demonstrate to the jury that the defendants were ultimately responsible for the criminal conduct and that they acted in concert."

"How can they do that?"

"Several ways. Any criminal conduct that they can link to the defendants will be important. We know that one of the defendants, Eric Miller, was present when the fatal shot was fired. His conduct leading up to the shooting is likely to be examined in detail. Any statement or conduct by the defendants encouraging violence by the strikers and any action or statement by the defendants ratifying or approving of acts of violence will be relevant."

"What does the defense need to do to disprove the charges?"

"Basically, to show that the defendants were good people who opposed violence and tried their best to stop it."

"Professor, what if the evidence shows that the defendants did not encourage violence but did not do enough to stop it. What would the result be?"

"That's hard to say. Under the law, the defendants should then probably be acquitted, but, if the judge permits the jury to rule on it and the jury feels that the defendants are morally responsible, they might well convict. Generally, the key to conviction is making the jury angry."

Bill did not find this analysis reassuring, but he reminded himself that the defense would get its turn.

When they entered the courtroom the next day, Don was sitting silently next to an obviously angry Frank Powe.

"Damn it," Powe said, hardly waiting for Bill to take his seat. "Do you guys want to be convicted? The last thing we need right now is Don going around on a soapbox. It's bad enough attacking Bradley and Alcott. But why on earth did he have to include the damn jury. Bill, for God's sake, talk to him — make him shut up until the trial ends. Then, when you're acquitted, he can say whatever he wants."

Bill smiled sympathetically. "Sorry, Frank, no one has the power to keep Don quiet when he thinks something unfair is happening. When he says, 'Whatever it takes for as long as it takes,' he's saying what's in his heart."

Powe shook his head in wonder. It was a lot easier to control murderers and rapists than these damn idealists.

The next witness for the prosecution was Professor Willard Tremain of the Wharton School, a wimpy, soft-looking man. Bill thought, what can he know? Armand Bradley first asked him about his academic and professional credentials, a question that allowed Tremain to list his seven books — two dealing with the issue of strike violence, over 100 articles on labor issues, plus many lectures and frequent testimony before Congress. He added that he was also a consultant to several large corporations who were worried about strike violence.

Powe objected to Tremain's testimony: "Your Honor, this is not appropriate expert testimony." The judge cut him short. "If a person with Professor Tremain's scholarly and practical experience isn't qualified to testify, there will be no way for me or the jury to learn the dynamics of strikes."

Several of the jurors nodded approval.

Bradley decided to get right to the key issue: "Professor Tremain, are all strikes violent?"

"Certainly not. There have been many strikes with no or very little violence."

"What in your view is the key element of violent strikes?"

"The key is the attitude of the union leaders. My research shows that strike violence is not a few isolated acts committed by a handful of 'loose cannon' strikers who can't stop themselves. In almost all cases, strike violence is not committed without the knowledge and complicity of top union officials. To most Americans, including most members of unions, beating, menacing, and extorting is outrageous behavior. But to many union officials, this behavior is considered normal and is routinely used as a weapon. Encouragement of violence is part of the folklore and tradition of many unions."

What a crock of shit! I wonder if he believes it. It looks like he does, but how can he be a professor and not know how strikes work, Bill wondered.

"Professor Tremain, can union leaders prevent violence if they want to?"

"Certainly, they have many ways to prevent violence. For instance, they can announce at the beginning of a strike that anyone engaging in violence will be fined and expelled from the union. They can and should conduct training exercises. They can remove angry, violent people from the picket line. They can refuse to put up scab lists, and they can avoid the kind of fiery rhetoric that invariably induces violence."

By now Bill was furious. Sons of bitches, that's what they were, a prosecutor who didn't care about justice and a professor who didn't care about truth. They looked sincere, wore nice clothes, and used fancy words, but they were jackals just like Don said.

Bradley continued in his well-modulated voice: "You mentioned scab lists. What are they?"

"They are lists of strikers who have crossed the line and returned to work, displayed prominently in the union hall."

"What is the function of such lists?"

"They are a way of targeting and increasing the anger toward the people listed. It's like announcing the start of hunting season on the people listed. Once a list is posted, you can be sure that the line-crossers will be subject to abuse, threats, and violence."

"Do you know whether the union in this case had such a list posted?"

"In preparing for this case, I visited the union hall and saw a posted scab list with a skull and crossbones drawn just above it. Any union that permits that sort of public identification and ridicule of people exercising their rights as American citizens to work is inviting violence."

He's full of shit, but he ain't dumb, Bill admitted to himself.

"In your experience, how do union leaders who believe in violence make this known to the membership?"

"In public meetings, they never advocate violence directly. But they speak in a code that will be understood by union activists. Sometimes the code will be subtle, such as encouraging the wearing of military garb, camouflage fatigues, as the union in this case did. Sometimes the message will be fairly direct, as when they reminisce about how scabs were treated in the old days. Don Foreman talked about that at one of the meetings. Another common way to incite violence is the constant use of warlike images, phrases, and metaphors."

"If a union leader were to refer repeatedly to a strike as 'class warfare,' would that be encouragement of violence?"

"Absolutely."

"What does the term 'class warfare' convey to labor experts like your-self?"

"We know it to be a phrase common to anarchists, socialists, communists, and others who advocate violence. Definitely likely to encourage violence and almost surely intended to have such an effect."

"No further questions."

By now, Bill's expectation that the trial was to be a ceremony of innocence vindicated had evaporated. Why had he been so certain of acquittal? How cleverly Bradley made his innocent behavior look suspicious. He looked at the jury. They seemed intent on every word the prosecutor spoke. I guess it will be hard for them to understand how I worked my ass off to keep the strike non-violent. You really had to be there to understand. Bill looked around the defense table. Eric looked especially angry, Don depressed, and Frank Powe like a man facing an uphill struggle.

Powe rose slowly from his seat: "Professor, have you ever been on strike?"

"No."

"Then how do you know what messages are intended to, or likely to, persuade strikers to use violence?"

"There is considerable literature on the subject that I have read, along with literature in the field of communication theory and practice. I have worked closely with professors Haggard and Thiebolt in developing their classic study of union violence. Similarly, I am a member of the Institute for Labor Law Research and helped to design their study and analysis of picket-line misconduct. And I have interviewed literally hundreds of people who have been involved in strikes."

"Do you think the use of metaphor of battle encourages violence?"

"I do."

"Do you think that Reverend Martin Luther King was secretly encouraging violence?"

"No, I do not."

"If I told you that he used such images frequently in his speeches, would that change your mind?"

"No, it would not."

"Can you explain why the use of images of battle are incitements to violence when done in a union context but not when used in support of civil rights?"

"Some of it is background. In the labor area, particularly where a strike is involved, you are calling upon a violent tradition. Secondly, when a minister uses such language, people are far more likely to understand that metaphor is being used. The war or battle is between good and evil and not an actual human conflict where victory can be achieved by frightening or intimidating the other side."

The son of a bitch is smart, Bill thought. But his anxiety grew. He did cheer up a little recalling that the union had an expert to show that Professor Tremain was wrong.

Bradley introduced recorded statements selected from union meetings in which fiery, angry rhetoric was used. Some of it seemed to favor violence towards replacement workers and scabs. The entire recording lasted fifteen minutes.

The state's next witness was Jordan Marcon. Through church connections, Jordan had found a new job and small house in Somerville near Ann's cancer specialists. They had left their house in part because Ann had faith in these doctors and in part to move their boys away from hostility to a place where they could be normal teenagers again. The "For Sale" sign on their lawn had attracted no possible buyers. It would be a long while before the townspeople considered it cleansed and ready for use again.

Marcon walked straight-shouldered behind the court deputy to the witness stand. He began by describing how he had prayed to God for guidance and had felt he heard God's voice advising him to reclaim his job.

"And you were a good union man before that?"

"Yes, and I would like to think I am still a good union man who is doing what he has to do to protect his family."

Arthur Poland, his eyes blazing, called out "Damn liar!" as murmurs of anger and sarcastic laughs came from other union supporters in the room. Laurie Poland poked Arthur in the ribs. Judge Alcott's face clouded, and the veins in his neck stood out as he banged his gavel angrily. "The jury will disregard any outbursts from the audience. And those of you who are here to support the defendants should know that if we have one more improper effort to influence the jury, I will clear the courthouse." Bill smiled at Arthur, who looked as embarrassed as a man who just farted noisily in church.

"Mr. Marcon, during the period that you were on strike, did you picket?"

"Yes, I did."

"Who was there with you?"

"Eric Miller and Ed Allen."

"Will you describe Mr. Miller's behavior on the picket line?"

"He was extremely aggressive."

"Objection."

"Sustained."

"Can you tell me what he said and did?"

"He shouted out insults, raised his fists, gave people crossing the line the finger, threatened replacement workers, and called them vile names. I'm embarrassed to repeat them."

"Just tell us what he said to the best of your recollection."

"I remember he called the replacement workers 'effing scabs.' He said they were shit. And I know he told one person 'When I find out where you live, I'm going to be there,' and then he called him a vulgar name."

"How did the man respond?"

"He just lowered his head."

"And during the time you were on strike, did you ever discuss the issue of violence with Don Foreman?"

"Yes."

"What did he say to you, and what did you say to him?"

"He said strikes worked better in the old days when scabs were in fear of their lives. I said I couldn't imagine hurting someone who was doing what he thought necessary to protect his family. He said I didn't understand labor history."

"Were you yourself, or your family, the victim of violence?"

"Yes, I have been threatened many times. My sons were attacked by members of the football team, and I had shots fired at my house that almost killed my youngest son."

"Thank you, Mr. Marcon. Your witness."

"Mr. Marcon, do you know who fired the shots at your home?"

"No, I do not."

"No further questions."

Bill and every former striker in the room felt a little ashamed as Marcon left the stand. But they still hated him.

The next witness was Ray Pinder, a superscab who testified that he had heard Bill Samson refer to the strike as "class warfare that had to be won." Pinder was certain he had heard Bill Samson say many times that the union should do "whatever it takes for as long as it takes."

"In fact, that was the union's slogan, wasn't it?"

"Sure was. Some of them are still using it."

"What did it convey to you?"

"Just what it said. That the union should stop at nothing. After I crossed over, I was pretty damn scared."

"Objection."

"Sustained. The jury will disregard the last remark."

The prosecution then called a security guard who had made a detailed study of Eric Miller. He mentioned five specific threats, Miller's reference to replacement workers as "roaches," and his assault on two guards at a local convenience store and his behavior during the drive-by. He stood up well under cross-examination.

When the next prosecution witness, Gary Sanborn, was announced, the strikers in the audience reacted with expressions of shock and anger. Judge Alcott banged his gavel angrily and threatened to clear the courtroom. Bill had learned almost a month previously that Gary was to be called. He was stunned when he first heard the news from Powe. "I know he's an asshole, but I never expected Benedict Arnold." But after thinking about it a while, Bill was sure that either Gary's testimony would help to exonerate him or else he would expose himself as the lying son of bitch that Bill knew him to be. Bill looked quickly around the courtroom. Every former striker in the audience was staring angrily at Gary as he took the oath to tell the truth.

"Mr. Sanborn, are you a member of Local 34 and what, if any, office do you hold?"

"I am chief steward and a member of the executive committee."

"What role did you play in planning the union's strategy?"

"I actually had nothing to do with strike strategy."

"Did Bill Samson handle things by himself?"

"No, Bill worked real close with Eric Miller and Don Foreman. It was the three of them who made the key decisions. Many of which I would have disagreed with had I been asked."

"What decisions did you disagree with?"

"They brought in speakers to the Friday meetings that drove me crazy — radicals, anarchists, and socialists who talked about overthrowing the capitalist system. And they whipped people's anger up all the time with marches and slogans and talked about the old days when scabs were frightened."

"Did you feel they were encouraging violence?"

"Objection. Calls for a subjective conclusion."

"Overruled."

"Yes, I did."

"Were you surprised at the way the strike was conducted?"

"Yes, I was really surprised. Billy changed. He used to be proud of being a papermaker. After Don Foreman showed the movie _Matewan_, it seemed like he wanted to be a Mineworker. He even started speaking differently, like he was trying to get everyone worked up. I couldn't believe it when he began to preach class hatred. That's not the paperworker style."

"What is the film _Matewan?_"

"It's about a violent strike by Mineworkers that ends with a lot of people being shot."

"Do you have any idea of why Mr. Samson changed so much?"

"Objection."

"Sustained."

"No further questions."

Powe approached the witness angrily. "Mr. Sanborn, are you saying that Bill Samson was intentionally encouraging violence?"

"No."

"Well, I must be dumb because it sure sounded like that to me."

"What I'm saying is that Billy — Mister Samson — conducted the strike in a way that he should have known would lead to violence."

"I thought you were his union brother."

"I would be happy to be his union brother again. But when he started listening to Don Foreman, he changed. Foreman's parents were communists; he even told us so. When Billy started listening to him and taking his advice, he changed. Really changed."

"Objection."

"The jury will disregard the comment about Foreman's parents."

"No further questions."

Bill's stomach tightened up another notch. He noticed the faces of the jurors. A few looked over at him. Their expressions were neither friendly nor sympathetic.

Bradley asked for a short recess and then recalled Professor Tremain.

"Professor, did you hear Mr. Sanborn's testimony?"

"No, I did not. You asked me to leave the courtroom."

"Do you have any idea of his testimony?"

"No, none."

"Are certain unions more prone to use violence than others?"

"Yes, absolutely. We have data that show that two unions are by far more likely than any others to use violence."

"Which unions are they?"

"The Teamsters and the Mineworkers."

"In strike situations, which of the two is the more violent?"

"The Mineworkers, without doubt."

"So that if a union leader were to use the Mineworkers as his model, what conclusion could you draw?"

"That they were either secretly or openly encouraging violence."

"Thank you. No further questions."

"No cross."

"The people rest."

Powe quickly asked the judge to rule that the evidence didn't prove a conspiracy. Just as quickly, his motion was denied.

Chapter 32

The defendants' case began on the third day with Frank Powe's carefully crafted opening statement. Bill's spirits soared. Justice would be done. Powe seemed to change physically as he spoke. His shoulders stiffened, his chest expanded, and his face became more alert. He was the type of speaker that Bill envied. Each word was carefully shaped and enunciated. Bill could almost visualize them leaving the lectern and floating upward.

Powe's opening statement had substance as well as style. He pointed out that the union lost its chance to win the strike because of Edith Kent's death, and he told the jury that mistakenly blaming union leaders for strike violence that they did not cause had a long history. "The United States Supreme Court has made it clear that union leaders in a strike are not responsible for illegal acts by their fellow strikers unless they authorized, participated, or ratified the acts in question. There is no evidence of any such conduct by the defendants. To be guilty of conspiracy, the defendants had to work together to achieve an illegal goal, and it is clear that this never happened, either."

"You will soon get a chance to hear defendant Bill Samson. Listen to him carefully, observe him closely. Decide for yourselves whether he and the people who worked with him during the strike are criminals and conspirators who should be in prison. According to the prosecution, Bill Samson is the key to the conspiracy. He is the person whose involvement was crucial to the alleged conspiracy. Yet the evidence will show that he never once suggested either directly *or indirectly* to anyone that they engage in acts of violence. You will hear from a nationally renowned scholar in the field of labor law who will explain that Bill Samson's conduct — that the U.S. attorney seeks to use as evidence of crime — is legal, defensible, and part and parcel of our system of collective bargaining.

"Defendants Samson and Miller are guilty of fighting to preserve their way of life, a way that has existed for generations. Their parents and grandparents worked long and honorably for this same company. They are married men with families. Neither has ever been in trouble with the law. It is with their families, not in prison, that they belong. Don Foreman is guilty only of helping them. It has been his consistent habit to help people, not the rich or the powerful, but those who are vulnerable, those who are the victims of injustice in their battles against the rich and powerful. He spent years in Alabama helping to register black voters. He deserves our admiration. It will be a sad day in America when people like Don Foreman, genuine American heroes, are treated as criminals."

Bill could tell that the jurors were rightly impressed. He could back up Powe's words. *I can tell the jurors how things really happened — show them that the whole case against us is political bullshit.* Bill was the only one of the defendants scheduled to testify. The decision not to use Don Foreman and Eric Miller was much debated. Bill himself was uncomfortable about it. He knew that Don, articulate and self-assured, wanted the chance to speak his piece. Powe finally convinced them that Don carried too much negative baggage. That he went to Canada and did not fight in Viet Nam would not sit well with some of the jurors, and his connection to SNCC was potentially troublesome. Foreman had also been involved with the early Black Panther party, and he had been arrested in college for the takeover of the President's office. Also Powe feared that Foreman would be too preachy and sure of himself to win sympathy from a jury.

The decision not to call Eric Miller was easier. Eric had engaged in violence, could be said to have encouraged it, and justified it. He had a terrible temper that might be aroused by harassing cross-examination. Bill's record was the cleanest of the group, and his lifestyle one that ordinary Maine citizens could understand. Eric was instructed to sit as quietly as possible, wearing his old flight jacket and all the medals he was awarded.

During his direct examination by Powe, Bill kept himself in control. He reminded himself to answer only what was asked. Powe had warned him not to make a speech. Bill testified that he had begun the strike opposed to using violence for tactical reasons and that everyone in the union knew his views. The strike had led him to read about labor history, and his reading had convinced him that non-violent tactics, such as those used in the civil rights movement, were not only crucial to union victory during a strike, they made the union better with a more righteous appeal to the idealism of the workers. He talked about how much he had learned about non-violence by reading *The Parting of the Waters*. At virtually every meeting, he had insisted to the members that they were helping the company, not the union, if they were violent. The meetings had been taped, and Powe played a portion of one in which Bill spoke against violence.

Powe would have liked to elicit Bill's efforts to stop violence during the drive-by, but it would mean pointing out Eric's attack on Dickerson.

"That's why you need separate lawyers," he had grumbled in going over Bill's testimony.

Instead, Powe asked, "Is it true that Eric Miller, Don Foreman, and you were the group that ran the strike?"

"No, it is not."

"How were decisions made, and what role did Eric Miller and Don Foreman play in establishing policy?"

"Basic policy decisions were made by the executive committee. Eric Miller had one vote, so did Cindy Regan, Tony Lucelli, Emil Jean, and Gary Sanborn. Don Foreman had none. I spoke to Eric a lot. He is an old friend and a loyal union person. It was important to get his views on things because since he was a war hero a lot of the members respect him and lots of the brothers and sisters see things the way he does. I consulted with him, but I also consulted with lots of other people not on the executive committee, like Ray Allair, Joe Schulz, and Louise Adams. Don Foreman was a great help to me as an organizer. We worked together and discussed all kinds of stuff, but he did not set policy. I consulted with him a lot because he knows things about labor and strikes and law that none of the rest of us knows."

"Was Don in favor of the policy of non-violence?"

"Absolutely. It was from him that I really learned how important non-violence was to the civil rights movement. He told me we had to maintain the moral high ground — that's the term he always used — the same way the civil rights movement did. Said it would help us to win allies and public opinion. He even said the scabs…er…the replacement workers were the unorganized part of the labor movement."

"How about Eric Miller?"

"Well, Eric didn't see the need for non-violence at first. He was like a lot of the guys who came back from Nam angry, and the hiring of sc…permanent replacements really worked him up. He grew up in North Bethany. See, he's a mill brat. Making paper was what he cared about. And suddenly, there were these scabs doing his work. Like a lot of our people, he hated them. Made no bones about it. But I … we convinced him that it was necessary for the union to be non-violent."

"Why did you consider non-violence crucial?"

"We needed it to maintain our solidarity. If the union had favored violence, a whole bunch of our own members would have been turned off and might have quit the struggle. Also, Don gave me stuff to read that made me realize that we needed allies to win the strike. Our natural allies are church and civil rights groups. They would not support a violent union, but they supported us because we preached non-violence. The policy was working. We were winning the strike until Edith Kent got killed, and, then, just like Don predicted, our solidarity gave way and everyone was too busy feeling sorry for Edith Kent to care about the strike. I feel sorry for her myself."

"No more questions."

It was Armand Bradley's turn, and he approached Bill with an almost friendly expression. Bill had been instructed to say as little as possible on cross-examination, and he warned himself not to volunteer any information and not to become argumentative as Bradley approached him.

"Mr. Samson, you mentioned that some of your members would have been upset or furious with the union if you publicly favored violence. Am I right that it was important to you that these members continue to support the strike?"

"Absolutely."

"And these people were, by and large, the more religious members?"

"Yes."

"Are you yourself among the regular churchgoers in the union?"

"No."

"Were there members who favored violence directed at replacement workers?"

"There were some."

"And wouldn't these members, or at least some of them, have been disappointed in the union if they thought that the scabs were being given a free ride by the union?"

"What do you mean by free ride?"

"That they could cross the line without fear. In fact, didn't some of your members expect and strongly favor violence towards the replacement workers?"

"Some favored violence, but not killing."

"I'm not talking about killing, but maybe fists, jack rocks, eggs, and threats. You had members who thought that the union should be taking such steps, did you not?"

"Yes."

"So that the membership was divided about the use of violence, was it not?"

"Yes, I guess so."

"Is that 'yes?'"

"Yes."

"So, to maintain solidarity, the union had to keep the loyalty of those who favored violence and those who bitterly opposed it. True?"

"I guess so."

"Wasn't the best way to achieve that result to publicly oppose violence but to make sure that some occurred directed both at the replacement workers and at the company?"

Bill's jaw dropped. It was obvious that the question had taken him by surprise. He seemed confused for a minute. "I see what you're getting at. But the best way to develop lasting solidarity is to persuade everyone that non-violence is the best course for the union."

"That would have taken a long time, wouldn't it?"

"Sure."

"And you didn't have much time to lose."

"True."

"How did you get the message out that members were not supposed to attack the replacement workers?"

"At each meeting, I made it clear that our struggle was non-violent in the tradition of the civil rights movement."

"But some of your members continued to engage in attacks and to make threats against the replacement workers, did they not?"

"Some did."

"What actions did you take against those who violated your policy?"

"I let them know that such conduct was harmful to the cause."

"What if any official action did you ever take?"

"We told people about our policy over and over."

"Doesn't your union have a method by which charges can be brought against someone who takes action contrary to union policy?"

"I believe we do."

"I take it you never considered bringing charges against any of the people who violated your proclaimed policy of non-violence?"

"Not that I recall."

"Well, if you brought charges or seriously considered it, you would remember, wouldn't you?"

"Yes."

"Did you consider taking action against Eric Miller because of his attack on Mr. Dickerson?"

"No."

"Are you aware that some unions have special training programs to teach pickets how to avoid violence?"

"I am now."

"Did you have such a program?"

"No." Bill shifted uneasily in his seat. *Damn! What a tricky lawyer! He's making me look like all words and no action.*

"Would it surprise you to learn that people crossing the picket line were threatened and sometimes attacked?"

"No."

"Did you ever order an investigation?"

"No."

"Did you ever order anyone removed from the picket line?

Bill, who had been answering the questions in rapid-fire style, suddenly paused. He was lost in thought. Why hadn't he done more? Was he really to blame for being all talk and no action? But if I had done what he's asking about it would have torn the union apart.

Bradley waited a few seconds and then softly repeated the question.

"No. I left that up to the picket captains."

"And the head of that was Eric Miller, the person whose own behavior we have heard so much about?"

"Yes."

"Do you know if anyone was ordered off the picket line during the strike?"

"No."

"Did you ever seriously consider a single formal action against anyone who committed or threatened violence?"

"You don't understand. A strike needs solidarity, and I was determined…"

Bradley broke in, looking annoyed. "Mr. Samson. Please answer the question. It doesn't require a speech."

"But I'm trying to explain why…"

"Your honor, Please direct the witness to answer my questions and not make a speech?"

Judge Alcott looked sternly at Bill. "Mr. Samson, just answer the question. It calls for a simple yes or no. You can explain all you need to if your counsel thinks it necessary on redirect." Bradley repeated the question

"Not really."

"Did you approve the posting of the scab list?"

"Yes, I did."

"And someone drew a skull and crossbones next to it?"

"Yes."

"Do you know who did that?"

"No, I don't."

"Did you try to have it removed?"

"I meant to, but didn't get around to it."

"You didn't consider it important enough?"

"I never thought it meant anything serious."

"Are you aware that some of your members referred to the list as 'the hit list'?"

"I've heard the term used once or twice, but it didn't mean they should be attacked. We put it up so people will know who crossed and who didn't."

"Why would they want to know that?"

"So that they know who their friends are and who has betrayed the union."

"Did the union take any disciplinary action against any of the people on the picket line the day that Edith Kent was killed?"

"No, they're not killers. It was an accident. Rocky Louis has been punished enough and so have the others. They were only found guilty of a misdemeanor."

"So, as long as these gentlemen weren't convicted of a major crime, the union is not going to bring any disciplinary action against them. Did you contribute to the legal defense fund for Rocky Louis and the others?"

"Yes, I did."

"How much?"

"One hundred bucks."

"Do you know whether the payment of attorneys' fees was made from the strike fund for any of the members who pleaded guilty to destruction of property after the drive by?"

"No, I do not."

"Did you take part in interviewing the strikers discharged by CP for misconduct during the strike?"

"Yes, I did."

"Did you personally or did the union conclude that any of them were legitimately fired?"

"No, we did not."

"Did the union do anything official to tell any of those people that their conduct was unacceptable?"

"I reminded them all of our policy of non-violence."

"Were Don Foreman and Eric Miller the people you conferred with most during the strike?"

"Probably."

"How was Eric Miller chosen to be in charge of picketing?"

"He was chosen by the members."

"On your recommendation?"

"Yes."

"What responsibility, to your understanding, did the local officers have to monitor and prevent picket-line misconduct and violence?"

Powe stood up. "I object. The question seeks to elicit from this witness a legal conclusion he is not competent to give."

"I'm just seeking his understanding, and I want to know whether he felt legally or morally responsible," Armand Bradley said softly.

"Overruled. You may answer the question."

"As far as I am concerned, we had a moral responsibility to explain to our members the importance of nonviolence."

"Were you responsible in any way for the speakers recruited to your weekly meetings?"

"I had input, but mostly that was handled by the program committee."

"Are they the ones responsible for the radical speakers?"

"I don't know who you are talking about. We had speakers of all kinds. It was part of our effort to make common cause with other progressive groups."

"You had speakers from the Radical Socialists of America?"

"Yes, we did."

"And you consider them progressive?"

"I think they have something to say that our members might find useful."

Bill noticed Arthur wince. He glanced quickly at the jurors. They stared back without expression. Ray Allair had his head down.

Bill's anger was stoked. I'm trying too hard to follow directions and keep my mouth shut. Meanwhile, the son of a bitch is making me look like a hypocrite. No more Mister Nice Guy.

"According to an article in the Lewiston paper, you said at one of your Wednesday night meetings, 'I am here to tell you that I am a militant. I am going to stay militant. And I hope to make every one of you as militant as I am.' Did you say that?"

"Yes, I did."

"Are you a militant?"

"Yes, I am."

"What's a militant?"

"A militant is a person who, when he sees a wrong, tries to right it. I have done that as president of Local 34. I intend to continue doing it. Moses was a militant; Jesus was a militant; Martin Luther King was a militant; Gandhi was a militant. Robert Kennedy was a militant. I'm not putting myself in their class, but I try to follow their model."

"Did you refer to the strike as 'class warfare?'"

"Yes, I did."

"Regularly?"

"Yes."

"Do you agree that the use of such inflammatory rhetoric might make some people think that violence was acceptable?"

"I don't think so. I just wanted them to realize that we were engaged in a serious struggle and that the enemy was corporate greed."

"Do you advocate class warfare?"

"Not like a physical confrontation. But I want our members to learn what I learned during the strike — that workers always get the wrong end of the stick. That since 1980, 80 percent of workers are earning less. That we have forty million people without health insurance. At the same time, the salaries of CEOs like George Watts have increased by a thousand percent. He even got a five-million-dollar bonus last year.

"Working-class people are not getting a fair deal in America now. We need to make things better for working-class people. Those are things I am talking about in using terms like 'class warfare.'" Finally, I'm getting a chance to explain myself.

"Is it true that you have tried to model yourself after Cecil Roberts of the Mineworkers?"

"No, but I respect him very much. He has combined militance with non-violence, and I believe that is the right approach for labor leaders."

When he returned to the defense table, Don and Eric stuck out their hands eagerly and congratulated him. Powe smiled more enigmatically. "You had me worried for a while, but you finished up fine."

Armand Bradley also seemed content. "No further questions."

Bill was surprised that Powe chose not to ask him to explain his answers. "Maybe he doesn't want to make what we didn't do seem too important."

Bill was not sure how the jury received his testimony. Some of the jurors seemed to be smiling at him. But all of them avoided eye contact.

Chapter 33

When Bill finished his own testimony, he was eager to hear the union's expert witness, Professor Milton Schwartz of the Yale Law School. Everyone Bill talked to had heard from someone who had heard from lawyers and former students that Professor Schwartz was a brilliant man, a deep thinker, and a powerful speaker. The union had circulated his impressive biographical data, and just reading it made Bill feel proud. Schwartz had joined the faculty at Yale after completing a clerkship with Justice Brennan and had taught labor law for twelve years. He had written three books and over twenty articles dealing with various aspects of labor law. His most recent monograph, *Toward a Theory of Concerted Action*, dealt extensively with the legal status of the strike weapon and had been awarded several scholarly prizes.

Milton Schwartz, wearing a dark gray suit and striped tie, had a sharp profile, hawk-like nose, and deep, serious, eyes. He leaned forward in his chair looking like a cat ready to pounce. Powe led him quickly through his history, replete with honors and achievements. The jurors looked almost as impressed as Bill was. It was an honor to have so distinguished a person testify on his behalf. Powe addressed him with just a hint of awe in his voice. The key part of his testimony dealt with the relationship between the right to strike and the use of the RICO statute.

"Professor Schwartz, how important is the right to strike under our system of labor relations?"

"It is critically important. Under our labor law since passage of the Wagner Act in 1935, collective bargaining has been the preferred technique for establishing wages and other conditions of employment. Collective bargaining, in turn, is premised on the existence of a robust right to strike. As my book shows early on, during the Wagner Act days when we had a strong right to strike, the institution of collective bargaining thrived. Since employers got in the habit of hiring permanent replacement workers and courts got in the habit of restricting the right to strike, the institution of collective bargaining has been severely weakened."

"Professor, what is the relevance of your work to this case?"

"The use of conspiracy to weaken the right to strike has a long and unfortunate history. If these defendants are found guilty, I have little doubt that unions in subsequent cases will be fearful of striking. The strike and our entire system of collective bargaining will be threatened. It is crucial to the success of our system of labor relations that the right to strike remain vibrant and healthy. Prosecutions such as this threaten it. The use of conspiracy theory is only rarely justified, and this case is a perfect example of its potential dangers."

When Schwartz finished his direct testimony, Bill felt like shouting, "That's it! That's what I was trying to say!" He was a great professor, just like everyone said. He knew the truth, and he spoke the truth. Bill wondered how Bradley, who should have been more worried than he seemed to be, would be able to cross-examine someone so bright and so good with words.

Bradley began almost tentatively: "Professor, are you a member of a union?"

"Well, I'm a member of the American Association of University Professors known as AAUP, and I believe that in some places it engages in collective bargaining."

"But not at Yale?"

"Oh, no."

"Does AAUP have any official status at Yale?"

"No, I don't believe so."

"Has AAUP ever gone on strike?"

"I don't know."

"Have you ever been on strike?"

"No."

"Ever engaged in collective bargaining?"

"Personally?"

"Yes."

"No."

"Ever engaged in an empirical study of collective bargaining?"

"No."

"Have you ever done a factual study of strikes?"

Professor Schwartz's expression changed from amicable to angry. "What do you mean by factual?" he asked sharply in a voice that over a decade of students had learned to fear.

"I mean how they function in the real world and not learning about them by reading cases and law review articles."

"Well, I have not done an empirical study of strikes."

"Have you ever investigated the dynamics of a single strike?"

Schwartz's face now showed irritation. "No, that's not the kind of scholarship I do. But I've read several excellent accounts, one in particular by Barbara Kingsolver has helped me to understand the dynamics of strikes."

"Is that *Holding the Line?*"

"Yes."

"About Hispanic women strikes in Arizona. Is it?"

"Yes."

"Not a real discussion of the causes of violence in it, is there?"

Professor Schwarz's voice dropped. "No, I guess not."

"What kind of labor relations scholarship have you done?"

"I have analyzed the cases and legal doctrine based on common sense and what I have learned from the literature about contemporary strikes and strikes conducted at various important points in labor history. I've thought about it in relation to contemporary legal scholarship."

"So, you have no first-hand experience with strikes and have done no factually based scholarship about strikes. Have you ever interviewed strikers or members of management during a strike?"

"No."

"Ever done a study of strike violence?"

"No, not of the sort you are describing."

"So, all of your information comes from other people's writing about other strikes like the one in Arizona and your own assumption about what happens during strikes and collective bargaining. Professor, am I right?"

"I guess that's so. But one can learn a great deal by reading and thinking."

"No further questions."

Bill felt as though someone had hit him over the head with a long flat board. His ears were ringing. He could see some of the jurors shaking their heads. A few seemed to be barely holding back laughter. How in the hell could we have brought this guy on as an expert when he doesn't know anything and hasn't really studied anything? Damn, he sounded so good till Bradley started cross-examining him. Yale Law School, for God's sake! Don't they have to know stuff to be professors and write books?

It was a grim group of defendants and strategists that met for Friday evening drinks after the day's proceedings were adjourned.

Don Foreman looked resigned and openly contemptuous of the entire legal system. Eric Miller was angry; it was not clear at whom. Bill Samson was confused, and Powe was apologetic. "I should have investigated him more fully and prepared him better, but he seemed like such a natural when we met. We need an expert with a strong factual understanding of strikes and collective bargaining."

George Connerton, who had been silent up till then, suddenly brightened.

"I know a guy who might be willing to testify for us. He's an expert and he knows what CP has been up to. And he doesn't like it."

Bill Samson looked stunned. "You know of such a guy and you haven't mentioned it?"

"It has just occurred to me that he might be our guy, and I don't really know if he will do it."

"Who is it?" they asked at once.

"Thomas Gillian."

"You're kidding, right?" Don asked, obviously unsure how serious the proposal was.

"No, I'm not. I know him, I like him, and I know that he hates what CP did in hiring scabs. I'd bet my last dollar that he realizes how ridiculous this criminal case is."

Powe seemed confused. "Are we talking about the Gillian who is Director of Industrial Relations for CP?"

"That's him. Any reason why he couldn't testify for the defense in this case?"

"No, but I can't imagine he would be willing."

"I don't know if he would, but he might. If you guys agree, I'll call him."

It took only a few minutes for the group to agree that the idea was worth trying.

That evening, Connerton called Gillian at home.

"Tommy, I'm about to ask you something and before you say anything, I promise on the soul of my dead mother that anything you say will be kept confidential unless you give me permission to use it."

"Hell, George, I trust you without your swearing, but this must be important. What's it about?"

"Tommy, what do you think of the criminal charges against Bill and Eric?"

"Just between us, I think they are ridiculous and not in anyone's interest. The whole damn business infuriates me."

"That's what I guessed, which is what leads to my next question. Would you consider testifying as an expert witness for the defense?"

Gillian remained silent for almost a minute. "I don't know. I mean, would it be legal? In any case, I couldn't do it and stay with CP." Another long silence.

"It's tempting, George. I'm tired of playing games with my conscience. More and more I've been thinking of quitting this job and becoming a consultant for paper companies that want to get along with the union." Another long pause. "I need some time to talk it over with Laura. I'll get back to you before Monday."

When Gillian, his face troubled, raised the issue of testifying with Laura during Saturday breakfast, she was unwilling to share her opinion. She asked him first what he thought he could contribute. "I may be fooling myself, but I think that I could make the difference — see to it that they don't get convicted. I know about CP, I know Bill Samson, and I know that strike violence doesn't happen the way the prosecution witnesses say."

"Do you think you could testify and stay with CP?"

His expression became more thoughtful. "Oh, no. I've held back from saying and doing what I want out of loyalty. If I testify I would be telling Eastman, LeBlanc, Bradley, and their ilk how much contempt I have for them. Watts is different. I guess he's a man of principle, but he doesn't know what it's like to work with your hands for a living. What I mean is: his principles and mine are about 180 degrees apart." Gillian stretched his arms out wide to illustrate the extent of those differences. "Another thing, Laura, I'm not as worried as I was about getting another job. I could make us a living as a consultant to both unions and employers who wanted to make collective bargaining work. I've even thought about a job teaching at a business school. Teach these young people about the real world, about loyalty to workers."

"Would you be happier staying or going?"

For the first time in a long time, Laura saw Gillian smile with pleasure. Then he laughed. "No doubt about it. I want out. I'm sick of kissing Watts's ass, and I'm sick of being part of a miserable, anti-worker system. This sure would be a great way to go."

Laura echoed his smile. "Thomas Gillian, it's nice to be in love with a good man."

When Powe announced that Thomas Gillian was his next witness, Bradley objected to the calling of someone not on the witness list. This precipitated a hearing in the judge's chamber. Powe explained that he had not known of Gillian's availability until the weekend and had not realized that he needed him till after Friday's session. "I've only had a few hours to meet with him over the weekend. I believe that he is a reasonable and honest man. I'll be happy to let Mr. Bradley interview him during the morning, and we can begin with his testimony this afternoon."

Judge Harrington thought this a fair procedure and accepted it.

When Gillian walked to the witness chair, another buzz of surprise and confusion arose from the paperworkers present in the courtroom. Powe began questioning him matter-of-factly. "Will you state your full name?"

"Thomas Francis Gillian."

"For whom do you work?"

"Consolidated Paper Company."

"What is your current position?"

"Director of Industrial Relations."

Bill could see the heads of several jurors snap to attention as the significance of Gillian's testifying for the defense suddenly struck them. Why would the Director of Industrial Relations for CP be a witness for the defense?

For the next ten minutes, Powe led him through his professional biography, beginning as a union steward. He testified to his experience with strikes in his various positions.

"Mr. Gillian, do you believe that the union in this case deliberately used or encouraged violence in support of its collective bargaining objectives?"

"No, I believe that whatever violence occurred was the result of angry members who refused to go along with the union's policy of non-violence. When the company decided to hire permanent replacements, I warned them that violence was bound to occur. They ignored me. Some of the company's labor advisors wanted it to happen."

"Can you tell us who?"

"Professor Eastman. He knew violence would hurt the union."

"Are you familiar with Bill Samson?"

"Yes, I am."

"How long have you known him and in what capacities?"

"I have dealt with him as friendly adversaries since he became VP of Local 34."

"Do you consider him an honorable man?"

"Absolutely. If Bill tells you something, you can take it to the bank. He never lied to me, and I never had one of my subordinates report that he lied to them or did not keep his word about something he said he would do."

Bill felt like crying. What a brave, decent man Tom Gillian was. And I called him a liar and a union buster.

"According to Professor Tremain, strike violence comes from the leadership and not from the rank and file. Is that correct in your opinion?"

A slight, malicious smile crooked the corner of Gillian's mouth. "No, with all due respect to the professor, it is wrong—absolutely and totally wrong. When I was a union officer, I was always arguing with members who were angry and wanted to use violence — and that was not in situations where the company hires permanent replacements. The most difficult of all jobs for a union leader is to keep a strike non-violent when the company hires permanent replacements. This union, up to the tragic death of Edith Kent, did a fine job of keeping to the path of non-violence even after we hired permanent replacements."

"Did you favor hiring permanent replacements for the strikers?"

"No, I opposed it strongly. I knew, first of all, that we would lose excellent workers, and second, that it would lead to violence no matter how hard Local 34 tried to keep the strike non-violent. I warned my superiors. But my superiors saw it as a way of busting the union." The faces in the audience radiated confusion, anger, and then finally, admiration for Gillian. His testimony continued in this vein for about an hour. And by the time he was finished, the papermakers in the audience were radiantly happy.

Bradley cross-examined him relentlessly for about an hour. At one point, he asked Gillian if he was receiving a fee for his testimony. It was a serious mistake. "My fee is the return of my self-respect."

Gillian answered all Bradley's questions calmly without anger or unnecessary explanation. Bradley failed totally either to discredit or change his conclusion. When Gillian stepped down to a spontaneous burst of applause from the audience, the outcome of the case was obvious — the defendants would be acquitted. The jury was out less than two hours before returning with a "not guilty" verdict for all the defendants.

Gillian left the courtroom with Bill Samson. He knew that his days with Consolidated Paper were over, but he felt sorrier for the company and the replaced strikers than he did for himself.

Bill was weepy, touched by the sense of what Gillian had given up. "I won't forget this, Tom. I know how you love working for CP."

"Forget it, Bill. It's not an honorable company anymore. I'm going to do something different. I'm going to work with companies that want to develop cooperative relations with their unions. I've been thinking of setting up a consulting firm." His face suddenly brightened.

"You know, I'm going to need someone to work with unions, help them to understand the value of labor-management cooperation. I could use someone like you."

"Are you offering me another job?"

"Sure am."

Bill thought for a moment. "Damn, Tom, I can't do it. In a way, I'd like to. I'd like to help you, and I'm going to need to find another job. You should have made this offer before I became a radical."

Gillian looked confused.

"I don't want to convince workers to cooperate. I want to teach them how to fight. I'm not the same person I was before the strike."

Gillian felt sad. What a waste of talent and decency, he thought. "I see," was all he said.

They walked together to the parking lot. At Gillian's car, Bill put his arms around Gillian and hugged him silently.

About the Author

Julius G. Getman is a preeminent scholar in the field of labor law, where he pioneered empirical studies and continues to do extensive field work. He came to the University of Texas in 1986 from Yale Law School, where he was the William K. Townsend Professor of Law. He has also taught at Stanford Law School, University of Chicago Law School, and Georgetown University Law Center.

He is author of *The Betrayal of Local 14: Paperworkers, Politics and Permanent Replacements* (Cornell, 1998) and *In the Company of Scholars: The Struggle for the Soul of Higher Education* (Texas, 1992); and co-author of both *Union Representation Elections: Law and Reality* (Russell Sage Foundation, 1976) and *Labor Relations: The Basic Processes, Law and Practice* (Foundation, 1988). A former President of the American Association of University Professors, he is currently writing a book with former Secretary of Labor Ray Marshall (a faculty member at the L.B.J. School of Public Affairs) on the future of the labor union movement.